ILLEGAL

A Ripped-From-The-Headlines Romantic Suspense

K. J. GILLENWATER

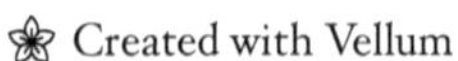 Created with Vellum

ACKNOWLEDGMENTS

Thank you to Sharon Abaud, from the Law Office of Sharon Abaud, an immigration attorney in Los Angeles, CA. She answered so many questions for me about immigration, illegal status in the United States, and the world of visas. I received invaluable information to make my book that much more realistic.

ॐ   I   ॐ

Twenty-four hours after Selena Hernandez had self-deported, she wondered if she'd made a gargantuan mistake.

Mexico City sucked.

The heat, the smells, the crowds, the garbage.

And the language. Selena had thought it would be easier. Somewhere deep inside her mind, the words were buried. The long-lost Spanish she'd been born speaking. But everything she dredged up was useless. Words she didn't need. Words she couldn't cobble together into a coherent sentence. Why couldn't the cab driver, who stared at her blankly, read the address she'd written on the motel stationery and take her where she needed to go?

The taxi, an old Volkswagen Bug, sat at the curb, its engine idling. Selena repositioned on the uncomfortable backseat, which had a large rip where the stuffing poked through. The driver reeked of cigarettes and body odor. Even with the window rolled all the way down, she couldn't escape the smell. The street outside her cheap motel room hadn't been any cleaner.

"I need to go here. *Aquí*." Selena leaned forward and pointed at her paper. "The US Embassy."

Her driver, a man in his thirties with dark skin and an appearance her mother would've called *indio*, glanced at her. "*Adónde?*"

On the edges of her mind, Selena knew what that meant. But for the life of her she couldn't remember. The last thing she wanted was to look stupid in front of a complete stranger. She briefly closed her eyes and took a deep breath. "Please, I want to go to the Embassy."

If Selena still had her smart phone, she could've figured it out. She'd only been able to afford a flip phone, which she'd purchased at the airport.

Her driver swiped to a translation app on his phone. He spoke loudly, "*Adónde?*" then held it up so Selena could hear.

"To where?" an electronic voice said in a stilted manner.

"The Embassy. The United States Embassy." A sudden lightness filled her.

Before the app could translate, her driver's eyes brightened. "*Oh, El Embasario de los Estados Unidos.*"

"Yes," Selena said, her mind at ease. "*Los Estados Unidos.*" Her accent was all wrong. Despite the fact her dark eyes, black hair and browner complexion echoed the appearance of others here, Selena had never been to Mexico. Silently, she vowed once she was able to leave, she never would come back. All she needed was an immigration visa, and she could return to Tucson and the life that waited for her there.

With the destination decided, her cabbie pulled away from the curb and into the maze of traffic. At two in the afternoon, the number of cars jammed on the road was a sight to behold. Multiple lanes packed with taxis, cars, buses of all sizes. Exhaust billowed from tailpipes that would've been forbidden in her home state of Arizona.

Selena scanned the mountains in the horizon and noted the

brown haze that settled over the valley. Out of the kingdom of the Aztecs, a massive, modern city had been built, which teemed with millions of people.

Selena hoped her time spent here would be short, barely memorable—a blip in her past to be forgotten.

The taxi zipped around slower vehicles. No signaling. No rearview mirror checking. Just move, move, move. Zip. Zip. Zip.

They approached a huge roundabout with multiple lanes and a towering statue standing in the middle. She'd read about it in the in-flight magazine on the plane.

El Angel De La Independencia. A golden angel alight a tall, skinny tower.

The driver navigated out of the roundabout, zoomed past the Sheraton Hotel, and made a right. *"Casi ahí."* He pointed ahead.

Selena nodded as if she understood. Butterflies filled her stomach. This stop had huge implications for her. She wanted to do everything right. Follow all the rules. Obtain a visa and then go back home, like the immigration attorney and the authorities had told her she could.

The driver pulled up to the corner down the street from the embassy building. Close enough.

Her appointment had been scheduled for 2:30—in fifteen minutes. She had to walk a half block and then locate the right office inside.

Selena handed the driver some American dollars, which he happily accepted, and climbed out of the hot, grimy taxi.

Everything had to go smoothly here. Her future depended on it. She clutched her handbag close to her body and made sure it was zipped closed. She'd heard about the crime stats in Mexico. Not good. Especially for someone who appeared to be a foreigner. Her black hair and olive skin might make her blend in momentarily with the locals, but the minute she opened her mouth, it was obvious she was American.

Or was she American? What exactly made someone an

American anyway? A look? An experience? A certain length of time living in the US? These questions had been ping-ponging around in her mind for a couple of weeks, and she had no answers.

The cab pulled away. Selena squared her shoulders, took a breath and tripped over her own two feet. She tumbled to the cracked sidewalk and hit her knee hard on the concrete. Instant embarrassment in front of a stream of pedestrians. Her emotions already on edge, she worked hard to keep in the tears that threatened to spill.

"*Señorita?*"

Selena flinched. The sun blinded her.

"*Permite?*" A hand grabbed her elbow and lifted her up.

The act happened so quickly, she hadn't had time to consider whether or not she wanted any help from a stranger. "*Gracias.*" She shielded her eyes from the bright sun.

A tall man stood above her. Dirty blond hair. Blue eyes. He didn't appear to be Mexican, but she'd been fooled before. Plenty of more European-looking people rounded out the citizenry in '*el D.F.*' or *Distrito Federal*—the common name for Mexico City.

His grip had been strong. Dependable. Nice.

He beamed at her. His gaze roved over her figure. Mutual appreciation of a sort.

Her thoughts grew muddied. "*Gracias,*" she repeated and flashed a fake smile. She repositioned the strap of her purse, which had slipped, nodded and went on her way.

The attractive man blended into the crowd.

His strong grip on her elbow had steadied more than her body. It reduced her level of anxiety several notches and boosted her confidence before she faced the most difficult situation of her life. A human touch made her feel normal again. She'd been so isolated and alone since her mother's arrest.

She strode forward to the embassy entrance. The building sat like a behemoth on the busy street. The ugly gray structure with a strange overhang and green awnings didn't fit in with the glass fronted Sheraton Hotel on one side and a more modern office building to the other.

A flicker of doubt glimmered. She couldn't do this. She couldn't go in. A mini panic attack struck. Her feet wanted to move forward, but she grew dizzy and short of breath.

This is stupid, Selena. Go inside.

She needed a moment to gather her thoughts, get herself together. She wanted to go into the building confident in what she was doing.

Glancing at her watch, she saw she had a few minutes. No need to rush. Time to calm down and slow her breathing.

Chill, chill, chill.

After dabbing at her knee using a tissue from her purse, she swept her hands down her skirt to straighten any wrinkles, fluffed out her hair, and retucked her blouse. The panicky thoughts faded. Her emotions finally in check, she took a deep breath and walked toward the entrance.

WYATT COULDN'T KEEP HIS GAZE OFF THE ATTRACTIVE Mexican woman he'd helped on the street. After six months at his new post, she'd been the first interesting thing to cross his path. In her red skirt and white blouse, she'd been hard to miss. And her practical flats had caught his eye. Most Mexican women higher on the economic scale in the capital city dressed to the nines. Fashion forward.

The stunner's shoes didn't match her outfit. He'd expected at least four-inch stilettos. When he'd helped her up, her short stature made the lack of heels even more intriguing.

The brunette headed in the opposite direction of his destination—the Starbucks in the next block. The office coffee tasted horrible. Too long on the burner, not enough grounds, and probably cheap to begin with. He shuddered at the idea of having to continue his day with mud in his mug. He'd taken his mid-afternoon break, set an appointment for exactly ten minutes on his phone, and sprinted down the street to pick up a Venti Mocha for himself and a Hazelnut Latte for Antonia.

The headache he'd had since waking up pounded in his skull. Only several shots of espresso mixed with hot steamed milk and chocolate syrup could cure it. His head throbbed in anticipation of its fix.

The US Embassy occupied one of the busiest sections of downtown Mexico City, only two blocks away from *El Angel de la Independencia*. Wyatt couldn't see the monument through the trees and manicured shrubs that lined *Avenida Paseo de la Reforma*, but he knew it was there. Standing tall in the center of the massive, multi-lane roundabout studded with traffic.

New to the city, Wyatt had learned to use the monument as his touchstone as he made his way throughout its myriad of streets. As long as he knew where *El Angel* was, he never felt lost.

Wyatt paused at the crossing, waited for the light to turn, and then made his way to the next block. At least Starbucks reminded him of home. Sure, he could find American fast food restaurants all over the city if he craved something familiar, but for some reason a Venti Mocha worked every time.

Wyatt entered the Starbucks. He queued up in line behind a well-dressed Mexican woman and a poorly dressed American tourist. He wished his Spanish were better so no one lumped him in with the latter.

"Venti Mocha y Grande Avellana Latte, por favor."

The tiny worker behind the counter bent her dark head as she punched the correct key. "Joor name?"

His attempt to blend in with the Mexican population had

failed. She'd pegged him as American even with his better-than-average Spanish accent. "Wyatt."

The woman scribbled his name on two cups and set them next to the short line by the Espresso machine. She moved on to the next customer

Antonia better repay him for the favor one of these days.

A *Proceso* magazine had been left on a table. The garish picture on the front of the news journal under the headline '*Narcotráfico Guerra*' caught his eye. Several limp bodies with ropes around their necks hanged from a highway overpass, one of them a middle-aged woman. He flipped through the pages to the story. Even with his limited Spanish comprehension he could get the gist of it—drug crime on the border had hit new highs. He closed the magazine and rubbed his hand over his shirt. Hard to believe the pictures depicted the same Mexico.

He glanced at the garish tourist and the well-dressed Mexican woman waiting for their orders, both of whom oblivious to the dangers that lay fifteen hundred miles to the north.

Wyatt checked his watch. He'd have to hurry back. His supervisor grew irritated when he didn't stick to the schedule. Exactly ten minutes. No more.

"Wee-aht." A second employee read one of the cups and set the freshly made drinks at the pick-up counter.

He gingerly took both hot paper cups. "Wyatt," he said under his breath. Not the easiest name to pronounce for a native Spanish speaker. No 'w' sound existed in Spanish, so the closest sound was a diphthong of two vowels with a bit of a "g" mixed in. He'd grown used it.

Wyatt hurried to the door, stretched his gait, and carefully carried the two steaming beverages. He wanted to take a sip of his drink, but feared he'd spill all over his blue oxford shirt and striped tie.

From a distance, he caught sight of a red pencil skirt and the figure in it entering the embassy building. He picked up his steps, hoping for another encounter with the beautiful woman in the practical shoes.

❧

Selena unfolded a piece of paper. The embassy lobby confused her. Signs pointed in different directions. She needed to find *Visas and Passports*. Maybe she should've done more research to better prepare. As a more intuitive person, she preferred acting on the fly. Taking time to think things through slowed everything down and resulted in talk but no action. A pet peeve of hers.

"*Necesitas ayuda?*" a deep voice asked.

Selena jumped.

The attractive man who'd helped her up outside stood next to her.

She'd blocked everything out and had been lost in her own thoughts and worries.

"*Lo siento.*" He held two Starbucks cups and had a concerned look on his face.

Now she felt the fool. She hadn't made it clear on the curb she didn't speak Spanish. If she wanted him to go on his way, she'd either have to be rude and ignore him or 'fess up to her fakery. "Are you stalking me?" She stepped back and tightly clutched her purse.

The man's eyes widened. "Oh, I'm sorry. I thought... Earlier, you were..."

"So you made an assumption about me based on my appearance? Bad idea, dude." She let out a snort. "Maybe think next time. I speak English. I'm an American." The nerves in her stomach twisted into sourness.

Her reaction drew the attention of the people milling around them.

The man backed away. "I was just trying to help."

Selena gave her best queenly look and marched down a hallway. She had no idea if she needed to go in that direction, but anything for a great exit.

❧

WYATT HAD REALLY MESSED UP. HE'D SEEN AN OPPORTUNITY to meet a hot girl, thinking he'd missed his chance out on the sidewalk. He truly did not know how to talk to women. Another check box in the column of 'clueless and incapable,' which he'd been accused of in the past. Attractive women usually made him feel that way. Maybe he should quit trying. Perhaps his mother had been right.

He wanted to shrug it off, but the feeling covered him like a cloud. His phone beeped to remind him his ten minutes was up. He wished he had time for an hour in the gym to burn off the bad vibes. Instead, he'd have to deal with an afternoon of customer service. Not exactly the dream career he thought he would have when he'd taken the job with the embassy: world travel, foreign people, amazing sights, new foods and experiences. But even working the easy cases at his desk while he learned the finer points of immigration law and passport rules, gave him the opportunity to find out more about the State Department and perhaps apply for the Diplomatic Security Service.

He followed the departure of the woman. Her confident walk revealed to him she had been out of his league. He took a careful sip of his mocha. The flood of caffeine into his veins soothed his damaged ego a bit, and the headache he'd had all day eased some. He let out a sigh and glanced at the big clock in the lobby. A few more hours of work, and he could head home. Maybe take a run around the neighborhood. Find a new place to pick up some tacos or a torta roll.

Wyatt headed for the employee entrance down the west hall.

A buzz of activity greeted him. His supervisor, Max Beltrán, nodded as he walked in. Antonia smiled at her drink delivery

He let out a breath, returned to his window, and took down the 'closed' sign. After several gulps of his mocha, he set it to the side. "Next."

❧ 2 ❧

"Hernandez?" called out a bespectacled woman who stood behind a glassed-in counter. Her dark hair had been pinned up in a librarian-style bun. "Hernandez?" She scanned the full waiting room.

Selena stepped forward. She'd been waiting in the uncomfortable chairs that lined the room for at least an hour. Her heart leaped at the knowledge she'd soon have her visa. Her nightmare would be over, and she could return to her life in Tucson. Her job might be gone, but she could find another. If she'd learned anything from her mother, it was to be resilient in the face of hardship.

Thinking of Maria Hernandez set her back for a second. Her mother had lied to her, kept things from her. She pinched her lips.

"Hernandez?" the embassy employee called her name again.

Get it together, Selena.

"Yes." Selena approached the window.

The name plate read: *Antonia Stewart*.

"Can I help you?" Antonia had the no-nonsense attitude of

former military or police with crisp speech, stiff shoulders, and a penetrating gaze.

Selena felt six inches tall. Out of her depth. Out of her comfort zone. Antonia held all the power. A stone of dread settled in Selena's stomach. "I'm here to apply for an immigrant visa." Selena handed over her documents and every bit of paperwork she had about her life and her place of origin.

Antonia thumbed through them. "Okay." She paused when she ran across Selena's birth certificate. A wrinkle marred her brow.

Selena had forgotten it was in her pile of paperwork. "Oh, yes, that's my birth name. Claudia Rios." Her face heated at the admission. She hadn't known the birth certificate existed until ICE had hauled off her mom to jail. "But I'm an American. That's why I'm here. To straighten all of this out. It's a mistake. A terrible mistake."

Even though the lawyer back in Arizona had explained it to her, the process of voluntarily leaving the United States, returning to her birth country, and applying to immigrate legally had been a blur. All she'd known was if she chose that path, she wouldn't be arrested. And arrested meant she'd have no chance of coming back to the US legally. The lawyer had convinced her it would be an easy process with her background, her education, her exemplary record. She was the kind of person the government wanted to let back in the country.

"I see." Antonia scanned Selena's face intently. The fluorescent lights created a glare on her glasses. "Well, unfortunately, you can't apply for that type of visa here. You have to visit a consulate office. We reissue lost or stolen passports, though."

"But I don't understand, I thought that was something I could do here. I made an appointment online." Selena's confidence deflated. It was as if she were five years old again. Small, awkward and stupid. She was sure the embassy website had explained it was an acceptable place to get a visa.

Antonia stared at the birth certificate. "I might be able to do something. Will you excuse me?" She swept all of Selena's papers into a pile and stepped away from the counter.

"Sure." Selena's stomach fluttered. Maybe Antonia Stewart would help her. Surely, she'd ask a supervisor what Selena should do. She tapped her fingernails on the counter and waited.

❧

WYATT'S HEARTBEAT RACED WHEN THE PRETTY GIRL HE'D RUN into twice that morning took a seat in the waiting area.

Most who showed up in *Visas and Passports* were tourists on vacation who wanted nothing more than to straighten out their situation and get back home. This girl had a different look and had arrived alone. Her red skirt and blouse emphasized her trim figure, and her hair flowed down her back in pretty, black waves. She didn't look like someone on vacation. A purpose shone in her expression. If he could find the right track to take, he could start over with her. Might make for a fun evening.

He leaned into his screen, muttered *please* under his breath and hit the 'Select' button to be assigned a new customer from the waiting area.

When the mystery girl ended up at Antonia's window, he let out a sigh. So much for luck possibly going his way.

He glanced at his computer screen for the next appointment on the list. "Steiner," he called out in a monotone.

A middle-aged woman and her husband shuffled up. The wife had a few extra pounds around the middle and bushy blonde hair, which she'd tied back with a loud-patterned scarf. A muumuu style dress hid her shape behind yards of pineapple print.

Wyatt had trouble keeping his gaze off the girl. Hernandez dipped her head, handed over papers, bit her lip, shifted her weight to her other foot. Restless.

"Will this take long?" Mr. Steiner, sporting a shaggy beard and wearing sunglasses, asked Wyatt, handing him a lost passport form. He smelled of sweat and sunscreen.

"Oh, Jimmy, leave the poor boy alone," said the wife in a thick Midwest accent. St. Louis or possibly southern Illinois in origin—an accent he knew well.

Wyatt focused on the couple in front of him and scanned their form. "Let me go make a few copies, and I'll be right back." He took their identification and headed for the shared copier.

Antonia stood off to the side, her back to the line. In her hand, she held documents and chatted on her cell phone.

Wyatt's curiosity was piqued. He couldn't think of a reason for Antonia to make a private phone call during work hours. If Max caught her, he wouldn't be happy. He crossed behind her to reach the copier.

"Yes, it's her. I'm positive," Antonia said. She took a quick glance back at the girl.

Wyatt placed the IDs on the platen, closed the copier lid, and hit *copy*. He snuck a peek at Antonia who was concentrating on her conversation.

She held a birth certificate, and he could make out one part of the name on it: "Claudia." "She won't be here much longer. If you hurry, you can grab her," she whispered into her phone. "Miguel said you'd pay up if I ran across anyone on that list."

The copier loudly spooled up and drowned out the rest of the conversation. In a few moments, it spat out a copy.

Wyatt grabbed the originals and the copy and headed back to his window. Antonia glanced at him as she slipped her phone back in her pocket. They locked gazes for a split second. She narrowed her eyes. Wyatt looked away.

Something wasn't right here. What list was she talking about?

He finished processing the paper work for the tacky tourists at his station. The blonde woman thanked him profusely. Her husband roughly grabbed her by the arm and headed toward the exit, his flip flops slapping on the tile floor.

Before moving to the next person in line, he pretended to click around on the screen in front of him, as if he were doing something work-related. He glanced at Claudia, who waited at the counter for Antonia. He had no idea who his coworker had called, but his gut told him he should do something.

His head, however, told him otherwise.

Don't get involved, Demko.

It was none of his business.

Antonia handed Claudia her papers and called out the next name on the appointment schedule.

Against his better judgment, Wyatt's mind raced. What sort of person would be willing to pay just to find out if someone showed up at their office? What would a birth certificate reveal? He thought through the possibilities. None of them seemed good. He'd lived in Mexico long enough to figure out almost the whole country ran on bribes and spies, from the local police to the highest levels of government. He'd be disappointed to find out his coworker had been compromised.

Most of the time, a foreigner in Mexico City or any number of tourist-laden towns would fare fine. Nobody watched, nobody cared. Mexico wanted to keep the tourist dollars flowing so they ensured criminal activities were kept to a minimum. An American could walk the streets of the capital city, cruise through the *Museo Nacional de Antropología*, or take a ride on the Metro and end up back at her hotel in one piece by the end of the day.

Claudia was different and she had no idea.

Surreptitiously, Antonia texted below the counter as her next customer approached.

Wyatt's gut told him something was about to happen, and it wasn't going to be good for Claudia.

On impulse, he grabbed his *closed* sign and set it on the counter in front of his station.

"I'll be right back," he announced to no one in particular. Max might be ticked he was stepping away again, but he didn't care. He needed a few minutes to see for himself that Claudia left the building without any problems. Maybe he was over-thinking it, but he had an overwhelming desire to be sure.

Claudia had vanished from the waiting room.

She'd arrived in a taxi; she'd probably leave in a taxi.

He should follow her to the sidewalk and make sure she safely got into one. The gentlemanly thing to do. She might never know about it, but he'd be satisfied he did what he could for an innocent woman who might have been set up.

When he exited into the hallway, doubts crept in. She hadn't exactly wanted any help from him earlier. A cold sweat took over. As the embassy lobby swirled with activity, he made for the bathroom. The unsettling feeling in his stomach was a familiar one.

Wyatt stood in front of the sink, a mirror reflecting his image. Pale. Weak. Pathetic. He remembered a time as a young boy when weakness would be treated with a smack.

He ran a hand through his hair and then noticed a spot on his shirt sleeve. That hadn't been there earlier. He turned on the faucet and grabbed a paper towel. He dabbed at what looked like a chocolate stain from his mocha, which the water only made larger.

"Dammit." Wyatt chucked the wad of wet paper towels at the garbage can. "What in the hell are you doing?" He gripped the sink with both hands, scooped up some water and splashed it on his face.

He let out a lungful of air and strode out of the bathroom.

Get your head in the game.

Sometimes he was glad to be in Mexico where nobody knew him, knew his faults, knew his weaknesses. He could be whoever he wanted to be here. He could be the hero. He could be the good guy.

An acute sense of purpose muted the negative voices in his head. His muscles tightened.

Wyatt headed straight for the exit. He hoped he hadn't missed his chance. All he'd heard was a snippet of a phone conversation and noticed some unusual behavior from Antonia. Did that really mean anything?

The afternoon August heat hit him. Mexico City sat at over 5,000 feet above sea level, but the sun could be brutal this time of year. He scanned the sidewalk. Although the embassy sat right on *Avenida Paseo de la Reforma*, one of the main thoroughfares in the city, large planters blocked taxis from parking near the entrance—an anti-terrorism feature. Most people hailing a taxi headed to the Sheraton Hotel down the street.

From fifty yards away, he spied her red skirt and white blouse. He picked up the pace. He didn't want to appear frantic, yet his stomach churned. He kept an eye on her figure, pushing past pedestrians, tripping over imperfections in the sidewalk. He crossed the street without looking. A car stopped short of hitting him. The driver honked. Wyatt tapped on the hood and waved. His movements quickened.

Within ten feet, he slowed. A taxi pulled up to the curb. Claudia casually stepped forward. He felt foolish. Nothing was happening. He had overreacted. He didn't know what to do.

Claudia raised an eyebrow and gave a glassy stare. "Are you following me?" She'd caught him in the act.

Wyatt reeled back. "I'm headed to the Starbucks." He pointed at the coffeehouse he'd visited earlier, which was located right behind them. "Too early for pumpkin spice latte, you think?"

"I don't know what game you're playing, but I'm not interested." Claudia reached for the door handle.

The driver had exited his taxi and looked disappointed she had no luggage. "*Señorita?*"

Wyatt paused. He could end it right now. He could let her

climb inside the taxi and drive away. Then he thought of that moment in the bathroom. The weakness he'd felt.

Not this time.

"Claudia, they know you are here."

"What?" She left the taxi door ajar and faced him. A puzzled expression darkened her features. "Where did you hear that name?"

The driver shrugged, checked his watch, and climbed back into the driver's seat.

A stocky man sporting a spiky haircut and wearing a black blazer and a white T-shirt appeared out of nowhere and interrupted them. "You need help, *señorita?*" he asked in accented English. "He bothering you?" He let his blazer hang open to reveal a handgun.

Claudia's eyes grew wide.

The stocky man grabbed her by the elbow.

Wyatt, acting completely on instinct, shoved the man with his shoulder. The man stumbled into the trunk of the taxi.

"Get in!" Wyatt yelled at Claudia.

A taller, leaner man with slicked-back greasy hair leaped up from the outdoor seating at the Starbucks. He tossed his drink aside. Hot milk and espresso spilled on the sidewalk.

Claudia stood frozen.

Both men had their weapons out.

Claudia sprang into action. In a flash, she grabbed Wyatt's hand and yanked him into the taxi. They landed in the back seat.

"Go!" she screamed at the driver. The door stood wide open.

One of the guns fired. A bullet buried itself in the well-worn seat cushions, missing Wyatt's knee by inches.

"*Pinche cabrón!*" The driver pushed on the gas.

"The door," Claudia yelled.

Wyatt scrambled and slammed it shut.

Tires squealed on the pavement.

Wyatt looked through the back window. The two men stood

in the street, watching as they drove away. The taller one pushed down the barrel of the gun his partner had aimed at the taxi, then tucked his own gun in the back of his pants and pulled out a cell phone.

"Damn!" Wyatt slammed the meat of his hand on the passenger's side headrest. He didn't like this stuff. High emotions. Out of control thoughts. The surge of energy flowing through his body made him want to run five miles without stopping. He liked calm. He liked controlled. He liked well-thought out. Cautious. No mistakes. And this whole event felt like one big mistake.

Claudia breathed heavily. Even though she'd saved his ass, she appeared just as surprised as he that they'd ended up in the taxi together. "Where do we go now?" she asked.

Wyatt took stock. "I have no idea." His brain wouldn't function. "But thanks for getting me out of there."

The taxi driver didn't seem to care they had no destination. He wove through traffic, checked his mirrors, and crossed himself.

"Yeah, I wasn't really thinking. I saw those guns and..." She shrugged.

His thoughts scrambled to understand how such a petite woman could act so bravely. Her instincts and quick actions were impressive.

"By the way, my name isn't Claudia," she said. "It's Selena Hernandez."

Wyatt took several deep breaths to still his rapid heartbeat. "Selena," he said, looking her straight in the eye, "I think you might be in some trouble."

$\maltese$ 3 $\maltese$

Selena's mind went blank. "What are you talking about?" The violence of the moment echoed in her head. People had shot at her. Tried to kill her. She wanted to tell the taxi driver to take her immediately to her motel, but his words caught her off guard. "Who were those men?"

"I'm not sure. All I know is, back at the embassy someone made a phone call after getting a look at your documents and mentioned you were on some list." The stranger glanced out the back window again.

"I don't understand." She couldn't make sense of it. A quasi-American from Arizona. Why would anyone make a phone call about her?

The driver glanced at them in the rearview mirror. His face had turned ashen. Selena didn't blame him and wondered why he didn't boot them out at the corner.

"Sorry, I didn't introduce myself. I'm Wyatt Demko. I work at the embassy." He awkwardly held out a hand.

Selena ignored the gesture and smoothed her skirt over her knees to calm herself. "Look, I don't know what's going on." Her voice sounded weak and shaky to her ears. She cleared her throat. She wanted to come across as strong, in control, completely capable of taking care of herself. "I've heard that Mexico has gotten more dangerous, but didn't really believe I'd see if for myself."

"They were after you." Wyatt furtively glanced out the back window "Those men."

Selena shook her head and laughed nervously. "Yeah, right. Really, I'd like to get back to my motel. Can you tell him I need to get to the Motel Real del Sur?" She leaned forward and said the words loudly, hoping the driver would pick up on her desire. "*Señor, Motel Real del Sur, por favor?*" The only thing keeping her from totally freaking out right now was the fact the driver had carried them far away from the armed men on the sidewalk.

"*Olvídalo.*" Wyatt met the gaze of the driver in the rearview mirror. "*Santa Rosa, numero diecisiete.*"

The driver nodded and glanced at her.

Sounded as if Wyatt Demko had given the man a different destination.

Wyatt faced her. "If I could, I would let you go back to your motel. I would."

"Let me?" Selena didn't like the sound of that.

"I might've screwed up back there."

"How so?"

"Antonia is going to figure it out soon enough. She's going to call whoever she was talking to and let them know that I'm with you." Wyatt's gaze went upward. "Shit, shit, shit."

"How do I know you're not the one they were shooting at? I don't know you from Adam." Selena leaned forward again. Despite what this strange man, Wyatt, might have said to the driver, she needed to take back control. "Pull over." She pointed at the curb. "Let me out."

"I know your real name is Claudia. I know someone wants to find you. And I know that they think I'm part of your scheme, so until we figure out the who of this scenario, I'm not letting you out of my sight." Wyatt grabbed her hand, laced his fingers with hers, and held on as if she were a trout about to flip flop off the hook.

Selena might've saved him from being shot, but that's where her help ended. "Let go of me." She yanked her hand out of his grasp.

Wyatt, if that was even his real name, didn't try to manhandle her a second time.

But as she pondered her situation, she realized her options were limited. She'd thought she was going to walk out of the embassy with a visa and a way back to Tucson. She didn't have the money to stay in Mexico City for long and had no idea what her next steps should be. Although her reaction to yanking Wyatt into the taxi had been impulsive, maybe he could be handy. If he was so determined she go to his apartment with him, she might as well give in and let him pay the cab fare.

❧

THANK GOD SHE'D GONE ALONG WITH HIM. WYATT DIDN'T know what else to do. Because he'd injected himself into the situation, he now had to worry about his own skin. And what about work? He'd taken off and hadn't come back. Max would be sure to notice.

He took his phone out of his pocket.

Claudia—no wait, Selena, she'd said—watched in silence.

"Max, it's Wyatt." Although Max was a stickler for the rules, he also could be a reasonable person in the right situation. Wyatt straightened his shirt cuff. "I'm not feeling so well. I think I've got to go home."

"Someone said they saw you in the bathroom a little while ago, and you looked kind of pale," Max said.

Wyatt didn't realize anyone had noticed him. Never thought

he'd be glad for his stupid insecurities. "Yeah, feels like a stomach bug."

Selena listened intently to his side of the conversation. He could sense her distrust, and he didn't blame her one bit.

"How long you been here? Six months?" his boss asked.

"About."

"Right on schedule. You must've picked the wrong street vendor. I told you not to get tacos off that truck yesterday." He chuckled. "Make sure you stay hydrated. Might take a couple of days to feel like your old self."

Although Montezuma's Revenge was an American joke, some of it held a grain of truth. He'd been told to be careful about where he ate in the city. Instead, he'd made a habit of preparing his own meals. "Thanks."

He put his phone back in his pocket. "We're almost to my place. Then we can talk. I need answers." He smoothed back a cowlick in his hair.

"I don't have any to give you." She crossed her arms.

Wyatt glanced at the driver. He might give the impression his English wasn't so great, but who knew if that was the truth? "We'll see about that."

His hand came into contact with the bullet hole in the seat cushion to his right. It had come within inches of striking him. If those men had wanted Selena dead, they could easily have continued pumping bullets into the taxi as it drove away. But he'd seen the taller man stop the stocky one from firing more than a single shot. Whoever was interested in Selena wanted her alive and talking. She must know something or these men wouldn't have come after her. And the money must've been good for Antonia to risk discovery right in the middle of the embassy.

The taxi drove west of downtown. Block after block. Farther and farther away from the center of the city.

"Where are we going?" Selena had stayed quiet for most of the trip so far.

"Not much further."

A phone rang.

Selena took an old flip-style phone out of her purse. Her eyebrows came together in confusion. "Nobody has my number. I picked up this phone the other day." She showed him the small screen with the number displayed. "Do you recognize it?"

The embassy.

"Answer it." He had a feeling it would be Antonia. Maybe they could get more information from her. Find out what was going on.

"I'm not going to do that." Spots of color entered her cheeks. "Someone shot at me."

"They were shooting at me."

"Why would they do that? You told me they were after me. That they'd seen my paperwork. Now you're telling me the bullet was for you?"

"Yes, Selena." He dug the bullet out of the cushion. "See this? They barely missed me before I got us into this taxi. If they wanted to kill you, they could've done it."

"Hey, don't get pissed at me." She frowned. "I never asked for your help."

"Well, you're the one that pulled me into the cab." Wyatt pointed out.

She let out a heavy sigh. "I suppose I did."

"Here's my apartment. You're going to tell me everything you know. Got it?"

Selena looked out the window at the unimpressive mustard yellow building. She said nothing.

Wyatt paid the driver and handed him an extra thousand pesos for the damage to the seat. The driver thanked him profusely, which made Wyatt wonder how rare it was to have a gun fired at a taxi in Mexico City.

❦

THE DRIVER OPENED HER DOOR. SELENA'S PALMS GREW sweaty. She had a fleeting thought about running away. She'd been athletic in high school, even if she was too short to compete in most sports. For five feet tall, she could pour on the speed when she wanted. Wearing a pencil skirt might slow her down, but she could hike it up her thighs, kick off her flats and tear down the sidewalk at a quick clip.

She took in the location around her. Three- and four-story apartment buildings up and down the block. An empty lot a couple doors down with mangled rebar and gravel piled high, trash scattered about. Cars zipped by and ignored the speed limit, which made her wonder what kinds of infractions the cops would investigate. Maybe none?

"We'll figure this out, Selena." Wyatt handed her a bottle of water that had fallen out of her oversized bag.

Wyatt's words stopped her. She took the water. If she did take off running, where would she go? She didn't really have a destination in mind beyond her cramped and dingy motel room. She'd be alone again to figure things out, and this time, she was clearly in a different kind of trouble. Would it be so terrible to use the man until she didn't need him anymore? He seemed eager to help and harmless enough.

She met his gaze. His clear blue eyes didn't hide anything. But she'd been fooled by her own mother, so maybe her judgment wasn't the best.

She uncapped her water bottle and took a few sips to wet her parched throat. "What do you know about getting a visa?"

Yes, he might be useful to her.

SELENA WAITED PATIENTLY WHILE WYATT ATTEMPTED TO unlock the door to his apartment. His hands trembled. Maybe too much adrenaline running through his system.

"So, who is this Antonia?" she asked.

"A coworker." He sighed and tried again.

Selena took the key from him, stuck it in the lock and turned. Although she'd experienced the same scare Wyatt had, for some reason, she'd recovered a lot more quickly. Wyatt seemed big and strong. She wasn't quite sure what to make of it.

Wyatt flipped a switch, and a single bare bulb lit up the living room. A few rag rugs covered the cement floor. He rushed to the window that looked out over the street and pulled the threadbare curtains closed. "They do that on TV, so I thought…" He shrugged and looked a bit sheepish.

"Do we call someone? Tell the police?" She perched on the edge of a worn padded chair.

The room seemed too orderly and neat for a single man in his twenties. Books were stacked in a perfect pile on the coffee table. Not a stray glass, plate or pizza box to be seen. She couldn't even detect a spot of dust.

Wyatt answered with a serious tone, "The police aren't your friends here."

The news reports always made Mexico's situation seem so dire with record numbers of migrants trying to cross the border into the US and drug cartels holding whole towns hostage while killing reporters and citizens alike.

"Oh." The idea of the police not being able to help shocked her.

"We are completely on our own. That's why it would really help if you'd tell me more about why you came to the embassy in the first place." Wyatt headed to the small, neat kitchen that took up one corner of the square room and filled a teapot with bottled water from the fridge. "You said tea, right?"

Selena was impressed he'd remembered. Observant. "Yes." His request for more information made her stomach turn in knots. "I wanted to go back home. That was all."

"And where's that?" He set the full teapot on the small stove and lit the burner.

"Tucson."

He nodded. "Did you lose your passport?"

"No." She sighed heavily and crossed her arms.

While the water heated, he leaned against the counter and twisted his lips. "Look, I'm trying to help." He caught sight of his shirt cuff. A brown stain marred the crisp fabric. He frowned. "Can you keep an eye on the water? I'd like to change."

Selena shrugged. The stain was barely visible from where she sat. He must be a bit fastidious.

Wyatt disappeared into the attached bedroom and left the door open. "I'd like to find out why someone is interested in sending two scary dudes with guns after you. And unless you can cough up some info, it's going to be awfully hard for me to guess."

"I need a visa, okay?" she snapped. "A visa to get back into the US legally."

Wyatt had removed the stained shirt, revealing a well-developed chest. He paused with a fresh shirt in his hand, his eyebrows raised.

She beat him to the punch. "I know, I know, I need to go to a consulate." Her face heated in embarrassment. She didn't enjoy admitting her ignorance.

He buttoned up his clean shirt without a word and tucked it into his khaki pants.

"So that lady, Antonia, gave me a list of consulates." Selena unfolded the paper. "Told me I should go north to one near the border."

Wyatt crossed the room and took the list. "Did you hand her your documents before or after you asked about the visa?" As he looked it over, he fixed the buttons on his cuffs.

Selena wrinkled her brow. "Before, I think." She replayed the scene in her mind. She had approached the counter, pushed her pile of papers at Antonia and told her story in a rush.

"Well, I guess it doesn't matter. I saw her looking at your

birth certificate and heard a bit of her phone call. Someone knew about you."

"But who would know I was coming to the embassy? Who even knew I was in Mexico?" Her mind raced, searching for answers. "That doesn't make any sense. I'm nobody."

"Well, to Antonia you were somebody. And you were somebody she felt worth risking her job over. Must've been a pretty good pay off."

Selena contemplated that idea.

"Let me see your documents." Wyatt set the list on the coffee table. "She was interested in Claudia, not Selena. Let's find out why."

From the sheaf of papers she'd brought into the embassy, she found her Mexican birth certificate. "Here."

"Claudia Garcia Rios," he read. "You were born in Quintana Roo. And you're an Aries...interesting." He smiled.

"So?" Selena didn't put much stock in astrological signs.

"Maybe you should look it up some time." He returned his gaze to the document. His face paled. "Your father is Felix Rios?"

"My father is dead." Selena watched as Wyatt paced the small living room.

"Are you so sure about that?" Wyatt said sharply. "If Antonia was willing to rat you out...."

Selena brought them back to the facts. "Yes, he is. My mother told me the whole story. He died in a car wreck when I was a baby."

"Didn't she also tell you your name was Selena Hernandez?"

"Yes, but..." Her mother wouldn't have lied to her about her own father, would she? Sure, Maria Hernandez had lied to Selena about her true identity so they could remain in the States all these years, but would she have made up a story about her father being dead, if he were really alive all this time? Doubt set in. The nervous energy coming off Wyatt in waves cranked up her own anxiety.

"I've got to pack. Antonia knows where I live." He went into the bedroom. A man on a mission. It was almost as if she weren't even there.

"Who's Felix Rios?" Selena followed him.

Wyatt had a backpack on his perfectly made bed. He carefully laid shirts, socks, and boxers inside. "Don't you watch the news?"

Selena froze. She didn't know what was happening. Why had Wyatt completely freaked out on her? "Tell me. Who is he?"

He took a break from packing. "Felix Rios is one of the worst drug kingpins in Mexico. They call him *El Señor de los Mares*—Lord of the Seas." He ducked into the bathroom and swept a host of toiletries into the open backpack. "He's known for smuggling drugs out of Mexico through the Gulf to the Caribbean, Florida, you name it." He picked up a newspaper sitting on his nightstand. "Here. It makes for good reading. The details will keep you up at night."

Selena took the paper—a Mexican daily newspaper in English—and scanned the headlines. "Quintana Roo Cartel Blazes a Bloody Trail in Its Rise to Power."

She glanced up at him with round eyes.

"Read it," Wyatt encouraged.

Selena focused on the words. "'Before they allegedly tried to assassinate Mérida's police chief, the foot soldiers of Quintana Roo's most powerful drug cartel already had left a bloody wake across the region. Felix Rios and his cartel have killed judges, congressmen, dozens of police officers and thousands of civilians. *El Señor de los Mares* controls the movement of more than a third of all drugs consumed in the southeastern United States, US officials say, and has expanded into the Caribbean.'" The story was accompanied with a shocking picture, thankfully in black and white, of headless bodies lined up on a jungle road.

Selena shivered. A blurry inset photo was labeled as, "The Elusive Rios."

Selena's heart beat sluggishly.

"No." She shook her head. "That can't be true. He can't be my father."

"His age is the right age. His name is the right name. And, besides, does it matter if he's not? Antonia thinks he is. That has to be why those men came after you."

It was as if the floor had dropped away. Her mind went numb.

He was right. It didn't matter whether or not her father was the drug cartel leader. The pieces had been set in motion on the game board, and she'd have to play out the game. Selena set down the newspaper. "What should I do?"

‍❊ 4 ❊

Wyatt felt disconnected from his body. He folded clothes and packed them in his bag, but his mind drifted elsewhere, floating somewhere between fear and panic. The situation had spun completely out of his control, and it made him sick to his stomach. He did not like that feeling. He liked orderly, structured routine. It didn't matter if he'd gotten himself into this. There was no way out of it now. He was inextricably tied to Selena and her possibly dangerous background. All because he thought she was pretty and needed his help.

"Stupid," he muttered under his breath.

"What?" Selena, unfortunately, had heard him. "I didn't ask for you to get involved. You threw yourself into everything. When I wanted to go to my motel, you brought me here. If anyone's stupid, it's you for butting into my life." She stormed out.

He didn't blame her. He finished packing, making sure to tuck his passport in his back pocket, zipped up his backpack and carried it into the living room.

Selena had vanished.

"Dammit."

The door to the hall stood wide open. She'd bolted.

He ran after her and slammed the door behind him. "Selena, wait!"

He couldn't let her out of his sight. His safety was linked to hers. Eyes and ears all over this city worked for Rios. A drug lord didn't remain in that position for over a decade without help. Lots of help.

Footsteps clattered in the stairwell. She might've gotten the jump on him, but his legs were a lot longer than hers. He took the stairs two at a time and bounded down to the first floor. He caught up to her at the bottom and grabbed her elbow. She fell backward at the force and smacked into him, sending them both to the tile floor.

She wriggled in his lap. "Let go of me." She wrenched away and scooted to the opposite wall. "Who do you think you are? You have no right to stop me from leaving."

Her eyes were wild and unfocused. She looked as if she wanted to wring his neck.

"I'm not stupid." With trembling hands, she twisted her long black hair into a knot on top of her head and then let it cascade back down. A nervous tic perhaps.

"I know." He took a few deep breaths. "I wasn't talking to you. I was talking to myself." He outstretched a hand. "Are we good?"

She looked up at him, paused for a few seconds, nodded, and accepted his help. "What now?"

"Where are you staying?"

"The *Motel Real del Sur* on Simon Bolivar."

"We'll need to get your stuff. Then maybe get you to the bus station." He hadn't really thought much beyond getting as far away from his apartment as possible, but when she'd turned to him for ideas, he felt compelled to build a plan of some kind.

"Antonia suggested the bus. That I go back north."

"Well, if she wanted you to go north, you should go south." Wyatt ran through the options. Puebla, Oaxaca, Veracruz. He quickly calculated the time it would take to get to each destination. The farther away, the better.

"Do you think it's dangerous to go to my room?" Selena interrupted his thinking. "I really don't have much there. I thought I'd only be in Mexico for a few days."

Wyatt marveled at her lack of knowledge about the visa process. Didn't sound like she'd had a particularly good attorney working for her. "It'd probably be better if we could go somewhere public, with a lot of people, figure out our next steps."

Wyatt's phone rang.

An unidentified number. He hesitated to answer. But they needed as much information as possible. What did they know about Selena? About him? What were their plans? "Hello?"

Selena's eyes grew wide.

"Lose the girlfriend or next time we won't miss," someone said in thickly accented English.

Click.

Wyatt's insides coiled up in a tight ball.

"Who is it?"

That uneasy feeling came back to him. "We've gotta get moving."

"My motel..."

Wyatt knew they had to leave his building now. Whoever had given his phone number to the cartel had probably also given them his address. He pulled the SIM card out of his phone and tossed both into the stairwell. "Come on."

Selena hesitated. She stared at his non-functioning phone. "What did he say?" Selena sounded more compliant, but also more fearful.

Wyatt held open the door to the lobby. Someone could be waiting outside. He scanned the sidewalk, the neighboring buildings. A dark vehicle was parked across the street. Too nice a vehicle for this part of town. His stomach roiled. "See that?"

Selena focused on the same car. "You think…?"

Two men exited the car—one tall and thin with slicked back hair and one short and stocky with a black blazer and a white T-shirt.

Time slowed down. "Shit." Wyatt didn't have time for her to dither about whether or not they were in danger. "Follow me." He led her to the back entrance, which opened into the alley full of trash and dog feces.

"Your stuff—you were packing…" Selena said weakly.

"Forget it." His scalp prickled. They needed to move.

Selena grabbed his hand. He liked the feel of it in his. Not so alone. Not so crazy if this beautiful woman trusted him with her life.

"Get me out of here," she said.

"I got this," Wyatt said with a confidence he didn't really feel, but something about Selena made him want to be the hero. A feeling he'd never had in his whole life, and he didn't want to let it go.

THE TWO OF THEM RAN THROUGH THE ALLEYS UNTIL WYATT brought them out to a main thoroughfare. He scanned the street in either direction. What did a cartel person look like? She wouldn't be able to tell. In fact, she could barely remember the two men who'd ambushed them. If she hadn't picked up on Antonia's dark intent for her at the embassy, what made her think she could pick out a bad guy from a street full of average Mexicans?

"I should've worn a different skirt." Red. What a dummy. Red could be seen from a mile away. It was as if she dressed this morning in a target.

"Come on," Wyatt urged. "This way." He led them to a covered area a half block down the street.

"No taxi?"

"I don't think we can trust anyone right now." Wyatt queued up in a long line in front of a green ATM-like machine. "We can take the Metro somewhere safe. More anonymous." He put his bank card in the slot, punched a few buttons, and the machine spat out a plastic card.

If she'd been on her own, she never would've thought of this or known how to buy tickets. Her decision to stick with Wyatt might have paid off. Even if she didn't quite know how much she could trust him. "Thanks."

"Come on." He waved the white card at her. "We can both use this one."

They exited the covered ticketing area and headed toward stairs that took them down to the Metro station below ground.

When they could no longer see the street, a bit of calmness settled in her. Somehow being visible in broad daylight was unnerving.

Below ground, they followed a surprisingly clean passageway to the orange line station platform. The crowds were light. But according to Wyatt, they were just shy of the major commuting time after work. An explosion of people could appear at any time.

"Where should we go?" she asked.

"I'm not sure yet, but the sooner we can get you out of Mexico City, the better, I think."

"Mmm." Selena really didn't know what else to say. She didn't want to think too far ahead. Right now it was about leaving those scary cartel dudes far behind. She still had a hard time believing she'd been shot at earlier. It all felt like a really bad dream.

"Hold up a minute." Wyatt stopped at a kiosk selling chargers and cell phones. He grabbed a cheap smart phone off a rack, handed the vendor some pesos, and then cracked open the plastic wrapping. He turned the phone on, captured a signal, and then shoved it in his pocket.

Before she could say anything, he looked up the track. "Come on. There's a train coming. I can hear it."

A Metro train approached. One of the older, orange models: square, utilitarian, dirty with city grime. The brakes squealed and squeaked, drowning out any conversation. Warm air rushed from the tunnel and brought with it the stench of oil and dust.

Selena was tempted to part ways. He didn't need this mess in his life. She could handle the situation by herself. No problem.

The Metro train doors slid open. She had to decide—take her chances alone and perhaps face the two men who'd shot at them or trust a complete stranger.

"Where to?" she yelled over the din.

❧

WYATT POINTED AT THE METRO MAP ON THE WALL OF THE train. "Tacubaya. Then we connect with the pink line to Insurgentes. La Zona Rosa. Loads of Americans there. We'll blend in." As he formed a coherent plan, the stress that weighed him down earlier disappeared.

In Mexico City, La Zona Rosa was the one place a foreigner could go where he wouldn't be noticed, tracked, remembered. A *discoteca*. Loud music. Crowds of people. Lots of drinking.

Wyatt had expertise with drunks. How they'd react. What they'd remember. He'd seen it up close and personal many times from a young age. By the time he'd made it to adulthood, he knew better than to rely on a drunk for anything. They couldn't be trusted in times of crisis. In fact, they'd force a kid to handle all of the difficulties of life without any support because they could barely keep their own shit together.

Wyatt remembered.

If he and Selena slipped into one of these clubs, they could blend in. In La Zona Rosa, foreigners were expected. They wouldn't stand out as much as they did on the neighborhood streets. They'd be Americans with a lot of money to spend. Selena would attract a certain amount of attention solely due to her beauty, but since she wasn't dressed for the club, flashier girls would distract.

They could wade through endless discos with dark lighting, hidden booth seating and stumbling fools who couldn't tell if their own shoes were tied after a few shots of tequila.

Hunkering down for a few hours in plain sight might be the best play.

The club pulsated with music. The rap tune in Spanish matched the rhythm of Selena's heartbeat...quick, too quick. Someone had wanted to kidnap her off the streets of Mexico City. It pinballed in her mind. She was nobody. She had nothing. Why her?

She and Wyatt had spent a couple of hours in a crowded restaurant a few blocks away mostly in silence. Slowly, they'd eaten appetizer after appetizer and ordered sodas and bottled water until the waiter dropped off the check before they'd even asked. The hint given, they needed to find a new place to hide out. Wyatt suggested a popular discotheque within walking distance. Pricey, but loud and crowded. Harder to be seen, followed, watched.

People parted around them as they passed through the crowd to reach an empty table near the railing along the dance floor. The music suffocated her in its loudness. The flashing, colored strobes confused her. She wished she were in her apartment in Tucson with her mother. She ached for what her life had been. The simplicity of it. At least up until her mother had been arrested and charged with ID theft and being in the country illegally.

Someone grabbed her arm, spun her into the crowd. A short, dark young man. "*Bailamos?*" He smiled, crooked teeth, full lips, black eyes.

Selena blinked rapidly.

"I don't think so, buddy." Wyatt curved an arm across her shoulders and led her away. "*Mi novia. Mi novia.*"

The man put his hands up in surrender and turned to another woman in the crowd.

"Um, thanks." Selena didn't know what the stranger had asked her, but felt compelled to be polite for Wyatt's intervention.

How long would his help last before she'd be on her own again? Even if Wyatt's interest in her was more about good old fashioned sexual attraction than anything else, she didn't care. Having to do everything on her own since she'd told the authorities she'd leave the United States had been tiring, defeating, lonely.

They arrived at the empty table, which was littered with empty plastic cups and cocktail napkins.

Selena stacked the cups and moved them out of the way. She frowned at the wet puddles on the table surface.

Wyatt took a napkin and wiped everything clean.

She flagged down a server making the rounds through the crowded seating area. "Excuse me, *por favor.*" She looked at Wyatt. "You want anything?"

"No." He pressed his lips together.

Selena gave the server her order, a margarita.

Wyatt set aside the damp napkin and grimaced.

She noted his expression. "What's your problem?"

"I don't drink." His jaw tightened.

"Okay." Selena drummed her fingers on the cleaned table

surface. "So what? Why does that mean you get to sit there and judge my order?"

"I didn't." Wyatt shrugged.

"You did. I saw it." Her mouth fell open. "That look. As if ordering a margarita was the worst thing I could do."

"I just think we need to be aware of our surroundings, on guard," Wyatt said, his tone sharp.

"One margarita isn't going to incapacitate me." She folded her arms against her chest. "I'm not a lightweight."

Wyatt scanned her body and raised an eyebrow. Then his mouth set in a line.

She focused her gaze on the clubgoers under the lights. "You stay here and sulk. If I'm going to be stuck here all night, I might as well have some fun."

Selena, without much thought, blended into the crush of people before Wyatt could object.

The music shifted to a new song. Something in English. A mash up of a classic 80s song with a modern drum beat.

As if on cue, a man approached her. Fit, tall, handsome, scruffy dark beard. "*Bailamos?*"

This time she understood it was an invitation to dance.

Why not?

She glanced toward their table. Too many people crowded around it to see Wyatt. Besides, she needed a distraction, a fun time, a bit of joy in an otherwise terrible, awful day. She shrugged and said to the stranger, "Sure."

He took her hand and pulled her into the center of the mass of dancing, writhing bodies.

"What's your name?" her dance partner asked in accented English.

"Selena." She smiled. She wanted to forget why she was in Mexico and the fear that had followed her all afternoon.

Her belief that if she self-deported her mother's past mistakes would be erased had been naive. Although discovering

Mexico had been her birth nation, it was a country and a language she didn't remember and felt no affinity for. She'd never even visited. The idea she might be trapped here for more than a couple of weeks spiked her adrenaline.

Stop it, Selena.

Stop freaking out.

"*Me llamo Carlos.*" Her partner's eyes glittered in the dim light.

Her heart pounded in her chest.

His arm slid from her waist to her ass. Before she could protest, he spun them both across the dance floor. The music rained down on them in an intense rhythm. The beat swallowed them up.

Selena stepped away from her partner in time to the music. She lifted her hands and twirled. She banished her fears. She was sick to death of worrying. Instead, she imagined herself back in Tucson. A night out on the town with her friends. Men buying her drinks. Dancing with whoever she chose. Having fun.

Her partner grabbed her by the waist again, and they swayed together. He breathed in her ear. The closeness felt good, comforting. She let him envelop her with his presence, not caring what promises this man felt she was making.

The song ended, and the music shifted to something new, something slower.

Carlos stepped closer.

Her partner was attractive enough. Although he wasn't much taller than she, his arms were ropes of muscle, and he had a winning smile that glowed under the black lights of the dance floor.

As she fell into the more seductive rhythm, she spied Wyatt sitting at their table with her massive margarita, scanning the crowd with a worried look on his face. She wondered for a moment about the cover charge he'd paid to get them both inside, plus the cost of the drink. Not cheap in La Zona Rosa. One more thing she owed this stranger.

She let Carlos move them through the crowd of dancers. She leaned into her partner and secretly wished Wyatt would see her hands all over the attractive stranger.

Would serve him right.

"*Eres muy bonita*," Carlos whispered in her ear.

She didn't know what that meant, but didn't really care.

She looked away.

Wyatt's gaze caught hers.

He scowled.

The song ended.

Selena smiled to herself, glad she had irritated him.

She let go of her dance partner. "*Gracias.*" She turned away from Carlos and pushed through the throngs of people to return to their table.

"Here." Wyatt slid her drink toward her. "More ice than drink." He surveyed the dance floor. "Having a good time?" His voice was laced with sarcasm, and he kept one eye on Carlos, who selected another willing dance partner from the crowd.

She slinked past, leaned forward, and planted a kiss on his cheek. "Jealous?"

Wyatt drew back in surprise and rubbed at the spot. "What the hell?"

She touched his knee under the table. "If you wanted to dance with me, why didn't you just ask?" She squeezed it. "Too shy?" For some reason, she loved making him squirm.

"The only reason I'm here is to keep us alive," Wyatt said with a growl. "I don't know what gave you the idea I was interested in something more than that."

She narrowed her eyes and stared into his baby blues. "Is that right?" Under the table she drew her hand away, but not without a lingering slide up his pant leg. She knew desire when she saw it, but maybe Wyatt was more uptight than she'd thought. "Look, you don't have to hang out with me. I'll be fine here by myself." If she wanted to dance, she was going to dance. This jealousy thing was stupid.

He fixed his gaze on her. "You think this is just about you? Antonia knows me, knows where I live, knows a heck of a lot more about me than she does about you."

Selena paused. "What?"

"What I overheard back at the embassy tells me she's dirty." Wyatt's words were filled with intensity. The silly cheek kiss barely a blip on his radar. "She recognized your name. Someone is interested in Claudia Rios—maybe a rival drug cartel trying to get at Rios, maybe somebody else. And now I'm involved, and my name is connected to *you*. I'm not about to let you wander off before I find out what the deal is."

Selena blanked. "I can't believe this." Her gut clenched at the very idea. The story in the newspaper at Wyatt's apartment about the violence in Quintana Roo came back to her. "They must've made a mistake. They must be looking for a different Claudia. Not me. I'm not even from Mexico!"

"Yes, you are. I saw your birth certificate. Mexican. Not American."

"What I meant was…I lived my whole life in Arizona. I don't care what a birth certificate says. I came here because I wanted to do the right thing—get an immigration visa and return legally." Although she didn't want it to happen, she felt the tears welling up. In her heart she was one-hundred percent American. "No stupid piece of paper is going to dictate who I am. Shove it up your ass."

Selena kicked at the stool and left the table. She headed straight for the bathrooms at the back of the club. Wyatt, despite his attractive exterior, was like all the rest of them. Prejudice bastards. Making her life harder than it needed to be. Why couldn't anyone look at her and see she was American through and through? It wasn't her fault her mother brought her to the

United States illegally. Wyatt had no clue. No heart. No respect for anything she'd been through. Why did she think he could help her?

"Selena!" Wyatt called after her.

She barely heard him above the din, and she didn't care anyway. She pushed on the door of the women's restroom. A horde of young women gobbled up the space in front of the floor-length mirror, brushing on mascara, teasing hair, checking out panty lines. She barreled past them into the only empty stall and locked it behind her. Wet toilet paper dotted the floor. The smell wasn't too pleasant either.

She leaned against the wall and thought it through. What was her next move? The embassy had been an epic fail. She'd been so dumb to believe she'd demand a visa and get one. The shame of her ignorance blocked out any other thought. What an idiot she was. How stupid. The lawyer had lied to her. The government had lied to her, too. They'd encouraged her to go back. Made it seem like a simple process.

A knock on the stall door interrupted her thoughts. *"Excúlpame. Por favor?"*

Selena wiped the tears from her face, slid the lock open, bolted past the girl who wanted to use the restroom, and ran right into the hard chest of Wyatt.

He grabbed her wrists. "Hey, don't run off like that again, you hear me?" Wyatt's eyebrows drew together. "You got me into this mess, and I'm not letting you out of my sight again until we figure out what's going on. Not sure about you, but I really don't want to end up dead in an alley somewhere."

Selena's heart raced. The panic she'd felt on the street when she'd seen the man with the gun returned full force. Her mind blanked. She'd hit a wall. No idea what to do. Where to go. Who to trust.

Wyatt must have recognized the fear, the panic. His gaze softened. He pulled her close and kissed her. A tender, sweet kiss that took over her mind and blanked out all other thoughts.

She slid her hands up his chest and leaned into his solid warmth. A few minutes ago, she'd wanted to punch him. Strange how a kiss could change everything.

They broke apart. People swirled around them. Selena couldn't read the look in Wyatt's eyes.

"Where are you staying again?" he asked.

"Th-the *Motel Real del Sur*. On Simon Bolivar." She wanted more from him than a kiss. Maybe he did, too. Her body flushed with warmth.

"Okay. That's not far." He squeezed her hand. "Let's go back to your place, figure this out."

Selena's heart dropped a little. Although a clear attraction existed between the two of them, Wyatt's thoughts didn't go beyond the kiss. She tried to hide her disappointment. She was grateful he wanted to help her make a clear plan. Fear had impacted her higher thinking processes. She didn't see herself as the kind of person who froze when in an extreme circumstance, but she'd never had her life threatened before by a gun-wielding lunatic. "Yes."

She let Wyatt take her by the hand and lead her to an exit at the back of the club. It opened into a filthy alley full of trash and smelling of urine. The music pounded behind them. The door shut automatically, and the noise disappeared. Selena stood in the alley with only the traffic noise. Her ears rang.

The sound of a lighter snapping caught their attention. Two people hovered in the dark of the alley. Someone lit a cigarette. The glow lit up the face of a pock-marked young man and his date, a thin woman in a skintight gold jumpsuit. Both paused and faced them. Hard stares.

Selena's leg muscles tightened. She was ready to run.

Wyatt grabbed her by the elbow and yanked her toward the street. He hailed a cab, and a beat-up Ford Focus pulled up to the curb. She climbed in, and Wyatt slid in next to her, his thigh hot against hers.

The couple from the alley stepped out of the dark. The woman in the jumpsuit took a long drag on her cigarette. The man put his hands in his pockets and scanned their taxi.

Selena's heartbeat raced.

Wyatt gave the driver the address for a restaurant several blocks away from her motel. Before she could open her mouth to correct him, Wyatt squeezed her hand. She slid a glance at him. He gave her hard stare.

Trust me, he seemed to be saying.

She closed her mouth.

Clearly, Wyatt didn't even trust the cab drivers. In a city as big as Mexico City, you'd think there'd be plenty of anonymity, but Selena was beginning to realize that the bad guys had eyes and ears everywhere.

As they drove away from the strange couple outside the club, Selena's fears diminished. She touched her lips, Wyatt's kiss still wet on her mouth.

❄   6   ❄

Wyatt sat in the cab next to Selena. Without thinking, he touched his lips and rubbed at the lipstick she'd left behind. That had not been in the plan.

Encounters with women were planned and relationships avoided because of the negative results he'd had in the past. He preferred control in order to stay focused and hold back his demons. Things never went well when he revealed his true self.

Selena had completely undone that.

When she'd come running out of the bathroom into his arms with fear and hopelessness so clear on her face, he had an overwhelming urge to kiss her. Her lips had been soft under his, and slightly boozy from the margarita.

Alcohol brought people nothing but trouble.

So he'd shut it down. Taking an emotional detour would cloud their judgment and alter their reactions. He took a step back and redirected into problem-solving mode. He didn't want to confuse her—or himself—with other feelings. The bad guys could be around the next corner, in a car tailing them, ready to pounce when they least expected it.

After he'd broken off the kiss, she'd tilted her chin down and frowned. At least, he thought he'd seen that before her features had gone neutral. She had to be over it, too. A mistake.

The taxi pulled up to a closed restaurant. A lit-up sign in the window read: *Cerrado*—closed. Wyatt paid the driver, and they exited onto the sidewalk. The streets were empty.

A block distant Wyatt could make out a faded, crumbling cinderblock building with a lighted sign that read: Motel Real Del Sur.

"That's your motel?" Wyatt asked.

They'd driven past blocks of trash-strewn streets lined with rundown two-story buildings. Electrical wires crisscrossed and sagged in a haphazard fashion. Although streetlights were visible, most were burned out.

Selena nodded. "I'm in room 323." She held a key card.

As they closed the distance between the restaurant and her motel, Wyatt found himself scanning the area for people—anyone who might be watching. They passed by an alley, and he made sure to step between Selena and the dumpster that blocked his view. Just in case someone hid behind it.

Light glowed beyond the glass doors of the motel. A place of safety in his mind. At least they'd be off the streets until they made a more definitive plan.

As they entered the lobby, their footsteps clicked loudly on the chipped tile floor. Dim yellow lights created a cave-like feel. A Hispanic couple, both short, rotund, older, sat in two faded chairs and avidly watched the news on a large television with a crack in it.

Although Wyatt understood and spoke Spanish at a certain level, the pace of the news anchor was well beyond his capabilities. However, the video the anchor introduced cleared up any confusion.

A white Toyota truck drove through the streets of Culiacán with a huge Barrett .50 caliber rifle mounted on a tripod in the back. A man wearing a bulletproof vest over a green T-shirt and with a bandanna over his face shot at a group of police officers and parked vehicles. Then, the screen filled with photos of three notorious cartel leaders in the northern part of the country. Across the bottom of the screen, the chyron read: *El cartel de Sinaloa mantiene su gigantesco poder.*

The Sinaloa Cartel maintains its gigantic power.

The video changed again with a shot of the Mexican army dressed in camouflage and armed to the teeth. They raced toward a fire in the middle of a busy street. People fled in all directions.

Stacks of money. Bricks of cocaine. Blurred out dead bodies lined up next to a pit.

Wyatt did catch one phrase used to describe the cartel's ability to strike fear into small communities: *ejército de sicarios.* An army of assassins.

He was reminded the risk he'd taken by befriending Selena. Although most of Mexico appeared peaceful, danger lurked around every corner. The federal government had a tenuous hold on the country, and many suspected everyone in higher office had been bribed to look the other way.

Selena stood next to him, stock still, her eyes wide as she took in the video. "Are they talking about drug dealers?" she asked quietly.

Wyatt didn't want her to know how the news had shaken the little bit of confidence he had. But he couldn't lie to her either. "Yes, the cartels up north."

She nodded.

"Let's go." He nodded toward the elevators with a new sense of purpose.

The elderly pair watched as they passed by.

When Selena was within range, the older woman grabbed Selena's hand. *"Buenas noches."*

Selena drew back. "Excuse me?" She glanced at Wyatt and bit her lip.

The woman scanned her figure, taking in every detail.

"Wyatt?" Selena frowned.

He wrinkled his brow and stepped between her and the couple. "*Déjala*." He loomed over them. "*Ahorita*."

The old woman let go of Selena's hand. She touched her throat.

Selena backed away.

Wyatt had perceived the discoteque as safe, so going to her motel now seemed like a bad idea. Was this an innocent move on the part of an elderly couple? Or something more?

"Come on," Wyatt urged. He touched Selena's lower back to move her along. The heat of her skin through the fabric of her blouse caught him off guard.

He checked over his shoulder. The couple remained seated, but never once took their eyes off Selena. A sour taste settled on his tongue.

SELENA'S ROOM WAS BLAND, DANK AND OUT-OF-DATE. EVEN with the lights snapped on, it was depressing and dim. She made a beeline for a ridiculous hot pink roller bag with a rainbow across it next to the bathroom.

Wyatt chuckled.

Embarrassed, she explained, "My mom bought this for me when I was twelve."

"I see." Wyatt offered a bemused smile. "At least it's easy to recognize on the baggage carousel."

Selena let out a huff, unzipped the suitcase, and rifled through an inner pocket.

Wyatt sat on one of the queen-sized beds. Tension eased out of him as he sank into the soft mattress. Ever since they'd been shot at, he'd made dumb choices based on fear. No more. "All right. What's our next move?"

Selena knelt on the floor next to her bag, a small pile of photos in her lap. She studied them with a slight smile.

Wyatt let out a sigh. "Hey, are you with me?" He snapped his fingers. "We've got to make a plan." The strangeness of the encounter in the lobby had set off alarm bells.

Selena looked up at him, unshed tears in her eyes.

Uh-oh.

He wasn't good with emotional stuff. His stomach tightened at the thought he might have to comfort her.

"I'm sorry." She sniffed and set the pictures on the desk. "This whole situation is so screwed up. It's not turning out like I thought. God, I feel so stupid." She rubbed her nose.

Wyatt sat frozen on the bed. What should he do? Say something? Go over there and give her a hug? No, that seemed creepy.

"And now I've dragged you into this...this...mess. Why can't someone just give me a straight answer? Is something wrong with me? Do I have a sign on my head that says, *pariah*? The lawyer was full of crap. The police were full of crap. That stupid woman at the embassy lied to me." The tears flowed.

Wyatt wracked his brain for the right response. The correct, normal response. Not the irrational response his mind threw out. "People suck."

There. That should work. Sympathy of some kind. A stating of the obvious. She couldn't get mad at him for that, could she?

She smiled, then snickered. "Yeah. They do." Selena stood and grabbed a tissue from a box on the dresser.

Wyatt mentally patted himself on the back for not saying something royally dumb.

Selena blew her nose a few times. Then, she sat on the bed opposite him, their knees inches apart. "I really never intended to drag you into this." She crossed her ankles, leaned back on her hands and bit her lip in a thoughtful pose. "I'm not sure why it got so messy. I thought I was doing everything right."

Wyatt thought about what he knew so far. The two names, the birth certificate, the scary dudes at the taxi, the threatening phone call. "You've grabbed the attention of some dangerous people, that's for sure."

Worry lines appeared in Selena's forehead.

"So you can't go back to the US?"

"No." Selena chin trembled. "It's a long story. I'm stuck until I get a visa."

Wyatt wanted to avoid tears, so he didn't press her on the issue.

"Well, if you can't go back to the US, you'll have to find a way to stay in Mexico until you can."

"I was afraid you were going to say that. I don't have anywhere to stay. I don't have much money." Selena sped up her words. "And I don't know Spanish or anything about Mexico. I've lived in the US for as long as I can remember. I don't know why I can't get a visa and go back to Arizona like they told me I could."

Yikes. She'd unloaded a lot of information he hadn't really asked for. But he posed a question to stop her flood of words, "Who told you that?"

"The immigration attorney." Selena's voice sounded thick with tears. She looked up, and her big brown eyes were wet.

Wyatt braced himself. Okay, this girl might've been attractive hours ago when he'd run into her outside the embassy, but that had been an instinctual reaction to a girl with a great figure and a pretty face. And although she'd been surprisingly badass when she'd yanked him into that cab, which he did find intriguing, he hadn't signed up for the emotional baggage that came along with it. He tried convincing himself their team situation was about survival—his survival—until he figured out who Antonia had sent after them. He was merely involved because Selena held the key to that.

He did his best to ignore his softening toward her predicament and changed the subject. "Well, you've got your things. So now let's decide what we're going to do." His knees almost touched hers. A fleeting thought ran through his mind. A stupid thought. He could console her. Envelop her in a quick embrace. Feel the warmth of her body against his.

Wrong. Wrong. Wrong.

He put up a huge mental hurdle in his mind—flashing red lights and big exes on a dark road to nowhere.

The sympathetic 'friend' routine, where he took advantage of a girl's emotional state for his own pleasures wasn't his thing. It would be so easy to do, but he knew where it would lead. More crying. More personal stuff dumped on him. Well, he didn't need it. He had enough of his own baggage.

Selena snuffled. Her gaze focused downward. "I don't have anywhere to go."

He switched beds, sitting right next to her. Her thigh against his. Although he wanted to avoid an entanglement with this woman, the interesting mix of quick thinking and capable-yet-vulnerable drew him in. But he could keep this on the up-and-up. Yes, she was beautiful. Yes, they had kissed. Yes, he was attracted to her spunk—no other woman in his life had risked herself for him like Selena had. But that didn't mean he had to follow through on anything. He had boundaries. He had self-control.

"Okay, so Antonia, she marked up some of the consulates where she thought you should go. One near the border, near Arizona where you're from, right?"

Selena nodded and rubbed the unshed tears from her eyes. Their gazes met, and she seemed to steel herself. "Nogales."

Wyatt contemplated the scenes of violence they had

witnessed moments earlier on the TV in the lobby. The border was a dangerous place for a single woman.

"Well, if she wanted you to go north, you'll go south." No way would he suggest she head right into the belly of the beast. That would be suicide. Wyatt opened up a public transportation navigation app he'd downloaded onto his new phone. "The only US Consulate south of the Mexico City is in Mérida."

She leaned in, curling her legs under her body. As she looked at the app on his phone, her breath heated his cheek.

He bit his inner lip for some control. Soft, warm body rubbing up against his? His baser nature couldn't help but react... uncomfortably. He straightened his pants leg when it became restrictive.

Lord, help him.

"Where's Mérida?"

"A long ways from here." He showed her the information displayed on the map. "Almost twenty hours on a bus." Wyatt had been impressed with the bus system in Mexico. It tended to be slow and not the most comfortable way to travel, but for short trips, he found it convenient.

"But inexpensive."

He let his phone go dark. "That's true. And I'll bet nobody would be looking for us there."

"How can you be so sure?" Selena's limpid eyes drew him in.

She, too, appeared to be thinking about the news. The dead bodies. The guns. The violence. They still had no idea who they were up against.

"I suppose I can't be one hundred percent sure." He took a deep breath and rubbed the back of his neck. Her nearness drove him to distraction. "But if these guys think you are headed north, they'll be staking out the other bus station across town." The slight panic mode he'd found himself in earlier ebbed away as their plans came together. He had something solid to depend on. Information. A decision. He could visualize the rest of the trip from here. His anxiety dropped, but his attraction for the luscious young woman cuddled up next to him grew exponentially.

"Look, you don't have to come with me. If you can take me to the bus station and point me in the right direction, I'll be fine."

Wyatt didn't like the sound of that for a number of reasons, many of which were not rational ones. "Hold on a minute. I stuck my neck out for you."

"I didn't ask you to get involved." She shrugged and leaned away. "Why can't you send me south and then go back to your life? Forget about me."

His mind raced. If he let her slip between his fingers, and she got caught... "I can't let you do that."

"Excuse me?" Selena glanced at her suitcase and then the door, giving away her plans.

She made a move as if to flee.

Wyatt grabbed her wrist.

She snapped back. "Hey." She twisted her arm.

He tightened his grip. "Don't." He stared down at her.

$$\text{❦} \quad 7 \quad \text{❦}$$

Selena struggled in Wyatt's grasp. The hair rose up on the back of her neck. This was her room, her stuff, her life, and she'd let a complete stranger step in and call all the shots. The intensity in his gaze made her worry she'd run into the wrong person to help her.

"Let me go." She tried a second time to free herself. "Do you want me to scream?" She screwed up her eyes and gave her most threatening look.

Wyatt searched her face. Then, as suddenly as he'd grabbed her, he let go. "I know you think you can do this by yourself, but I'm telling you, you can't. And, unfortunately, I can't risk letting you out of my sight until we know more about the men who came after you. You don't have to like me. We just have to work together."

Once he released her she used her suitcase as a barrier. It made her feel safer with that little bit of distance and a roller bag between them. "You want to call all the shots about where we go, what we do, when we do it. That's not how I operate. You're stifling me with your research and your apps and whatever." She gestured at his smart phone on the bed.

Wyatt ran a hand through his hair. "I only want us to make calculated decisions. Mistakes might get us both killed." He put his phone in his pocket. "Look, it's better if we're together. That way we can keep an eye out for each other. Have each other's backs."

"So why in the hell would you want to stick with me all the way to Mérida?" Selena was totally confused by his insistence on helping her. It didn't make any sense. "Why not put me on the bus, tell me what I need to know when I get to the consulate and…and…" Her mind flashed to the bullet embedded in the taxi seat. The bullet meant for Wyatt.

"And?" he asked expectantly.

Her hackles came back down. The intense feelings that had bubbled inside her suddenly deflated like a popped balloon. She huffed out a breath and fiddled with the telescoping handle on her bag. "You're right. We're in this together."

He let out a deliberate, quiet exhale. His features relaxed, which told her he was relieved, and it dawned on her he'd made her feel less alone and a lot safer since they'd been forced together. He was tall, fit, tough. He'd handled the emotional ups and downs of the day well. In fact, his rock-solid demeanor to her bespoke fearlessness. She'd never met a man quite like him before.

"Thank you for everything, really." Selena looked up at him. She bit her lip. He really was quite handsome.

His eyes crinkled at the corners. "My pleasure." He stared at her mouth.

Selena's knees went weak. The heat between them was palpable. Her mind went back to the unexpected kiss in the club. How much she'd liked it.

THEY STOOD A FOOT APART, A SUITCASE BETWEEN THEM. Selena made the first move and kicked it away with her foot. She took a tentative step toward him. Her lips parted, and her eyes glossed over, losing their intensity. Her honey skin flushed.

He captured her mouth with his. He couldn't help it. He curled his arm around her waist, drew her in close to his body. The erection he'd been trying to hide now obvious between them.

At first, she felt stiff in his arms, but then she melted against him. The kiss deepened, and he liked it. Too much.

He knew he needed to end it, to keep from going down a bad road he'd gone down before, but his baser instincts wanted this. All of the planning and processing and logic couldn't stop him. One touch of her mouth against his was enough to end all controlled action. Every worry he'd had about their situation, his history of failures, his knowledge that he would never be good enough for a creature such as Selena got buried beneath a desire so hot, so out of control, he set everything else aside for one moment of bliss.

When Wyatt had acted distant after the kiss in the club, she'd assumed he'd changed his mind about her. But now she had no doubts of his attraction to her. She felt it against her stomach.

She touched the rough scruff on his cheek. So blond, so light, she hadn't noticed it was there until she felt it for herself.

She gently thrust her tongue in his mouth.

He groaned.

He scooped her up in his arms and laid her on the bed. "This is a bad idea, isn't it?" His face inches from her, his breath hot on her cheek.

"Yes." Her skirt rode up her thighs. Her blouse came half-untucked. "It's the worst idea I've ever had."

His lips curled into a devilish smile. "So, so bad."

Her insides warmed at the passion clear on his face.

Their kissing intensified.

He rolled over on the bed and took her with him.

She laughed.

It was good to laugh. Her life had been a series of terrible events lately. One after the other. It felt good to be free. To be sexy. To be loose and wild and out of control. The rules of everything weighed her down, made her feel hopeless. But this moment in her motel room with an attractive man who'd thrown himself into her life? It felt natural, carefree, amazing. She wanted it to go on and on. She wanted it to never end, so that she didn't have to deal with the truth of what was outside the motel room. What lurked on the streets or around the corner or in the next car that drove by. She wanted to be free of worry and fear again. Wyatt was offering that to her, if only for a moment.

She straddled him, hands on his chest, her hair hanging down in a curtain around her. "Who are you, Wyatt Demko?" she whispered.

"Does it matter?" He reached for the buttons on her blouse.

"Maybe." She helped him. "So back there, at the club, why did you stop?" Her tone grew serious.

He paused with half the buttons unbuttoned. "I don't know."

A noncommittal bullshit answer if she'd ever heard one. She arched a brow. "Really?"

He settled his hands around her hips. The moment growing cool. A strange look passed over his face. "I'm not great with relationships, I guess. Screw them up every time."

"We're not in a relationship." She took off her blouse, letting it flutter to the floor. She wasn't about to let this uptight, yet seriously hot man, end things quite so quickly.

What red-blooded male would turn away from that kind of offer?

He lay there for a moment.

"You can't be serious." Selena couldn't believe it. She'd offered herself up on a plate for him, and he had to hesitate. Way to make a woman feel less than wanted. She unhooked her bra. "Maybe this will help you make up your mind."

He slid his hands up her naked torso. "Yes, I'd say that helped."

Selena let go of everything and imagined she was a thousand miles away. She fell into the rhythm of their lovemaking. No more words. Only the physical. Because if she stopped for a moment to think about her actions, to analyze her situation, her fears might end it all, and she'd have to face the truth.

She was in serious trouble.

⁂

THE PHONE STARTLED THEM BOTH. THE RED LIGHT ON ITS face flashed, and the ring would wake the dead two rooms over.

Automatically, Selena sat up in bed it to answer it. She clutched the sheets around her naked body.

"Wait," Wyatt whispered. He touched her arm.

It sent a shiver through her body. She paused. He was right.

That couldn't be good.

Instead, she changed course, grabbed her discarded clothes off the floor, and began to dress. As if they were acting on the same unspoken plan, Wyatt did the same.

The moment between them in bed had to be set aside. The fantasy had ended, and real life had punched its way back in. Everything in her mind focused on escape, running, getting away. The unknown enemy who pursued her hadn't paused for a minute. They'd found her somehow. Maybe the older couple in the lobby had been spies. Or maybe the word had gotten out on the street.

After putting on her shoes, she whipped into the bathroom and scooped all of her toiletries into a Ziplock bag.

The phone rang incessantly.

Wyatt had finished dressing and unzipped a pocket in her suitcase.

She shoved in the Ziploc. "Let's go."

Wyatt grabbed the suitcase and headed to the door.

Selena snatched up the photos and papers from the desk and shoved them in her large handbag. She scanned the room one last time and then followed him.

The phone continued to ring. Even after the door closed, Selena could hear it, echoing down the hall, chasing them.

She grabbed hold of Wyatt's hand and squeezed. He was something real to hold onto. Their kisses had been real; their bodies had been joined together. If only for that one moment, they'd been like one person. Thinking, breathing, acting as one. She drew on that to find some courage. To beat back the fear that stuck in her throat and threatened to choke her.

❧ 8 ☙

Four main bus stations existed in Mexico City. Each station serviced a different section of Mexico. Since Mérida was south of the city, they would have to buy tickets from the *Terminal Central del Norte* station.

Wyatt hoped when they fled the motel through the back exit nobody had seen them. His nerves were on edge after the mysterious phone call. Selena's motel had one good thing going for it —bad street lighting, which made for a good escape.

Wyatt held tight to Selena's hand. In the crowd of people rushing around them, he didn't want to risk losing her. Her palm was sweaty against his. Uncomfortably so. He wiped his hand against his pants and put an arm around her shoulder. Then they'd look more like a couple anyway.

Selena leaned in, as if she'd been expecting the closeness.

He wanted to say something about what happened in her motel room, but a fleeting worry passed through his mind that she'd think it had been a moment of bad judgment on her part. Better to say nothing than to put a foot in his mouth. Let her be the one to bring up the topic. Didn't women like to talk about their feelings all the time? He'd avoid it until she felt comfortable with it. Safer that way. No chance to screw it up.

Wyatt scanned the large open space that made up the ticketing area of the station. As they approached the video screen with the upcoming departure times, people's heads turned. He stood a half-a-foot above most of the crowd, and his blond hair stuck out like a llama in a pack of horses.

He spied a vendor. "Come with me."

"Don't we need to buy tickets?" Selena studied the screen intently.

"We gotta do something first." Wyatt pulled her toward the kiosk of goods.

"What?" Selena queried.

He picked out a floppy hat and a pair of sunglasses with bright blue frames and then donned them to see if it gave the right kind of coverage. "Buy a disguise." He hunched down and attempted to look at himself in the two-inch by two-inch mirror made of reflective plastic in the sunglasses stand.

"*Mil pesos, señor,*" said a squat woman with a dead stare who sat on a stool next to the kiosk. She put out her hand.

Wyatt ignored her and selected a brightly striped shawl with neon pink fringe. "Here, put this on."

Selena wrapped the serape around her head and shoulders. "How do I look?"

She'd chosen to wear a very red, form-fitting skirt and a white blouse, which meant not only did she catch the attention of every male under the age of ninety in the bus depot, but she could be seen from a mile away.

He stepped back and took in Selena's altered appearance. Less curvy, more lumpy. Also it hid her face well. "That should help." He turned to the vendor. "*Cuánto para todos?*"

"*Dos mil.*"

Selena's lips curled slightly. "Thank you."

Wyatt handed over the money for the items. "No problem." Her anonymity was paramount to his survival. Anyone could be after her. Guns weren't easy to come by in Mexico. One had to have connections—and those connections weren't good ones—criminals, drug cartels, crooked police. Even a small caliber gun had to be registered with the army and couldn't be carried on the street. He had no interest in becoming the next torture victim in the American newspapers as a testament to the dangers of Mexico.

Drug dealers and their cohorts had burned, stabbed, shot, chopped, and boiled their enemies. For now his security was dependent on her security. He put on the sunglasses, adjusted the hat and then joined the end of the ticketing line. Selena followed closely behind.

"I don't know when I'll be able to repay you for all this." Selena tucked her long hair under the shawl, but the fringe kept getting in the way. "When I go back to the States, and I can go back to work..."

"Don't worry about it." Repayment was the least of his problems.

A woman in her late forties, pudgy, with an earnest, round face and dull brown hair stood in front of them in line. "Are you American?" She smiled widely before either had a chance to answer. "We've never done this before and don't speak a lick of Spanish. Do we, James?" She elbowed the man in front of her.

Great.

The last thing they needed was a nosy stranger to butt in and ask too many questions.

A middle-aged man with a receding crew cut turned to face them. He munched down on a street taco. Embarrassed, he quickly finished chewing and held out a hand, while gripping his half-eaten taco with the other. "Oh, hey there. You guys trying to go the non-tourist route, too? Melanie wanted to see the 'real Mexico' before it grew too dangerous. You know, the news and all. Our kids didn't want us to go, but we stuck 'em with

Grandma for a couple weeks and now here we are...we finished up with the pyramids today. Have you seen them? Man, they are amazing. We really wanted to climb the Pyramid of the Sun, but my knees couldn't take it." James did a couple of squats.

Wyatt thought he looked fit enough. He didn't really want to engage with these people.

"Yes, we're from the US." Selena smiled and kept on chatting. "Just trying to get to Mérida the cheapest way possible. You know how it is...taking a gap year after college before I get a job. Trying to see as much as possible without busting the budget."

Wyatt couldn't believe it. Why in the heck would she fabricate some ridiculous story? Better for them to buy their tickets and stick to themselves. He didn't like the idea of making up something on the fly and then having to remember it. Not his style. Things should be more methodical, thought out, discussed between them. Selena's shoot-from-the-hip way of doing things might be hard to manage.

"Well, what a coincidence," said Melanie, her eyes alight with excitement. "We're headed to Cancún, so we should be on the same bus, I think." She pointed at the departures board in the distance. "Are you going first class or...?"

Before Wyatt could open his mouth, Selena rushed in to answer. "Oh, yes, first class all the way."

Wyatt didn't think Selena even knew the difference. He glanced up at the ticket prices on the screen and totaled up the costs. The tension rose in him as the conversation continued.

"Right? I mean, it's so humid down there, you need trustworthy A/C and the seats are a thousand times more comfortable," Selena's new, brunette best friend continued. "We took a cheaper bus to Acapulco, and my Lord, we'd never do that again. Would we, dear?" She prodded her balding husband with a pointy elbow.

James gave a broad smile. "Never."

Almost too broad.

"Oh, I'm so sorry, how rude of me. I'm Melanie Brewster. From Minneapolis. And my husband, James, as I mentioned earlier." Melanie's purse strap slipped off her shoulder, but she'd clutched it so tight to her side, her pudgy arm kept it in place as she stretched out her hand. "And you are...?"

Wyatt swooped in before Selena could open her mouth. "Oh, babe, that window opened." He pointed at the new ticket window where the worker had slid the sign from *cerrado* to *abierto*. "Come on, before someone else notices." He gently pushed at Selena's back to move her into the other line and away from these chatty strangers.

Selena gaped like a fish. "What? Oh." She picked up her feet and flowed with Wyatt away from the Brewsters from Minneapolis and toward the open window. "Bye, Melanie. So nice to meet you."

Wyatt kept his eyes on the path they took rather than see how Melanie accepted their somewhat rude behavior. He didn't care what the lady thought about him or the way they skedaddled out of line. They were never going to see them again, if he had any say in it.

"Was that really necessary?" Selena hissed at him as they approached the window. They'd be the first in line because of Wyatt's quick thinking.

He snatched up her hand to make sure she didn't decide to make friends with some other random stranger. "*Dos boletos a Mérida. Hay cabidas?*" He set several bills on the counter. Cash only if possible for everything from now on. He wasn't sure how sophisticated Selena's pursuers were, but he didn't want to take any chances. Cartels and criminals had bribed their way up into the police and the government. Who knew what they had access to?

"*No hay boletos.*" The bus employee had sleepy eyes and spoke in a monotone.

Damn. Sold out.

The next bus to Mérida didn't depart until six the next morning. They couldn't wait that long.

Wyatt scanned the schedule. *"Dos boletos a Puebla. La diez y media, por favor."* The 10:30 bus left in ten minutes.

Without saying a word, the employee took his cash and handed him two tickets.

❦ 9 ❦

"What was that back there?" Wyatt gave Selena a quizzical look.

They followed the signs to the correct gate to wait for boarding.

Selena tilted her head and pursed her lips. "What do you mean?"

He pulled her aside to let other passengers bypass them. "That ridiculous story you told those people," he said in a harsh whisper.

"Melanie and James?" Selena took a step back. She didn't understand why he sounded so pissed off.

"Yes, Melanie and James," he snapped. "We didn't talk about any of that." He rubbed the back of his neck.

Selena made a face. This dude was uptight. Hard to believe after what had happened in her motel room. "I didn't know we needed to." She shrugged off his criticism and continued toward the gate at a faster clip than normal.

"Of course we needed to." He trotted to keep pace with her. "If we were going to tell people some story, don't you think you should've consulted me first?"

"Chill out." Selena planted her feet and faced him. Travelers dodged the two of them as they now blocked the flow of traffic. "I mean, really, it's just a little lie. They aren't going to interrogate us about it. In fact, we are probably never going to see them again." She was beginning to get a glimpse of the deeper person inside the handsome figure—rigid and cold. Not the man she thought she'd just slept with. He'd been passionate and, well, pretty hot. Where had *that* Wyatt gone?

He frowned. "Next time we discuss it."

"Don't worry," Selena said under her breath. "There won't be a next time." She thought ahead to Puebla. A couple of hours away. Maybe at that point, she'd cut him loose. Fade into the crowd and buy her own damned ticket.

They both silently approached the gate, the heat of their argument palpable in the air.

"Hey, guys," a chipper voice called out. "We're on the same bus!" Melanie strode up to them, flapping a paper ticket.

"I thought you were going to Cancún?" Wyatt asked in a monotone.

The woman's round face shone with sweat. "We almost thought we weren't going to make it."

James joined his wife. "We didn't want to be stuck in the city for another night. No buses to Cancún until tomorrow morning. Puebla should have a connection."

A pit grew in Selena's stomach. She scanned her brain for the details she'd spat out at the ticketing area.

Melanie gushed, "Tell me more about the two of you. Dating long?"

Wyatt's lips curled into a sardonic smile.

Selena gritted her teeth.

"*Ahora embarcando: autobús a Puebla,*" said a voice over the loudspeaker. "*Ahora embarcando.*"

"Oh, time to board," said Melanie.

Wyatt leaned in. "Lucky for you."

Selena forced a smile. "Where are you sitting?"

James scanned his ticket. "Row six."

"Oh, too bad." Selena let out a deliberate exhale. "We're in row fifteen."

"Yes," said Wyatt. "That's too bad."

Selena wanted to sock him in the arm. Once they arrived in Puebla, she needed to ditch Wyatt, buy her own ticket, and solve her problem. She didn't need his help or his judgment.

FIFTEEN MINUTES INTO THEIR TRIP, SELENA HADN'T SPOKEN one word to him. She'd stared out the window at the dark nothing outside, as if she were looking at the most interesting landscape in the world. He'd been right about the strange couple they'd met, and she couldn't stand it. He smiled to himself. He'd gotten a bit of a kick out her reaction when Melanie and James showed up. Her face had turned pink. She knew he was right.

As the silence continued, his triumph turned to worry. Sure, it had been fun to see her squirm at the bus station, but her unpredictability could be dangerous. What if she talked to the wrong people? What if the next thing she did put both of them in danger? Although he was glad to hear the bus engine work hard to climb out of the valley and into the mountains that surrounded Mexico City, he knew that two hours wouldn't make a big difference to someone determined to find Selena.

What had he gotten himself into? The whole day had been a blur. He'd thought Antonia was bit uptight, a bit closed, but she'd warmed up to him over the last month. Offering to buy her coffee drink that morning had been his way of a friendly gesture. But boy, had he judged her wrong. How much had someone paid her for the information about Selena, and why would she risk her job to do it?

. . .

EVEN THOUGH THE HOUR WAS LATE, SELENA WAS WIDE AWAKE. They'd taken their assigned seats, and Wyatt had been kind enough to offer her the window seat. She turned over in her mind what had happened in the motel room. What Wyatt might think of her.

"I'm not the kind of girl who does...you know...that with just anyone," Selena spat out. "Like, I'm not into one-night stands." She slumped in her seat. "God, that sounds so awful."

"Okay," Wyatt said warily. "Good to know."

"Good to know?" If that wasn't the understatement of the year. "That's all you have to say? You followed me around before we got into this mess."

His eyes widened. "I didn't follow you around."

"You kind of did." She bit the inside of her cheek to hold back a few choice epithets.

Wyatt let out a breath. "Okay, you're right." He licked his lips and stared fixedly at the seat back in front of him. "I inserted myself. But before, on the sidewalk...I only wanted to meet you." He added in a teasing tone, "But you were the one that pulled me into the taxi."

"True."

"I honestly didn't know what was going on when I went after you...I just knew it wasn't right." He rubbed his neck. "Antonia's a former Marine. I didn't see her as the type to take a bribe or whatever. Something was up. I felt I needed to warn you or watch you." He sneaked a quick glance at her.

"Watch me?" She sat still and clasped her hands in her lap.

"Okay, that sounds a bit creepy." He picked at a stray thread on the sleeve of his shirt. "I wanted to make sure you were okay."

"Oh." His nervousness surprised her. Selena wanted to understand his motives. She wanted a deeper reason. Nobody had stuck his neck out for her like this before. Not even her longtime friends. "You have some kind of hero complex?"

He bristled. "Should I have stayed inside the embassy?"

"No, I guess I'm glad you didn't." She thought about the two men with guns on the street. What they might have done had Wyatt not showed up. Where she'd be now. She shivered.

"Can I see your birth certificate again?" Wyatt asked.

Selena's brow wrinkled. "I guess." She dug through her big purse. "Here." She unfolded the yellowed piece of paper.

Wyatt let down the tray in the seat back and smoothed out the certificate. "Felix Rios. Pilar Rios. Hospital General de Valladolid."

Selena removed a handful of postcards, letters and pictures and dumped them in her lap. As Wyatt viewed the details on the document, she categorized her pile—postcards stacked neatly between her thigh and the arm rest, letters tucked between the seat and the window, and photographs in her lap.

"The date is definitely before he went to prison."

"For what?"

"Drugs, probably. Just know he was in there for awhile. Then after he got out, he reestablished himself on the Yucatán, the Cancún area. I'm sure because of the tourists. Anyway, somehow he worked his way up to controlling all the drugs on the peninsula."

"It's hard to believe my mother would marry a man like that."

"Maybe that's why she went to the United States? To get away from him?"

She played with the idea, the facts she'd been told about her father. Her stomach rolled. "That does make some sense. But... so unbelievable, too. Out of all the men in Mexico, could it be true?"

"Perhaps she thought she needed to protect you, hide you away. Even back then, drug cartels were dangerous."

Selena's mind was a jumble of thoughts. "Maybe." She flipped through the photos to remember happier times.

A toddler-aged Selena in a blue dress, smiling widely, two

buck teeth visible, chubby legs like sausages. Five-year-old Selena in front of a birthday cake with candles aflame. Two neighbor boys flanked her. One boy had stuck his fingers in the cake. The elementary school play when she'd dressed as a sheep in Little Bo Peep's flock: white pants, white sweatshirt covered in batting her mother hot glued in clumps.

"Is that you?" He picked up the birthday party photo.

"Yeah." She smiled at the memory of that day. "Those stupid Gomez boys. I don't know why my mother invited them."

"At least they came."

"I suppose."

"I have a December birthday. Nobody wants to celebrate right before Christmas."

"Aw, that's sad. I'm sure your mom made it special anyway."

"If by *special* you mean getting drunk and falling asleep on the couch by six o'clock." He handed the picture back to her. "Whatever. Forget it. Birthdays are stupid anyway." He laughed shallowly.

"Yeah, stupid." Touchy subject. Time to change the topic. "This is my mom." She showed him a picture of a young woman in a watermelon-red dress with crochet detail around the neckline. Her hair twisted into two braids and pinned to the top of her head. Palm trees blurred in the background.

"Wow, you look at lot like her."

"I do?" Selena studied the photo. Maybe something in the smile, the nose. But they'd always had distinctly different eyes— her mother's were deep set and rounder; Selena's had an almond shape to them.

"She was a beautiful woman." His skin flushed.

Selena shrugged, unsure how to answer.

WYATT CRINGED INTERNALLY. HIS CHEEKS WARM. SHE'D SEE right through him if he wasn't careful, and that's how people got hurt—exposing their weaknesses to others. He focused his attention on the birth certificate. "Parentage aside, the facts are the facts: you were born in Mexico. When did you find out?"

"A week ago."

He blinked rapidly. Not the answer he'd been anticipating. "And a lawyer told you to self-deport and apply for a visa?" Wyatt reviewed what he knew about the visa process. He'd taken a training course about immigration law during the onboarding process. One of many dry topics. He couldn't quite remember all the details. Something about Selena's predicament didn't seem right.

"I swear I had no idea. Nobody seemed to want to believe that." Selena's voice sounded thick with emotion.

He rushed to reassure her, "I believe you. Really. I do."

She let air escape out her nose. "Okay. Thanks. Ever since my mother got arrested, I've had to fight that perception...police, neighbors, the attorney. Everyone assumed I was in on the lie." She turned her head to look him in the eye. "I never knew. I went to school, college, got a job... I don't even know how my mother managed it, to be honest."

"They arrested your mom?"

She nodded. "At work. Some kind of employment raid. Bad social security numbers." She took a deep breath. "I want to be able to talk about this without losing it."

He touched her arm. He couldn't help it. Ever since they left the motel, he'd wanted one more feel of her soft skin. "You're doing great." She'd put her trust in him, and he wasn't about to mess that up. She was so alone and isolated. Her mother was in jail, and she knew no one in Mexico. Maybe he'd remember the details from that training course, if he gave it a little bit of thought.

She shot a quick smile at him. "I'm just glad I was given this chance to fix my mother's mistake, you know? I want to be a real citizen, a legal resident. That's it. I never did anything wrong. I just lived my life in Tucson. I love my country—and that's what America is: my country." She gestured at the birth certificate. "Should a piece of paper be the only thing that makes you an American?"

"You'll work it all out, I'm sure." Wyatt wanted to be supportive.

"Yeah, I can fix this." Selena's attitude brightened. "I'm really grateful for your help." She crossed her ankles, and a postcard tumbled to the floor. "Oops."

"I got it." Wyatt picked it up. On the back of the postcard was written in Spanish: *Pilar, Recuerda nuestro día especial. Te quiero. Felix*

He flipped it over. An ancient ruin stood on a tropical shoreline. '*Tulúm, Mexico*' was printed at a diagonal across the front.

He handed it back to Selena.

"Thanks." She took the card and placed it in the pile on her lap. "Enough about me. What about you?"

He shrugged. "There's nothing that interesting about me."

A gentle laugh escaped her lips. "Everyone has something interesting in their background. Come on." She nudged him with her elbow. "For instance, how did you get the job at the embassy?"

Wyatt mentally ran through the messiness of his youth and hesitated. "It's a long story."

"I've got at least ninety minutes to kill." She pointed at her watch.

Not many people asked about his past. Mostly he avoided opening up. But Selena had been willing to share her problems, and it might feel good to unload his own. "I wanted to start over fresh. Clean break, you know?"

"What happened that you felt you wanted to start over?" Concern knit her thin black brows together.

He paused. "I didn't have the best childhood." He cracked his knuckles. "I've been on my own for a long time."

"Oh. I'm sorry." She touched his leg.

Her sympathy stirred something in him. "Not your fault. I learned how to look out for myself." He laid a hand on top of hers. The connection felt right. "I worked hard to get where I am. Harder than most."

"I get that." Selena nodded. "Nobody's going to look out for you, but you." She pulled her hand away.

He offered a weak smile. "Right."

"I used to hate school when I was little." Her features were smooth and expressionless.

His body quickly tensed at the admission. It hit close to home. "I don't know that there was ever a time I'd say I liked school." Snippets of a life he'd hidden away rose to the surface of his mind. "I liked getting away from problems at home, though. Why did you hate school?"

"Kids can be mean." Her lips pressed together.

"Yeah." He knew when not to push for more information. He'd spent his younger days keeping secrets.

"But my mom was always there to be that soft landing, encouraging me to keep trying. Never give up." She picked up a picture of her mother, and a slight smile appeared.

"Your mom sounds nice."

Selena nodded. "I miss her."

"It'll be okay." He scanned her profile.

"I hope so." She dabbed under her eyes and sniffed. "Hard to see that right now. Everything is a mess."

Gently, he touched her shoulder. "Well, I'll make sure it's the least amount of mess it can possibly be."

She faced him. "I appreciate that, Wyatt."

The bus driver turned down the lights. Two women across the aisle crossed their arms and closed their eyes.

"Guess it's bedtime," Wyatt said. He stretched and yawned.

"I'm not that tired. But don't mind me. I can entertain myself." She gestured at the photos and other items in her lap.

"Wake me when we get to Puebla."

"You got it."

Wyatt felt tired in his mind and his body. Getting some shut eye before the bus arrived in Puebla might help. He couldn't think straight. On the one hand, he wanted to go back home, forget about today and pretend he hadn't helped some girl escape the clutches of a drug cartel. On the other hand, he knew he couldn't. It was too dangerous. And besides, he liked getting to know Selena. They had a bit in common, which surprised him. He hoped they could find some sanctuary in Mérida and blend in with the morass of American tourists on the Yucatán Peninsula while they figured out her problem.

He closed his eyes for a moment as the rumble of the bus lulled him to sleep.

WYATT HAD TIPPED HIS HAT OVER HIS EYES AND APPEARED TO be sleeping.

Selena set her attention back on the photos in her lap. Pictures of people she didn't recognize. One of her mother, very young, maybe eighteen or so, her hair teased high with dark lipstick and baggy jeans. A young man had an arm around her shoulders, and her mother leaned into him. Palm trees in the background. The man had a hard to read expression as he wore sunglasses. Could that be her father?

As she flipped through the small stack, she came across a few more of her mother at various ages. Some of people she didn't know...an older couple, a very elderly man in chair smoking a cigar, a gaggle of young children playing soccer in an empty lot. But no more photos of the mysterious man with the sunglasses.

Selena went back to that photo and scanned the blurry features. Pictures hadn't been as crisp or clear back then. She wanted to recognize some feature in the man that corresponded to her own face, but could find none.

Her mother had told her Selena's father had died long ago. His name had been Pablo. There had been an accident. She'd been left to raise Selena alone. After what Wyatt had told her about Felix Rios and what truths she knew about her mother, the idea that this man could be her father seemed more and more real, and it frightened her.

With mixed emotions, she put the pictures and other items back in her bag. She was left with a single faded postcard. The face of the card had an ancient structure made of big stones—a wall with a tower rising out of it—sitting near the edge of an empty sandy beach with a blue sky in the background. Luscious tropical greenery surrounded the ruins. In the bottom right-hand corner was script writing that read: *Tulúm, Mexico.*

She had no idea where Tulúm was located. Had this been a place her mother had visited?

She flipped the card over to read the note on the back. It was all in Spanish. Selena let out of breath of frustration. But she did notice it was addressed to *Pilar* and signed *Felix.*

Pilar—her mother's real name. For Selena's whole life she'd known her mother as Maria Hernandez, but the name on her birth certificate proved her mother's real name was Pilar Rios. She wished she knew Spanish so she could read what he said. Maybe Wyatt would know.

She flipped it back over and smoothed her hand across the shiny surface of the laminated postcard. The picture looked so peaceful—magical, really. She wondered what it would be like to climb to the top of the stone tower, look out over the turquoise waters, and take in the fresh sea air.

A tear slipped across her cheek. She hadn't intended to get emotional. She'd wanted only to find out more about who she was, what her mother had been hiding from her and why. Everything had been pulled out from under her, and she felt as if she were drowning. Not only that, but for some reason bad men had come after her. Wanted to snatch her off the streets of Mexico City in the middle of the day and whisk her away to who-knows-where.

If her father really was a drug cartel kingpin, were these men enemies of her father? His henchmen?

She looked up from the postcard and saw her new friend, Melanie, pass by her on the way to the restrooms. The older woman gave her a big smile.

Selena put her finger in front of her lips to warn her against waking Wyatt. Melanie covered a giggle.

It made Selena's heart a little lighter knowing nice people were on board with them. Someone else who spoke English, who might be a resource at some point during the trip.

The bus sped up, its loud engine drowning out the conversation going on around her. She wished she could lose herself in the view out the window, but it was dark and the windows only mirrored her reflection back at her.

She knew what she needed to do. Although her throat constricted at the idea, it was the right choice.

❦ 10 ❧

"All right. I wrote everything down." Wyatt's self-esteem went up several notches as he relayed all the details they'd need to follow in applying for her visa. He liked making lists, organizing things. "What to do when we get to Mérida." Wyatt handed her a brochure that had been blank on the back, which was now covered in notes.

Only a few minutes more, and they'd be arriving at the station.

"Um, okay." Selena reviewed it and nodded. She set it in her lap without another word.

She didn't seem impressed with his step by step instructions. Wyatt hated to admit it, but that hurt a bit.

"I should probably give you my cell number, just in case we get separated." He took her flip phone off her lap and added his number.

"Thanks." She stared at the new contact he'd created. "Wyatt Demko. Demko..."

"It's Polish."

"Doesn't sound Polish. I thought Polish last names were all *ski* this and *ski* that. Wayne Gretzky. You know, Polish."

"My dad was Polish. My mom was Swedish, I think."

"Demko. What does it mean?"

"I don't know."

"At least you know your family history," Selena said darkly.

"So you really had no idea you'd been born in Mexico?" he asked.

She shook her head and focused her gaze on her flip phone.

"I'm sorry that happened to you. It must've been upsetting to find out." Wyatt thought about his own upbringing. To him it would've been a relief to find out he was someone else, could live a different life. The burdens of a screwed-up family could sometimes be too much to bear. "I'm sure you've got someone who cares where you are."

"Friends, I suppose," Selena said. "They don't even know I'm here."

"Why?"

"I didn't want them to find out." Her voice became thick with tears. "Didn't want them to know."

Wyatt tightened his jaw. "They don't have to know." He hoped he could help her find a way to get back to Arizona as quickly as possible. The sooner she could leave Mexico, the safer she'd be. He was determined to keep moving and keep working toward her goal. "If we follow the steps I laid out, it'll be okay." He touched her shoulder.

She leaned into him.

He liked it.

She hid her face in his neck. The warmth of her breath arousing. "Thank you for caring."

"Uh, sure." Thoughts rushed back to him from that first meet on the sidewalk, the kiss in the disco, the sex in the motel room. His notion that maybe she'd been worth pursuing. But relationships never worked out for him. He'd discovered long ago he was good looking enough to draw women in, but didn't do well when things became serious. Epic failures, in fact. He liked neat. He liked orderly and planned. But as he much as he wanted to dismiss his growing feelings for her, he couldn't deny the attraction had only deepened as he'd gotten to know her better. Last night flashed through his mind. He wished he had more time to repeat that experience. His nerve endings tingled.

Selena pulled away and gave him a sheepish look. "That was embarrassing." She sighed. "I guess I'm not used to relying only on myself. My mother was always my fallback position...and now I have to get used to something different."

Wyatt wanted to empathize with her, but that would mean opening up about himself and he was not going to go there. That always messed things up. "It's okay."

They sat in awkward silence.

Somewhere, out there, some bad people were looking for him, looking for Selena. Although he wanted to set aside any worry, one niggling little part of him wouldn't be quiet. Wouldn't relax.

They spoke simultaneously.

"I don't know if I can do this," she said.

"You can totally do this," he said.

They both laughed a bit.

"You think so?" Selena brown eyes shone. "I've been thinking about those men and if we are really safe."

"I'll make sure you're safe." He wanted to share his fears for her safety, but didn't want to spook her. He could be strong for the both of them.

It was outside his nature to stick his neck out for someone else. He'd been burned enough that he'd made a conscious decision years ago to pursue only his needs, his desires, his dreams. But for some reason this woman made him act differently. Made him want to be someone...better.

"Okay," she said. Her demeanor brightened, and she repeated more confidently, "Okay. Thank you."

She squeezed his hand.

His heart thawed just a little bit more.

A sensation of weightlessness filled Selena after Wyatt had reassured her. After looking at the detailed notes he'd handed her, she didn't know if she could pull it off alone.

The world had felt large and scary when she'd boarded the plane in Tucson. Navigating a whole different country, a different language, a different way of doing things...even getting a bus in Mexico seemed out of her realm of comprehension. Nothing was the same down here. Nothing at all.

She didn't realize how much she'd come to rely on Wyatt in the few short hours they'd been together.

Selena surveyed Puebla at night. Lighted signs. Empty sidewalks. Clumps of people outside bars. They rolled through town, stopping at a series of stoplights down a main artery, and headed toward the bus depot. Their only companions on the midnight streets were taxis and *combis*—volkswagen vans turned into multi-passenger vehicles.

"Let's hope we don't have to wait too long for a bus," Wyatt said. His knees bounced in a nervous gesture.

"Yeah, I hope not." Her heart warmed, knowing she had someone to travel with, someone to navigate the foreign world outside, someone to share the burden.

He unbuttoned another button on his shirt and dragged his hand through his hair.

Although he'd said he'd wanted to help, she wasn't so sure he'd come to terms with his decision.

The bus station stood eerily empty. They entered the massive building through the arrival gate. *La Terminal Central de*

Autobuses Puebla, or CAPU, had the appearance of a modern airport with clean tile floors, wide hallways and windows all around. As they followed the signs toward the ticketing station, Wyatt hoped at least one food cart would be available. A few tacos and a coke would be just the thing.

He glanced at the attractive woman walking next to him. So innocent. So naive. She had no idea how bad it could be out in the Mexican countryside with no protection.

They entered the ticketing area. Bus company signs lined the walls on either side.

Although most disembarking passengers weren't traveling any farther, everyone had to pass through the rotunda. Voices bounced off the tile floor and hard surface walls, echoing and clashing.

Wyatt pulled Selena aside. "Here's the schedule." He scanned the big screen for bus departures from Puebla to Mérida.

"When can we get out of here?" Selena scanned the increasingly empty space.

"Looks like the first bus leaves at 6:30 am." Wyatt checked his watch. "That's almost five hours from now." He didn't love the idea of spending the night in the station, but it made the most sense. "We can't buy tickets until they're open." He noted the darkened windows at every major bus company. A janitor worked a push broom near the exit.

Selena rubbed a hand across her face. He could see her tiredness. He probably looked the same. Exhausted. Drained. They'd been on the move almost nonstop for twelve hours.

"Where do you suggest we sleep?" Selena asked.

"There's some chairs over there." Wyatt pointed out some uncomfortable-looking metal and vinyl chairs. "Or the floor." The hard tile didn't appeal.

"I'll take a chair," Selena said resignedly.

WYATT AWOKE WITH A START. HE'D HAD THE DREAM AGAIN. The bad one. The one that always reappeared when he was under stress. He could still hear his mother's voice. As if it was yesterday, and he was the same little boy.

"DO IT."

Wyatt cried. He was scared. He didn't want to.

"If your momma tells you to do something, you do it."

Wyatt could smell the liquor on her breath. The rank odor sickened him. He wanted to run away and hide. Under the truck. In the ditch. Away from the angry woman his mother always seemed to be.

She shoved the lighter into his chubby six-year-old hand. "He's a rotten, no good, son of a bitch." She pushed him toward the pile of belongings his father had left behind.

He held the lighter, trembling. The smell of gasoline made him sick. He didn't want to do it. It was wrong. He knew deep down it was wrong.

His mother kicked at a cardboard box full of random objects—a football trophy, pair of well worn sneakers, T-shirts, shaving kit, papers and letters.

"Do it, Wyatt, or you're no better than him."

Wyatt had no one else. His father was off to jail. His mother was all he had, even though she scared him half the time. Even though she was mean, and yelled, and drank all day, she was his mother. He stepped forward, lighter in hand. He'd never used it before, but he'd seen his dad use it plenty to light his cigarettes...at least he called them cigarettes, even though they didn't look like the kind the neighbor lady smoked.

Wyatt flick, flick, flicked with his thumb. The lighter made a snapping noise. The ridges on the mechanism hurt the soft skin.

Tears ran down his face. He didn't want to look back at his mother, knowing she'd make fun of him, knowing she'd say terrible things about him.

Flick, flick, flick.

"Oh for God's sake. Give it to me." His mother grabbed the lighter out

of his hand, flicked it once, and a flame popped up. "You can't do anything right. A loser just like him."

She tossed the lighter on the pile out in the yard.

With a huge whoosh, the fire erupted.

Wyatt's eyes grew wide. He stepped back at the intensity of the heat. The flames climbed higher and higher in the sky. An acrid, black smoke arose in the air.

"There," said his mother, backing away from the hot flames. "Now it's like he never existed. We're better off without him."

Wyatt wiped at his eyes and runny nose with the back of his hand. He hoped his mother didn't see. He also hoped she didn't see he'd peed his pants. There would be a spanking.

He watched everything burn down to the last scrap. Long after his mother had returned to the trailer for another beer, Wyatt sat in one of the broken folding chairs, the flames dancing in his eyes, and wondered if he'd ever see his father again.

Selena's neck had a crick in it, her ass had fallen asleep, and the air conditioning in the station had been too cold. She'd wrapped up in the serape, but it hadn't helped.

She checked the clock. "Almost time to leave."

Wyatt stretched out his legs. Then he tilted his hat back on his head.

"You had one heck of a dream last night."

"I did?" Wyatt shrugged.

She nodded. "I didn't sleep too well." Selena scanned the station and the early morning travelers who arrived. "Looks like the Brewsters must've decided to get that motel room after all. I don't see them."

Wyatt rolled his head around on his neck. "Kinda wish we had, too."

"Let's go find our gate," Selena urged. "At least I know the bus seats are more comfortable than these."

. . .

SELENA AWOKE WHEN THE BUS TO MÉRIDA SLOWED, AND THE brakes hissed. Hours of travel were behind them. Bright midday sunlight streamed through the tinted window and blinded her. She looked at her watch. Noon. Thick vegetation lined the two-lane highway. Different look than the road outside desert-like Puebla.

She sneaked a glance at Wyatt. Fast asleep. He hadn't noticed the change in speed.

The bus slowed and turned off the road into a dirt and gravel rest area. A few food stands lined the edge of the parking lot.

Her stomach growled and her bladder was uncomfortably full. Although the bus had its own restroom, it had been out-of-service. She hoped the restrooms were large enough where she could put on a pair of pants. The A/C had chilled her over night, and even the serape couldn't keep her warm enough.

She dug through her bag. The motion woke Wyatt.

"Are we already there?" he asked sleepily, his hat blocking his eyes from the midday sun.

"No, looks like we're at some kind of rest stop." Selena stood. "I've gotta pee."

"Chill out. We'll be here for a little while."

"Easy for you to say." Standing made her discomfort worse.

Wyatt squinted at the sun. "I'll get us something to eat. What do you like?"

"Food." She squeezed past him, jeans in hand, and exited with the rest of the passengers.

A line had formed in front of the restrooms. Garbage and food waste littered the area. As she stepped closer to the open doorway of the women's restroom, the smell of urine and feces became overpowering.

Oh boy.

Selena girded herself. Just when she thought her bladder

would burst, her turn arrived. She squished past the large woman who exited, a piece of wet toilet paper on her shoe.

The bathroom was dimly lit. Probably a good thing. She breathed through her mouth and tried to think of pleasant things.

Holy hell, what a nightmare.

She pushed open the stall. The door had been kicked in at some point, and a huge hole gaped where the lock should've been. Everyone would be able to see her doing her business. But at this point, she was so desperate to relieve herself she didn't care. She carefully hovered over a toilet seat that was covered in grime and unidentifiable liquids. Flies buzzed lazily in the air. The floor around her was dotted with used toilet paper.

She finished and was glad a few squares of toilet paper came out of the dispenser. Gingerly, she stepped out of her skirt. As quickly as possible, she shoved her feet, shoes and all, into her jeans.

She zipped and snapped her pants, balled up her skirt, and exited the stall for the next travel-worn woman to use. Eager to wash her hands, she balked at the non-functioning faucets. One dribbled a bit of water, but no soap existed. Resigned to the fact she would have to walk out of there as filthy as the bathroom itself, she passed her hands under the drips, wiped them on her pants' legs and quickly headed back to the bus. She had a small bottle of hand sanitizer in her bag, and she needed to use it ASAP.

She strode past her friend, Melanie, who unluckily waited at the very back of the line. "Good luck," she said as she made a beeline for the bus.

❦ I I ❦

Wyatt watched as Selena lined up for the restrooms. He didn't have the heart to tell her what she'd encounter. Having lived in America for most of her life, she had no idea how other people lived south of the border. She was about to get a pretty harsh lesson.

As he analyzed the events that caused Selena to end up in Mexico, a stray thought came to his mind. The training he'd attended. He'd forgotten about it, and now it came to the forefront as if he were reading the notes he'd taken in his training binder. If an illegal immigrant exited the country and then tried to re-enter, they'd have a ten-year penalty applied. At the time it had been glossed over by the trainer, as running into a case like that would be rare. Most immigrants in the States worked with attorneys and knew the penalties.

But why hadn't Selena's attorney? He thought it through. Could it be possible that she'd been lured over the border? Would the government have lied to her in order to start this chain of events?

No matter the reason—lawyer incompetence or deeper plot

—Wyatt needed to tell Selena what he'd remembered. But first, they needed to eat.

He scanned the food choices. Three vendors were set up: tacos, a drinks-only stand, and fresh fruit cut and served on a stick. Although the bright red watermelon, yellow pineapple, and green melon cut into chunks, looked tempting, the preparation area turned him off. Gnats buzzed over a wooden chopping block, and the small, bronzed man who cut the fruit handled everything with bare fingers.

Wyatt queued up at the taco stand. At least the meat was cooked and killed off any germs. He hoped. His stomach rumbled. Regardless of food quality or the potential for E.coli, he needed to eat. The best he could do was pray everything went down without a hitch and stayed down.

Half the bus stood in front of him, but since this might be their only stop, he had to wait.

Unlike America, where a bus company had some control over its employees, a Mexico bus trip could change on the fly. It might depend on the needs of the driver and his replacement, rather than the needs of the passengers. And, unlike an American bus line where drivers were unionized and limits on the number of driving hours existed, a Mexican bus line was staffed with multiple drivers, so turns could be taken and the bus could continue operating. A twenty-four hour bus ride was literally that...twenty-four hours of travel time.

Wyatt's attention wandered away from keeping track of Selena and focused more on the possibility of food. Each step closer he got to the front of the line, his stomach ratcheted up its demands. A breeze drifted his way, and the rich smell of cooking meat filled his nostrils. The wait grew unbearable. A woman at an outdoor grill cooked the unidentified meat—beef, possibly pork. The meat sizzled and spat fat as it cooked. Wyatt's mouth watered. Then, the cook generously filled a hand-rolled corn tortilla with meat, topped it with some beans, cotizo cheese and some pica de gallo and fresh cilantro. She wrapped the order in brown paper and handed it to the couple waiting for it. They already held their drinks, poured from glass bottles into plastic baggies with straws—a 'to-go' drink out in the rural Mexico. To grab the plastic baggies so that the liquid didn't spill out was an art.

Before he had a chance to order, he thought to text Selena about her preferences. Just because he liked street tacos with all the fixings didn't mean she did.

He touched his pants pocket.

No phone.

Shit.

Luckily, it was a burner phone and hadn't cost him much.

His stomach told him to stay in line and stop worrying about a cheap cell phone.

"*Señor?*" the woman behind the counter called. He'd turned into the last taco customer.

James Brewster stood in line at the fruit stand. They noticed each other and exchanged nods.

Wyatt picked several things off the menu. Did Selena eat traditional Mexican food? She had been ignorant of the culture and language in Mexico, so he doubted himself. Best to order a couple chicken tacos with cotizo only. Girls always liked chicken. Especially the plainest, most boring chicken imaginable.

As he sipped on a bottle of orange soda, he fixed his gaze on the grill. He couldn't wait to slam down the four pork tacos he'd ordered.

The rush of pure sugar immediately woke him up, and the tired, fuzzy feeling in his head disappeared. He felt a hell of a lot more like himself. The tacos would be the cherry on top.

Selena returned to her seat and reached for her bag to find the hand sanitizer. She'd pee in the jungle next time, if it came to that.

She glanced out the window to find Wyatt. Her stomach could use some food right about now. Not sure what kind of meal was available at a roadside stand in the middle of nowhere, but she trusted Wyatt knew more about what was safe and what was edible.

"*Documentos, por favor,*" a loud voice demanded from the front of the bus. "*Passaportes, documentos.*"

A man in a dark green uniform that appeared to be the police stood next to the bus driver.

The passengers grew silent. Chattering, excited voices were replaced with a serious quiet that unnerved her.

People in the front rows handed the man their papers. As he reviewed them, he looked up every now and then searching faces on the bus.

Selena's gut clenched.

She dug through her bag to find her Arizona driver's license. The couple across the aisle from her were young, indio, and serious. They held IDs ready to comply.

The officer stepped closer. He scanned each item the passengers submitted.

Selena wished her new friends, the Brewsters, were on board. They could've helped her navigate the situation. She glanced out the window one more time. Her stomach full of acid.

Wyatt, where are you?

At the very last minute, she changed her mind. She dug in her bag for her birth certificate. That should work, right? A Mexican citizen riding the bus. No crime there.

The officer leaned over her. His shadow made her shiver. "*Documentos, señorita.*" He held out a hand. His thick mustache twitched.

She froze. The woman back at the embassy—Antonia—she'd

recognized the Rios name on her birth certificate. Maybe this wasn't such a good idea. Wyatt had said the police were dirty—controlled by the cartels and bribes.

"*Señorita?*"

She pulled out what remained of her cash. A few twenties. American. They liked American dollars, right? She'd never bribed anyone before, she didn't know the procedure. Shoving the wad into the officer's thick-fingered hand, she begged, "*Por favor.*" She had no words in her head—in English or in Spanish—to get across her desperation, her willingness for him to do almost anything to skip her over, let her go, ignore her.

The officer slapped her hand and tore into her with a flood of Spanish.

Her insides grew cold.

She'd made a terrible mistake. "I'm sorry. Here. Here." She handed him her driver's license. What an idiot. What a fool. She'd come to this country so damned naive about everything.

Memories flooded back. An experience she'd spent her youth tamping down, forgetting about, leaving as far behind as she could. The day all the kids laughed at her and called her stupid because her English had been poor in kindergarten. Spanish she no longer remembered. She'd felt the humiliation of being different, which had made her feel inferior.

And here she was again in a similar situation she where knew no one and didn't speak the language. An authority figure loomed over her, demanding she comply. He let go a stream of Spanish words she couldn't understand.

Where was Wyatt?

Panic spread like wildfire throughout her body. She willed Wyatt to appear from behind the bushes. He'd fix this. He'd straighten it all out.

The couple across from her interceded, realizing her predicament. "*Americana?*" the woman, dark eyes wide, asked.

"*Sí!*" Selena said.

Okay. She'd be okay. This woman would help her. Everything would be fine.

The woman spoke in rapid Spanish to the officer, who held onto both seat backs, allowing no one to pass.

The uniformed man listened, raised an eyebrow, and a slow smile came across his face. He took Selena's driver's license, scanned the info on it, studied her, and handed it back.

"*Gracias, señorita.*" Instead of continuing down the aisle, the officer turned on his heel and headed to the front.

Selena let air out of her lungs. Her limbs trembled. She tucked her driver's license into her bag. Her hands shook. She leaned back in her seat and then twisted her hair into a knot on her head. Sweat beaded on the back of her neck. Wyatt would be back any minute, and she could eat something. That would help.

The officer in green leaned in close and spoke to the driver. The driver looked over his shoulder, met Selena's gaze, and quickly glanced away. The officer handed him a roll of bills. The driver swept it into his jacket pocket.

When the officer stepped off of the bus, the driver closed the door with a rapid hiss.

Selena cringed.

The bus driver, sans his driving partner, pulled away from the curb and sped up to get back on the highway. A rumble of displeasure ran through the passengers. Most were on board, but not all. A few were still in line at the food stands.

Wyatt, Selena thought. *What about Wyatt?*

She stood. She wanted to scream at the bus driver to stop. What was going on? Why were they leaving?

The woman across the aisle grabbed her arm. "*Siéntese. Siéntese. Los carteles.*" Then, she shook her head, a grave look on her face.

Los carteles.

Selena swept her gaze across the passengers who rode with

her, hoping for someone to be her champion. To stop the bus. Let her off. Let her get away.

The bus fell silent. Once friendly faces turned to stone.

She'd been handed over to the cartel right under Wyatt's nose, and no one could help her.

❧ 1 2 ❧

"Hey, the bus, it's leaving!" James Brewster dropped his freshly prepared fruit on a stick and trotted toward the road. "Did you see that?

Wyatt tucked some paper towels in his back pocket. "Where's Selena? Do you see Selena?" An unwelcome flush of adrenaline tingled throughout his body.

Melanie Brewster walked toward him, cleaning her hands with a travel-size bottle of hand sanitizer. "Grossest pit stop I've ever made." She grimaced.

James had disappeared.

"Do you know where Selena is?" Wyatt froze in place. He had an inability to focus.

"Haven't seen her. Mmm, those look good." She eyed his order, which sat on the counter.

"The bus left without us. I have to find Selena."

Melanie's expression went from relaxed to fierce in a flash. "What? Where's James?"

"He ran after the bus. Is this normal?" Wyatt's six months in-country weren't doing him a lot of favors. Why would the bus leave? He reached for a cell phone he no longer had. "Damn."

"James!" Melanie called out, circling around the food carts. "Fucking hell," she said under her breath.

Pretty harsh words coming from the kindly, middle-aged woman.

James appeared from behind the brush, which blocked their view of the highway. "It's gone." He scanned the few remaining people at the bus stop. An older couple flagged down a car, and a young man crouched near the highway as if in wait for something. That left the three Americans.

"Selena?" He prayed James had spotted her.

"She's gone, too." He grabbed his wife's arm and pulled her close. They spoke to each other in low tones.

It didn't make any sense. Everything had been moving along according to plan. Then, poof, the bus takes off.

Doubt crept into Wyatt's mind. How well did he really know Selena? He'd stupidly left his passport on the bus and his phone, which was a better model than the flip phone Selena had. And she happened to be the only one of the four of them not at the bus stop?

Stop it. Just stop it.

But he couldn't help the feeling of shame, the feeling of failure. No matter how much he tried to create perfect plans, an organized life, methodical routines, he could never seem to escape making major goddamn errors. He couldn't control everything, and it dragged him right back into feeling like that scared little boy left to fend for himself Again. And again. And again. No matter how many times he tried to reinvent himself or fix something he didn't like—his clothes, his body, his job, even down to a stain on his shirt—he failed. Just like his mother had warned him. Laughed in his face. He couldn't escape her because he was exactly like her. Whiny, needy, shallow, hungry for love.

For the last six months, he thought he'd broken free. He'd been happier and less muddled in his mind. The job had come easily. He'd built a routine that worked—gym, work, home. Over and over every day. Repeat. Repeat. Repeat. Not one foot off that path until...

Until he'd met Selena. Then he'd thrown his carefully arranged life out the fucking window and run after her like a puppy dog. He'd dropped everything. All out of a need to prove himself to be a good man.

She'd used him until he had no more use to her. He'd given her a path to follow, the information she needed to get her visa squared away; he'd even fronted the cash for her goddamn bus ticket.

He looked at the food in his hands. He'd even bought her tacos and worried about whether or not she would like them. What a fool. What an absolute, stupid fool. He'd wanted so much to believe she liked him, needed his help. That he mattered to her in some way. And now she was gone. She'd let the bus take off without him and hadn't looked back.

He wondered how much she could get for his passport. One good forger away from a US Passport and a new life in California for some migrant, he'd guess. Enough to keep herself afloat until she found the next gullible idiot. His mother had been right.

His appetite disappeared. He dropped the whole of his order in the overflowing trash can. The baggie of soda bled over every-thing. He watched dispassionately as flies gathered lazily above the cooked meat.

❧

SELENA'S STOMACH KNOTTED INTO A MASS OF NERVES. HER usual quick thinking and spur-of-the-moment decision-making couldn't help her here. She was trapped on a bus and, even if she could get off, she would have nowhere to go, no one to help her. She was in the worst trouble of her life. Even worse than when the agent from the Department of Homeland Security had contacted her about her mother having been arrested.

Sure, she'd been shocked. Her mother had lied to her about her citizenship her whole life. Her decisions had destroyed Selena's dreams for a career, marriage, a family of her own. It had been humiliating to have her landlord help her box up her belongings. Selena had had to make a flurry of important decisions in a short span of time.

But now she was actually worse off. She'd been threatened with jail time in Tucson...but here in Mexico, she might lose her life. She hadn't fully believed Wyatt's crazy idea that she was some long-lost daughter of a Mexican drug lord. That couldn't be possible.

Her heartbeat thrashed in her ears.

But look where she was. On a hijacked bus deep in Mexico.

Her mind filled with the news stories she'd seen. Women and children killed, people beheaded or hanged from a freeway overpass for crossing the cartels who dotted the country—small ones, big ones, everyone wanting a piece of the drug pie. And the authorities couldn't be trusted.

No wonder the couple across from her said nothing as the police had slipped their driver some money. The bus driver had no choice. Neither had the passengers on the bus. If someone wanted Selena, they were going to get to her.

She and Wyatt had been stupid for thinking they could run away. The cartel likely had their eye on her the whole time. When they'd gone on the run, hidden in *La Zona Rosa*, the cartel had bided their time. The bad guys knew they'd move. And that had given them the time to stake out every bus stop from here to the border.

The bus rumbled along. The earlier quiet conversations and gentle laughter ended. Seriousness settled over the passengers like a death shroud. They knew they had no choice. They had to go along with it. They knew what might happen if they helped the *gringa* get away.

The sun sank lower in the sky. Selena's body had stopped

pumping adrenaline, and a heavy tiredness took over. She stared out at the jungle around them and swathed herself in the bright serape. She wanted to disappear inside of it. Hide away.

Dense trees and vines lined the two-lane highway. Selena wished she could pretend she was somewhere else, anywhere else than right here, kidnapped in broad daylight.

Maybe she could leave a note.

She searched the pockets in the seat backs in front of her for a scrap of paper...a magazine, a forgotten newspaper.

Wyatt's cell phone.

Shocked, she looked at it. He'd left it here. Why?

She switched it on.

A blank screen welcomed her.

No signal.

She racked her brain for a reason Wyatt would leave his cell phone on the bus. A mistake?

The bus squealed to a stop.

Passengers screamed.

Bags and boxes rained down from the shelves above the seats at the violent movement.

Selena looked up. Two dark SUVs blocked the road. Her stomach dropped.

A host of men in jeans and T-shirts, each armed with a semi-automatic rifle, emptied from the vehicles.

Terror overtook her.

Her limbs shook uncontrollably.

The couple across the aisle backed up against the window, their eyes round, dark holes. The entire bus grew silent.

The bus driver opened the door. Two large men entered.

Selena quickly shoved Wyatt's cell phone in her bra and prayed.

$\maltese$ 13 $\maltese$

Wyatt sat on a rock near the highway. He had no passport, no phone, but had his wallet. Luckily, he had cash, a debit card and a couple of credit cards with no balances. He could return to his apartment and then figure things out from there.

The minutes ticked by. He willed the bus to turn around, come back, pick them up. Selena would greet him with a smile and a laugh. All a big practical joke.

But that was a fantasy. He'd been abandoned like a bad blind date after a bathroom break. She'd played him good. The big brown eyes. The sympathy. The oh-woe-is-me and "I don't know anything about Mexico." And he'd fallen for it—hard.

He'd had his head so far up his own ass, he hadn't seen the truth.

The kiss at the discotheque. The passion between them in her motel room. It had seemed so real, so intense, so right.

James Brewster sat on a sister rock and clapped him on the back. "Don't worry. I'm sure she'll find her way back to you. You've got her number, right?"

Wyatt picked up some pebbles from the side of the highway and chucked them one by one. "I left my phone on the bus."

"Oh." James let out a sympathetic sigh. "You can come along with Melanie and me."

Wyatt shook his head. "Nah, I'm gonna go back to the city." He could lick his wounds there. He'd have to apply for a new passport at work. How embarrassing.

"I'm sure another bus should be coming along in a couple of hours. Might not be going to Mexico City, but at least you can head in the right direction. If you've got some cash, the driver should give you a seat if there are any empty ones."

Although buses in Mexico had destinations and typically didn't stop like a city bus would, if a passenger wanted to disembark along the route, the driver would oblige.

"Yeah." Wyatt didn't feel much like talking. The last two days had been a whirlwind of crazy. Every single impulsive decision made him feel more and more out of control. He hated it.

"Well, if you change your mind, you know where to find us." James gestured at Melanie who stood under a tree. "Looks like rain." He stood up, wiped his hands on his pants, and joined his wife.

Wyatt chucked another pebble. Cars zipped by. He set aside his thoughts about Selena and directed his thinking toward his normal, everyday, routine life. He could do some laundry when he returned. Oh, and unpack the bag he'd been forced to leave behind. Then he remembered he'd left his door unlocked.

Shit.

Who knew if any of his stuff would be left?

He threw the next pebble with extra oomph. It bounced into the tire of an approaching bus headed toward Mérida.

The wrong direction.

The door hissed open. Passengers emptied out and repeated what he and Selena had done only a couple of hours ago. Some queued up for food, others headed toward the toilets. Still others strolled around to stretch their legs.

Thunder rumbled.

The sky grew darker overhead as the sun set, and the rain rushed in.

The new arrivals grumbled en masse. They were likely tired and hungry. Now they would add wet to their description.

The rain began with a wallop.

People darted to and fro, using jackets and scarves to protect themselves from the downpour.

Wyatt, in a funk he couldn't shake, sat on his rock and let the rain soak him through to the skin. For some reason he felt he deserved it. A punishment for making a foolish choice. Something his mother would've done…make him run five laps around the Rolling Hills Trailer Park, scrub the toilets with a toothbrush, rake the gravel under the carport until all the leaves and debris were gone. She had a multitude of punishments when he did something dumb.

The Brewsters passed him on their way to the bus, hunkered under a jacket James held over both of them.

Melanie glanced at him and nudged her husband. "Come on, Wyatt. We've reserved a suite in Mérida. You can stay with us. Maybe she'll turn up." She smiled sympathetically.

The rain fell so hard, it splashed up from the ground and drenched shoes, pants legs, everything.

Out of the mist and darkness, a red-and-white bus pulled up with *Distrito Federal* on its marquis. A bus heading back to his life, his work, his home. He could put this whole thing behind him and forget, forget, forget.

More passengers flooded out and mixed with those from the Mérida-bound bus. A morass of human beings pummeled by the torrential rains. As the day grew later and later, odds were high these would be the last customers of the day for the food stands. Likely the last of the buses to stop for the night.

"Well?" Melanie frowned at the downpour. She gripped the edge of the jacket closer to her head.

Although his appetite had left him, he was exhausted and soaked to the skin. At this point, he was closer to Mérida than home. He imagined sitting on the Mexico City-bound bus—or maybe standing, if there weren't any empty seats—with wet clothes for hours. Alone.

Did it really make a difference where he licked his wounds? Mérida or Mexico City?

Then, he realized he could avoid embarrassment at work and apply for a new passport at the consulate in Mérida. The idea sounded better than the alternative. He already felt like shit. Better to confess his mistake to strangers than to his coworkers and boss.

Wyatt stood and brushed off the back of his pants. "Why not?"

❧

THE TWO MEN DIDN'T BOTHER TO SAY A WORD TO SELENA. One grabbed her by the arm and yanked her out of her seat. She clung to her bag. The only things she cared about were in it.

"Hey, what do you think you're doing?" Even though she knew why they were here, she couldn't believe it. Her gaze grew unfocused. Her thoughts scrambled.

One of the men, in a dirty white T-shirt, grabbed her by the hair and twisted it painfully. "*Cáyete, puta.*"

Fear shot through her. She grew still.

He yanked open her bag, pawed through it, found her flip phone and stuck it in his back pocket. Then, he nodded at his partner.

Silently, Selena thanked the Lord she'd managed to hide Wyatt's cell phone elsewhere.

The Mexicans around her shrank back, not wanting to be the next target.

A disconnect grew between her mind and the reality that played out in front of her—as if she watched a film. Headlines she'd seen at the bus station newsstand popped into her head:

Mexican Policeman Killed in Cartel Ambush

3 Journalists Murdered in Less Than a Week

More Than 61,000 Missing in Mexico Amid Spiraling Drug Violence

Selena wondered what it would be like to be number 61,001. She would be another illegal sent back to Mexico and never heard from again. Some in the US might even say, "Good riddance." The topic had become so volatile these days.

One of the men spoke to her in rapid Spanish. Harsh. Loud. Angry.

Her scalp burned as the man tightened his grip. These men, although they weren't tall, were strong, wiry, scary. Both had bandannas covering the lower halves of their faces. Both were armed to the hilt...pistols at their sides, long knives in their belts, semi-auto rifles slung across their backs.

Intimidating as hell.

The whole bus grew so silent Selena thought she could hear her own heartbeat.

Patter-patter-patter.

Louder and louder and louder.

Her armpits became sweaty.

A cold wave ran through her.

She closed her eyes. The whole situation overwhelmed her. She wanted it to go away. She wanted to be somewhere else. She wanted to be back home on the living room couch texting with her friends, putting off doing her laundry, avoiding cleaning the kitchen.

Then, she tripped on the steps while exiting the bus. Her eyes flew open. Hair ripped from her head. She cried out in pain.

Rain had begun to fall in cold sheets. She fell to the wet pavement. The rough surface tore a hole in the knee of her jeans, and her serape slipped from her shoulders. In horror, she watched as Wyatt's cell phone tumbled out of her bra.

The phone.

She flopped forward onto it, praying her captors hadn't seen it in the murky rain. In a quick move, she crammed it back into her bra.

One of the men grabbed hold of the back of her blouse and hauled her up, which caused several buttons to pop off, exposing her bra beneath. Her serape fluttered to the ground.

Her first thought was the phone. They would see the phone. But she'd managed to tuck it in far enough to one side that it remained hidden.

The passengers pressed their noses against the window glass, watching the spectacle.

Shame and fear washed through her. She wanted to cover herself, but the men held her too tightly.

The door of the bus closed.

One of the SUVs backed up and let it pass.

The bus gunned it down the highway and disappeared into the rain as if she'd never existed. As if nobody cared the bus driver had been paid off to let the cartel kidnap a helpless young American in the middle of nowhere in the dark of night.

And nobody did care.

"Where are you taking me?" Tears flowed down her cheeks. "Why?"

The man in the dirty T-shirt leaned in close and drew his arm across her middle. In accented English he said, "You don't want to know, *puta.*"

His breath was hot against her ear, and his arm tightened across her midsection.

Her lungs wanted to burst for lack of oxygen. She was paralyzed at the thought of being raped by these two burly men on the side of the road, in the deepening twilight, in the rain.

Every choice she'd made to get to this point in her life flashed through her mind. Where had she gone wrong? Had Wyatt been the one to betray her?

Her stomach heaved. She was going to be sick.

They dragged her toward one of the SUVs. The back door stood open. A black maw. Instinctually, she yelled and bucked backward.

Her serape lay on the ground. A strong gust of wind picked it up and carried into the compact shrubs at the edge of the jungle.

As the men forced her into the vehicle, it was the last image she had in her mind.

❦   14   ❦

Selena lay sprawled on black leather seats at the mercy of the two men who loomed over her. She brought her knees together in a protective motion.

The man in the dirty T-shirt laughed. "Maybe you get lucky next time." He kicked at her feet and threw her bag inside.

She drew her knees into her chest.

He slammed the door shut. Immediately, the child-safety locks clicked. She had a desire to be still and let the relief sink in.

A darkened glass panel blocked her view of the driver's compartment, but she felt eyes on her every move. She pulled the edges of her blouse together.

The passenger windows were dark tinted. In the gloom of the evening storm, she could see nothing outside but rain and gray.

She itched to switch on Wyatt's phone and call someone.

But what good would a cell phone do with no numbers to dial and no one to come to her rescue?

She should've known better than to trust Wyatt so easily.

Out of all the buses, all the directions they drove, all the people they carried, somehow these men had known exactly where to find her and when she'd be most vulnerable.

Her own mother had let her down, lied to her, disappointed her. Now Wyatt had done the same. He made it seem as if he cared, as if he wanted to help her.

She'd put her trust in a stranger. She'd even thought he was interesting enough for a roll in the hay. What a fool. He'd snowed her good. She'd believed every word of what he'd said, even though she hadn't seen any evidence of his claims. The coworker who supposedly made a phone call about her...she'd never witnessed it. All information had been given to her by Wyatt. He'd been the one to direct where they'd gone every step of the way, now that she thought about it. None of the choices had been her own. The only choice she'd really had was whether or not she wanted to sleep with him, and what a foolish, irresponsible decision that had been.

Tears welled in the corners of her eyes. The same way she'd felt all those years ago in school. The stupid Latina girl who didn't know English.

Her mother had duped her. Wyatt had duped her.

Who *hadn't* screwed her over for being too trusting, too kind?

"Dammit!" She kicked the seat in front of her.

The humiliation weighed her down. Every idea she'd had about Mexico had been wrong and now look where she was.

Clutching her bag to her chest, she curled up into a ball in a corner of the back seat. The tears came strong and fast. Her nose ran.

Why care anymore? She didn't even have the energy to think about it.

The car continued down the road. Rain pelted the roof, sounding like a hive of angry bees.

Selena emptied out everything until she was numb inside.

Let the cartel have her. Let them do what they wanted. It didn't matter anymore. Not one bit.

THE BUS TO MÉRIDA PULLED AWAY FROM THE REST STOP. Wyatt stood near the front by the driver. There hadn't been enough seats for the three of them, so Wyatt had volunteered to stand for awhile. They'd switch out seats every few hours. Maybe he'd eventually get some sleep.

The Brewsters had been kind to invite him to travel with them. They could've left him to fend for himself. Guess they felt sorry for him after Selena had left him behind.

Whatever the reason, he didn't care. At least when he arrived in Mérida, he would have a place to crash for a night or two. Then, he could go back to what he liked to do: plan. He wanted to have a routine again. The quiet routine he'd had in Mexico City. Everything normal, regular, no surprises, same thing day after day after day after day.

A flash of Selena ran through his mind. Her long, black hair strewn across the pillow, her eyelids half-closed, her lips parted slightly. He shivered.

All a lie. He had to keep reminding himself. She'd scammed him out of his phone and passport. She'd used him for information and help and money until he couldn't help her anymore. She'd probably never expected him to go with her to Mérida. She thought he'd turn around in Puebla and go back home. But, no, he'd insisted. He'd set himself up for more than a free ticket to Mérida.

He flushed at his gullibility.

The bus shifted into a lower gear.

Wyatt lost his footing and gripped the pole at the top of the exit steps.

The bus headlights caught something oddly familiar in the brush next to the shoulder. A colorful scrap of fabric.

The bus whizzed by before he could process what he saw. A familiar striped pattern of bright blue, pink, green, and white.

But that wouldn't make any sense. He must be dreaming. She'd disappeared like every other woman he'd cared about in his life. He wanted it to be real. He wanted to think she still needed him. That she was out there somewhere hoping he'd find her.

Wyatt shifted his weight, sighed and zoned out, waiting for his turn at a seat.

The rain clouds departed, and the sun sunk low in the sky. Selena had lost of track of how long she'd been a captive in a cartel SUV and had run out of tears. Thank God she'd used the toilet back at the bus stop.

They slowed down and made a right turn. Headed south.

The vehicle bounced over rough pavement and a series of winding turns, which gave her motion sickness.

Where were they headed? Why off the main road?

Selena didn't like the thought of that. She bit her lip. More invisible. More distant from civilization. Farther away from a potential cell signal.

Every minute that went by, her nausea grew.

She dug through her bag to see if she had a stick of gum or a protein bar to help her through. At the bottom, she came across some of her extra clothes—her favorite T-shirt. A faded one with butterflies scattered across the front. It had been a gift from Rosemary, her best friend in high school. She'd gone to college out east, and they rarely kept in touch any more. Funny how that happened. She used to tell her everything, but when Selena found out her illegal status, she'd been too embarrassed to reach out. The minute her mother had been arrested and the truth revealed, nobody wanted to talk to her. Nobody cared. In fact, she'd received more dirty looks from neighbors in her apartment complex than sympathies.

She had been a proud Latina girl with an LPN degree one day, and the next day she had become lower than dirt...an illegal who deserved everything she got. Nobody had wanted to hear her side of the story. Nobody had wanted to hear she had been as surprised as everyone else that she hadn't been born in this country, that she wasn't a citizen, that she'd broken the law for years without even knowing it. She'd lost more than her name the day of her mother's arrest. She'd lost her whole world.

Selena glanced up at the darkened piece of Plexiglas between her and the driver. She couldn't do very much to shield herself from prying eyes, so she whipped off her blouse and donned the T-shirt.

Her cheeks heated.

Even if she couldn't see beyond the tinted barrier, she felt watched, exposed, humiliated.

She shoved the blouse into her bag.

At that very instant, a loud bang rang out. The SUV swerved left to right and back again.

Selena screamed.

Her bag flew from her hands. The contents spilled all over the back seat.

"*Jesucristo!*" the driver swore.

Before she could orient herself, the SUV rolled. Selena lost all control as she bounced around inside. Her head hit the ceiling. She had a fleeting though about seatbelts and how stupid she was for not wearing one.

The SUV slid on its side along the road. One of the windows cracked. After a few terrifying seconds, it came to a stop.

Shouts outside. Gunshots. Screeching tires.

Selena lay motionless for a moment, taking stock of her body.

Nothing broken. Arms and legs moved. Her head hurt a bit. She touched her scalp and felt some blood.

The broken-out left-side passenger window was her new ceiling.

She attempted to push the door open, but she wasn't tall enough. The Plexiglas divider had held up during the wreck, offering no avenue of escape.

Her belongings—mostly letters, paper work and pictures—lay scattered all around her.

She wanted to run from her captors, hide in the jungle, and let them battle it out without her.

More gunshots, so close they exploded in her ear.

A thud, thud, thud as a few hit the SUV.

She balled up against the back of the driver's seat...the farthest she could get from the noise and bullets.

Terrible thoughts ran through her head. She was going to die here. Whoever was out there shooting would eventually find her. Or nobody would look for her, and she'd be left in this SUV to starve and rot on some deserted road in the middle of the Mexican jungle. Her mother would never know what became of her. She'd be forgotten. Another dead body in the war on drugs in Mexico.

She thought about the news report at the motel. The violence people were capable of. Killing women, children, whole families without a care or concern. These people had grown hardened and cruel. They had no qualms about chopping off heads or leaving a victim to hang.

The control some of these cartels had over the people of Mexico was frightening...and she'd become caught in the cross-fire. A pawn of some kind. She hadn't asked for this. She hadn't had any idea what she'd agreed to when she'd flown into Mexico City. That seemed an eon ago—a totally different place and time...and a totally different Selena.

"*Aquí! Aquí!*" a youthful voice called out. Close.

The shooting had stopped.

Selena felt a rush of fresh air.

She looked up.

A young teenager with a kerchief over his nose and mouth appeared in the window opening and shone a flashlight into her eyes.

Selena raised a hand to block the blinding beam.

"*Claudia,*" he shouted. "*Está Claudia*!"

❧

"So, Wyatt," Melanie said after he'd switched to a seated position. James had been kind enough to take a turn standing up front. "You hungry?"

She unzipped her bag and pulled out a sandwich baggie filled with peanuts.

Wyatt shook his head. Although at the rest stop he'd been starving, his appetite had disappeared.

"How about a bottle of water then?" She handed him one of several bottles he could see stashed in her bag.

"Thanks." His throat was a little dry and maybe it would fill the empty hole in his stomach.

"So what do you think happened with your girlfriend back there? Did you two have a fight or something?"

"She's not my girlfriend." An image of her naked body flashed through his mind. His gut clenched at the deception. "I was helping her out."

"Oh?" Melanie took a handful of peanuts and munched on them while she avidly searched Wyatt's face.

"I met her at the embassy in the District. She needed help with a visa." That moment on the sidewalk seemed so far away. "Long story short, she needed to get out of the city, so I offered to escort her."

Melanie scanned his face, blinked a few times, and then took another handful of peanuts. "Well, that was kind of you. Sorry it ended so abruptly."

"Yeah, that's what I get for being snowed by a pretty face, I guess."

Melanie munched thoughtfully and took a sip of water. "We've all been deceived by someone we've trusted. It's part of life. You live. You learn. Guess your bag was on the bus, too?"

Wyatt's clothes had dried out some in the air conditioning. "I didn't have a bag."

Melanie stiffened. "Ah, okay."

Yeah, that came across kind of odd. Why would he get on a long bus ride and not bring anything with him? No change of clothes. No toothbrush. "We, uh, left in a hurry. I really didn't expect to be going this far."

"To Mérida?"

"Yeah."

"Why did she need to go there? What was wrong with Mexico City?"

"She needs a visa. It's complicated. One of those DACA people. Parents brought her over the border when she was a kid. She didn't know it. Now she's trying to figure out how to get back to the United States."

"Huh. Weird. Sounds like quite the pickle." Melanie took a long drink out of her water bottle. "Can you excuse me? I'm going to use the restroom. I think the one on this bus is actually working."

"Oh, sure." Wyatt vacated his seat and let Melanie into the aisle.

All around him, passengers had fallen asleep. The day grew later and later. They'd be arriving in Mérida early the next morning. Maybe once there he could find a store to get a few things. Thank goodness he had his wallet with his ID and social security card. A few identifying documents should help him replace his passport. But first he'd have to find a local police station to report the stolen one. Otherwise, they wouldn't process his request for an emergency replacement.

He sighed at the hassle. He wanted to go back home.

His mouth became dry, so he unscrewed the cap on the bottle of water and downed half of it. Selena had made it very clear she didn't need his help anymore, didn't want him around her. As much as he wanted to pretend he'd gotten over the shock of what had happened, he felt deeply wounded. Another life mistake that would follow him around. Every time he thought he'd made some progress, he made another blunder.

Maybe relationships were never going to work for him. His mother had never figured it out. Why did he think he would? Damaged goods. Messed up in the head.

He leaned his forehead against the seat back in front of him and took several deep breaths. His heart thudded dully against his chest. He willed himself to concentrate. Put out of his mind all the negative thoughts, to push forward and go back to what was familiar.

A schedule. A list. Organization. Neatness. Control.

All of these things seemed out of reach in his current situation. He focused on the destination and his new plan of action. That's all he had. Everything else, every worry, every doubt needed to be exorcised from his mind. All emotions, all fears— gone. Or he'd be paralyzed. And he didn't want to be in that place again. Ever.

The bus would arrive in Mérida. The Brewsters would give him a place to stay. The consulate would help him get his passport. Then he could go back to the life he'd made for himself in Mexico City. Boring, yet routine. Stable. Normal. Regular. All the things he'd discovered he needed to surround himself with to keep from spinning out of control.

He sat back in his seat feeling less defeated. He glanced out the window, his gaze following the driving rain sliding down the glass. Melanie's cell phone sat with her bag of peanuts and her water bottle on her seat.

An idea crossed his mind. He couldn't let it go. He should want to move on and forget about Selena. But she'd hurt him, and he felt the need to hurt back.

He picked up the phone and entered his cell number.

Would she pick up?

It took a few moments for the phone to connect to a cell tower. Maybe the signal wasn't so good out here.

It rang.

He waited.

He broke out in a cold sweat.

A few rings and it went straight to voicemail. He hadn't set it up, so it just beeped.

He didn't know what to say. All of his anger and embarrassment made him tongue tied. "Screw you, Selena."

He hung up, cleared the number out of the history, and set it back on the seat.

He didn't have the courage to say more than that to the woman who'd used him. Would she even notice there was voicemail?

He felt stupid.

Why had he done that? It had served no purpose. Even if she'd picked up, what power did he have to force her to give his passport back? None at all.

His cheeks heated.

"Excuse me again. Sorry, Wyatt." Melanie pulled a frown.

"No problem." He stood and let her slide back in.

"I'd suggest you avoid the bathroom if you can." She bugged out her eyes, and she pulled her lips back in a grimace. "Pretty grim in there. Emergencies only."

He gave a half-hearted smile.

"Do you like to play hearts?" Melanie flashed a box of playing cards.

"Sure." He hadn't played hearts in probably ten years. Since he was a kid, with his neighbor. "You might have to remind me of the rules."

Melanie's eyes lit up. "Not a problem. Jimmy's always beating the pants off of me. Maybe this time I'll have a chance."

Jimmy.

The way she said it sounded vaguely familiar, but he couldn't place it.

Wyatt glanced at her husband who stood up front, his hand securely around the metal pole, his back straight, his legs hips' width apart. Like a military man would stand.

Melanie snapped Wyatt out of his thoughts as she dealt cards on the tray in front of her. "Okay, we each get thirteen cards... each heart is worth a point. The queen of hearts is worth thirteen points..."

Wyatt focused on the vagaries of hearts and put Selena as far back in his mind as he could. He needed to forget they'd ever met. Move on. She wasn't worth it.

But as he reviewed his hand of cards, he couldn't help but let his thoughts drift to those deep brown eyes that had been full of passion when he'd been inside of her.

❦ 16 ❦

The young boy beamed and used his fingers to make an ear-piercing whistle.

All the tension released from Selena's body, and she swiftly accepted his identification, "*Sí!* Claudia." She tapped on her chest and smiled.

She didn't care who had rescued her or why—she wanted out of the vehicle that had become a temporary jail cell.

The boy's head disappeared. She heard a whoop of celebration outside.

Using Wyatt's cell phone as a flashlight, she quickly gathered her spilled documents: an explosion of pictures, letters and postcards that made up a mysterious past she still needed to unravel.

A man in his thirties, with long black hair held back and a bandanna-style mask, and a woman about the same age, with a bright pink buff with *Yucatán* printed across it in rainbow colors, appeared in the window. They hung over the edge and held out their hands to Selena.

She threw her bag over her shoulder and accepted their aid. Each grabbed an arm and pulled her up. Her torso dragged painfully against the edge of the door, but she was glad to be free.

She sat on the edge of the overturned vehicle. Her rescuers hopped down, and the man encouraged her to jump into his outstretched arms. She needed no prompting.

Around her, in the deepening gloom of the evening, stood a group of about a dozen people—mostly men. Some with gray hair, some barely out of their teens, and then the youngest who'd spied her first.

"*Gracias.*" She had so much more she wanted to ask, but didn't know the words.

Spanish came at her from multiple directions. Joyful cheers and shouts, whistling. Automatic rifles raised above heads. These rescuers were laden with bullets on belts, knives, pistols. Even the youngest of them.

One older woman in a purple T-shirt and long pants pulled at her hand. "*Señorita, señorita, vénganse.*" She tugged her toward a jeep with no top.

Unsure of what to do, Selena followed. That's when she spied the bodies, some of which were bullet-riddled in the SUV behind hers. She recognized one of her captors, his eyes wide open, his arms thrown back, and a bullet hole in the center of his fore-head. Her posture stiffened. Her muscles grew rigid. The horrible scene couldn't be real, her mind told her.

Other bodies were scattered about on the muddy road. In a heap behind the SUV, one body lay with half his head gone. A big red blob with torso, arms and legs. She recognized his clothes.

Her stomach heaved. She bucked out of the woman's grasp. These people were killers. Stone cold murderers. These weren't saviors. They were vigilantes of a kind, armed to the teeth, willing to kill. All for her? Why?

The older woman soothed her. "*Cálmate, cálmate.*" She stroked Selena's bare arm with her wrinkled hand. "*Segura.*

Segura." She pointed at the host of people surrounding her. "*Amigos todos.*"

Friends.

This woman wanted her to believe they were friends. She'd never in her life asked a friend to murder people for her.

Her thoughts flashed to Wyatt. He had been a friend, or so she'd thought. For a split second she remembered his hands on her body. The warmth and gentleness he'd shown her. It was hard to believe he'd given her up to a mob of narcoterrorists.

She'd barely had a moment to rest since she'd arrived in this godforsaken country. She wanted desperately to believe the woman in front of her, who had a mild resemblance to her own mother. The comforting hands. The quiet words to soothe her. At least this woman had cared enough to rescue her from the roughness of her abductors.

Selena wanted to trust her and her cohorts. Exhaustion and hunger had reduced her thinking to the basics.

"*Amigo.*" Selena repeated with a slight smile and a nod. She couldn't possibly make it on her own in the middle of the jungle. If these people were willing to help her, she had no choice but to accept their help, no matter how dangerous they appeared to be.

The woman smiled and revealed an absence of teeth. "*Amiga, sí.*" She led Selena to the unprotected Jeep. "*Tiene usted hambre?*" The woman understood the language barrier and held her fingers up to her mouth. "*Hambre?*"

"*Hambre.*" Hungry. Her stomach growled in response. "*Sí, hambre.*"

The woman snapped her fingers and fired off some rapid Spanish in a much harsher tone than she'd used with Selena. The young teen and one of the younger women scurried away.

"*Me llamo, Patricia,*" the woman told her. "*Patricia.*" She held a hand against her chest. "*Patricia. Se llama, Claudia.*" Gently, she pressed her hand against Selena. "*Claudia.*"

"Gracias, Patricia." A name. She'd learned a name. And, although she'd never been called Claudia in her life, Selena accepted the moniker. She copied Patricia's phrasing, *"Me llama Claudia."*

Patricia smiled.

If they knew her as Claudia and that was why they'd rescued her, she was willing to be Claudia as long as they needed her to be.

She climbed in the Jeep. The seats were dotted with rain. Patricia handed her a waterproof poncho that smelled of mildew and cigarettes, but she gladly layered it over her damp clothing. Her hair hung in wet strands around her face, and she shivered in the cooling evening air.

The group, including Patricia, moved the undamaged SUV off the road, deeper into the darkening jungle. Not much could be done about the crashed one. It partially blocked the road, but they could drive around it. The bodies were dragged into a pile. Selena shifted her gaze down the road. She couldn't watch the gruesome work. She caught sight of a bright yellow orchid clinging to a palm tree, which reminded her of another life. A life she wanted to return to.

Her graduation from high school. Her mother in her best dress: a floral print with spaghetti straps and a long skirt. She'd been proud of how beautiful her mother had been. Her figure still youthful, her hair styled and piled on top of her head all held together with bobby pins and hairspray. Selena had helped her with it. They'd been close in that way. They'd dished about the neighbors, the girls in her graduating class, her mother's long-time boss, even the lady at the nail salon who'd given them matching manicures the day before.

On the drive over to the ceremony, her mother had handed her a clear plastic box that held a perfect pink-and-white orchid corsage. "I'm so proud of you, Selena." Her mother's eyes had filled with tears. "A high school graduate."

The young teen boy who'd spied Selena in the SUV returned from his food scouting trip. He handed her a tinfoil package.

Selena snapped back to the present and took it gratefully. The smell of fresh-made tamales made her stomach jump in anticipation. "Thank you."

The girl who'd accompanied him handed her a glass bottle of bright green soda. Warm, but still welcome after having been without food and drink for so long.

The girl cocked her head and scanned Selena's face. "You are Claudia?"

English.

"Yes." She unwrapped her meal. "You speak English." She took a massive bite. Even though the food was simple, it tasted delicious.

The girl nodded. "Some. I work on the beach last winter in Cancún. *Turistas.*" She smirked.

Selena took a sip of the soda. Sickeningly sweet, but it slaked her thirst. "What's your name?"

"Yolanda." The girl hovered near her and opened up to more conversation.

Selena was only too happy to befriend the girl. "How did you know where to find me?"

"*El jefe.* He knew. He tell us to get you."

"*El jefe?*"

"*Tu papá.*"

"My father?" Selena paused. "My father is dead."

She still clung to the facts she knew. Her mother had repeated the story a thousand times since she was little. Her parents had come to the United States for work and a better life. Selena had been born in California. Her father had been killed in a car accident on his way to work in the avocado orchards. Maria, Selena's mother, had moved to Tucson to escape from the bad memories and to raise her daughter in a less violent environment.

"*Muerto?*" Yolanda laughed. "*El Señor de los Mares* is very much alive. And he's been looking for you for many, many years."

"Yolanda!" Patricia, who'd been helping move bodies off the road, signaled to the girl. "*Ayúdame.*"

Selena had so many more questions, but her new friend joined the older woman in her work. Although in normal life, the idea of eating while around a half-dozen dead men would've repulsed her, Selena gobbled up the tamales in record time.

❧

THE CARAVAN OF VEHICLES DROVE THROUGH THE JUNGLE, bumping over the muddy road, which was pitted with tire tracks and ATV trails. On and on and on and on without end. It grew later and later, but at least the rain had stopped.

Yolanda shared the back seat with Selena, Patricia sat up front in the passenger seat, and Silvio, the name of the teen boy who'd first recognized her, drove. Despite his age, he navigated the road as if he'd traversed it for years. He knew every turn, every slope, every straightaway—even in the dark with headlights bouncing off the jungle surrounding them and barely lighting up the road.

Although they were sandwiched between two larger trucks of fully armed men, Silvio seemed to think he was the one in charge. He whistled loudly whenever he knew they were approaching a particularly sharp turn or gestured wildly when he thought they should speed it up on a straight piece.

The rough roads didn't do much for Selena's need for sleep. Her eyelids grew heavy. She'd asked Yolanda many times how much farther they had to go, only to get a shrug or a half-smile. "*Casi, casi,*" she'd say, as if scolding Selena for asking.

After what seemed like hours, they broke through the trees into a dark clearing. Ahead, Selena could see lights, people, and animals. A small village arose from out of the dense trees and vines. If she'd seen this village upon first arrival in Mexico, she would've considered it a rundown, pathetic place. But after what she'd been through since, it looked like heaven.

She prayed for a shower, a bed, another bite to eat. Although Patricia, Silvio and Yolanda had been friendly to her, it seemed as if they were following orders more than performing some random act of kindness. They had been told to treat her well. She'd been placed with the least scary people for a reason—to feel safe.

She bit the inside of her cheek.

"*Venga, venga,*" Patricia urged. The Jeep had parked next to a house on stilts. Simple wooden slats served as a ladder that led to a tiny porch and a front door. Under the platform, which made up the floor of the house, an old hand-crank washing machine, a few tires, a banged-up scooter and a couple of skinny dogs took refuge.

The trucks full of men had driven farther into the village. A remote place didn't require much security.

Selena followed Patricia. An old woman appeared in the doorway lit up by a lantern in her hand. She'd wrapped her small frame in a brightly-colored serape, similar to the one Selena had lost on the road. For a moment she thought of Wyatt and wished desperately he were here with his thoughtful, calm planning and solid frame. No matter what he'd done to her, he'd be a comfort now in this strange place.

Yolanda stuck close behind. Silvio had disappeared.

Is there where *El Señor* lived?

Her gut clenched at the thought of meeting Felix Rios.

Her breathing accelerated.

The old woman at the top of the steps scowled and shook a broom at them. She argued with Patricia. Clearly, the old woman was angry, yet her voice trembled. Selena sensed very quickly they weren't welcome here.

Yolanda appeared at her side. "This is where you will sleep."

Selena glanced at the old woman. "I don't think she wants me here."

"This is where you will sleep," Yolanda insisted and pushed her toward the steps. "Go."

Selena stood at the bottom.

Patricia grunted, grabbed her arm in a pinch grip and forced her up. "Here. Sleep."

The old woman gripped the broom across her front, blocking entrance. Fear etched deep lines around her mouth.

In a flash, Patricia whipped out a long, serrated knife from a holster on her hip.

The old woman melted into the house and let them pass.

The room was lit by a single battery-powered lantern. The shack was one-room with a bare wood floor scattered with well-worn blankets. A small wooden counter in the corner served as the food preparation area with a camp-size propane stove and a basket full of lemons, limes, bananas and a small mango. Against the wall farthest from the door were two lumpy looking mattresses with mosquito netting hanging from the ceiling. A beat up small bureau between them. On the wall hung a cross and numerous depictions of the Virgin Mary and the baby Jesus. Candles surrounded a small, framed version of *La Virgen de Guadalupe*. Clothes hung from a rope strung across another wall —threadbare dresses and dingy blouses.

The old woman sat in a rusty metal chair by the kitchen. Her eyes glittered in the lantern light.

Patricia shoved Selena toward one of the mattresses. Selena lay on top of a faded blanket and curled up with her arms around her bag. She wanted to jump up, run out the door and flee into the jungle. If she could run away from here, she could pull out Wyatt's cell phone, hope to connect to a signal and...

Wyatt's image flashed in her head. He would slow down and make a realistic plan. He wouldn't run off into the jungle alone without thinking it through.

She funneled her own thoughts into something more achievable. No more mistakes. No more decisions without a plan. Mérida was her goal. Now, how to make that happen?

Someone else joined her on the mattress. She looked over her shoulder to see Yolanda. She was grateful it was the chatty girl versus Patricia, who had a bit of a mean streak.

Yolanda gave her a quick smile and lay on her side. "We will leave in the morning. Sunrise."

"Where are we going?"

She held a finger to her lips. "Quiet." She thrust her chin in the direction of Patricia, who stood on the opposite side of the room, whispering to Silvio, and occasionally taking sidelong glances at Selena. "You need to sleep. *Duérmate.*" She said the last word more loudly, perhaps for Patricia's benefit.

Selena rolled from her back to her side so they faced each other. "At least tell me who those men were. The ones who took me."

"*La policía comunitaria.*" Yolanda thought for a moment. "The police...from the town."

"The police?" Selena was confused. The police were the ones who had helped get her off the bus, but it didn't seem as if those who kidnapped her were one and the same.

"No," Yolanda corrected. "*Policía comunitaria*....the community police. *Autodefensas*. People who no like the cartels."

Patricia crossed the room and sat on the mattress opposite them. "Yolanda."

The young woman rolled over. "*Sí?*"

Patricia spoke in rapid Spanish.

Silvio had disappeared, and the old woman, who owned the hut, had crafted a pallet on the floor out of blankets.

Selena doubted Yolanda's explanation about a vigilante group coming after her. They had been so scary and brutal. Their tactics more criminal than anything.

The idea she might be a drug lord's daughter chipped away at her. It would explain why her mother had lied about her father all these years. Maybe the truth existed in her bag full of papers and pictures. The things her mother had held onto about their past. Maria Hernandez might have provided her with puzzle pieces of a mysterious past that she needed to put together.

Every mile they covered put her one mile closer to Felix Rios and the danger of a Mexican drug cartel.

Selena scanned the back of Yolanda as she chatted with Patricia. Yolanda had been willing to share information with her. If she played her cards right, perhaps she could find out more about Rios, his past, and what his plans were for his supposed long-lost daughter.

❦ 17 ❦

Selena woke up to the smell of coffee. Her stomach growled. The older woman, who had given up her modest home for a cartel gang, still sat on her chair in the corner of the hut with dull, wide eyes. Her wrinkled, pale face displayed a hard life in every line.

Selena averted her gaze.

Yolanda had mentioned the *autodefenses*...vigilantes who tried to protect the average villager from the violence and forced participation in the drug trade. The *autodefenses* were used as pawns when cartels wanted to pressure innocent people into letting their crimes slide. A fine balance between the law abiding citizen who wanted to be left alone and the cartels who needed places to operate in secret.

A small village like this one, deep in the jungle, would be invisible to the police or anyone who cared to hold the cartels accountable. Although the news Selena had seen back in Mexico City indicated a veritable war had exploded in the northern border towns of Mexico, the south had remained relatively quiet —until now.

El Señor de los Mares in the Yucatán, as Wyatt had explained, operated more stealthily, so that the authorities ignored him and focused on his larger, louder and more violent cartel cousins near the border. Rios had figured out a way to keep his operation going without arousing the ire of those who would try to stop his drugs from flowing.

Yolanda handed her a plate of fried *plátanos* and rice and a metal mug of coffee.

Selena curled her legs underneath her and drank deeply. Using her fingers, she shoveled food into her mouth. Although the *plátanos* had the consistency of a banana without much sweetness, her stomach didn't care. She cleaned off her plate in minutes.

The door to the hut stood open, but the dense jungle blocked the sunlight. She didn't have any concept of time. It could be eight in the morning. It could be noon.

"*Dónde está Claudia?*" a male voice called from outside.

Selena had an urge to push open the single window between the beds and leap out of it.

Footsteps clamored up the steps. "*Patricia, dónde está mi hermana?*"

The figure that appeared in the doorway made Selena freeze. The slicked back hair, the sunglasses, the slim body...one of the two men who'd first attempted to kidnap her in Mexico City.

Instinctually, she backed into the corner and put a pillow between her and the man. As if that would protect her. Any minute a gun might appear, a shot might be fired, and the searing pain of a bullet might enter her body.

The man turned her way.

Selena tensed.

He slid his sunglasses down his nose.

His eyes, almond-shaped, were like hers.

"*Es Claudia?*" he asked to the room.

Nobody answered.

Selena slowed her breathing, trying to get control of her emotions.

"Claudia," he addressed her in perfect English. "I am your brother, Miguel."

❧ 18 ❧

"Wyatt, we're here." James Brewster roused him as they pulled into the Mérida bus station.

Wyatt yawned. "Thanks." He scanned the view outside in the early morning light. Vibrantly painted homes and business lined the street with palm trees planted between. The storefronts had exquisite Spanish colonial facades with columns and decorative trim. Everything grew green and lush. The sky, though the sun had barely risen, was a bright clear blue. If he'd arrived on vacation, he would think it looked like the perfect day for an adventure.

But Wyatt had slept little. He'd taken his turn standing at the front of the bus, but when he'd been relieved around three am, he found he couldn't turn off his mind. Stray thoughts ran endlessly. Worries about his job, his apartment, his future. Worries about what he'd gotten himself into...the missing passport, the stranger who'd called his cell phone with a threat. Worries about his own judgment...the instant trust he'd placed in Selena. The ease with which he wanted to believe her story, take care of her, help her.

He liked to think three moves ahead. But everything about the last few days had been a mess.

"I'm looking forward to checking in to our hotel," said James.

Wyatt pasted on a smile and forced himself to maintain eye contact. "Your offer still good?" It bothered him to accept their hospitality.

"Of course. Of course. Until you get on your feet and figure things out. We were going to be here for a few days at least... Chichén Itzá and Uxtal aren't too far from here. Have you been to any of the pyramids?" James didn't wait for an answer. "The beach. We were thinking of a night in Celestún. Kind of nice to stay away from the typical crowd in Cancún, you know? We like to see the real Mexico. The people. The food. All of it. Not that tourist trap shit."

Wyatt scanned his companion, almost a perfect depiction of an American tourist...loud shirt, overly chatty, hat, reflective sunglasses. "I've never been this far south. Haven't had much time to travel since I got here."

"Oh yeah, that's right, I keep forgetting you work at the embassy. How long have you been doing that?"

"Six months."

"Right. Right. Must be a pretty cool place to work."

"Not really, actually."

The bus made a turn. Ahead Wyatt could see the bus station. Compared to the beautiful, colorful architecture they'd driven past, the bus station was a disappointment. An ugly, gray block that took up a whole chunk of property right in the middle of downtown.

"They're turning this into a shopping mall," James said.

"Oh really?" Wyatt found it strange a tourist would know such details, but shrugged it off. Maybe James was a curious sort. The Brewsters revealed they had a very detailed itinerary in mind.

"I was hoping they'd knock it down entirely. Hideous." James trailed off and kept staring at the building as they approached. Then, he snapped his head back as if hitting the reset button. "So you don't like your job?"

"Right now I'm doing desk work. I'm looking for something with a little more excitement." After the last two days, Wyatt didn't know if that was so true anymore. "And Mexico wasn't exactly my first choice."

"Excitement, huh?" James rubbed the side of his nose. "I might have some connections."

"Oh? What do you do?" Wyatt asked out of politeness.

Melanie came down the aisle toward them as the bus turned into the station. She gripped the seat back to steady herself.

"Let's talk later." James winked. "I might have something that would interest you."

"Sounds good." Wyatt stretched.

"Who wants breakfast?" Melanie said in a singsong voice.

She was entirely too perky for someone who'd spent the last three hours before sunrise standing in the aisle.

⊛

THE HOTEL THE BREWSTERS HAD CHOSEN WAS A BOUTIQUE hotel in an historic building near Central Plaza. The tropical climate resulted in a proliferation of greenery around it. At one end stood a white cathedral with two towers climbing into the sky. Impressive and beautiful. The streets around the cathedral were lined with Spanish colonial-style storefronts decorated with curving street lamps made of wrought iron. Crisp white paint delineated the trim around doorways and balconies that looked over the streets lining the plaza.

Wyatt lay on the bed in only a towel. His naked back pressed against the cool blankets. He'd taken a shower first thing. He had no clean clothes, so he loathed to get back into his sweaty, stinking button up shirt and khakis. The shirt had become hopelessly wrinkled and the stain on the sleeve prominent. He'd hung it in the bathroom while he showered, but the steam hadn't done much. He felt out of sorts. He wanted clean lines and smoothness to combat his anxieties and clear his mind.

"Wyatt," called out Melanie after a knock on the door. "You decent?"

He'd found it odd the Brewsters had a reservation for a suite with an extra bedroom and bath. Seemed extravagant for a couple who traveled Mexico by bus. But maybe after being married so long, they liked their space. Wyatt didn't really think it was his place to ask and gratefully accepted the private extra room. He'd thought he'd end up on the couch or even on the floor. This had been a surprise.

"Hold on." He'd seen a couple of bathrobes in the closet. He dropped the towel from his slim hips and padded across the floor naked.

Melanie opened the door. "I have a shirt of James's you can wear." She barged in.

Wyatt froze, bare-assed. "Shit, Melanie." He grabbed the towel and covered himself.

Melanie reddened and averted her gaze. "I-I'm sorry, Wyatt. I didn't hear you. I thought you said 'come in.' Oh, God, oh, God." She dropped the shirt and ran out of the room.

Wyatt quickly put on the less wrinkled khakis and the borrowed shirt, a white-and-blue pin-stripe that was too large in the neck. But it would work. He had a long list of tasks he needed to accomplish as quickly as possible. Besides, he needed to get out of his hosts' hair and head back to Mexico City ASAP. He didn't need to meddle in their vacation...and it was clear they didn't know what to do with him either.

He slipped on his brown loafers and used the mirror above the dresser to check his appearance. Unshaven, hair wet and slicked back, shirt baggy. He tucked it in as best he could, tight and smooth. He took a deep breath, grabbed his wallet and left his room to enter the shared living space and micro kitchen that made up part of the suite.

James sat on the couch, his feet up on the coffee table, and flipped through the channels on a large TV affixed to the wall.

"Thanks for the shirt, man," Wyatt said.

"So Melanie walked in on you, huh?" Even though his gaze focused on the screen, he grinned.

Wyatt shrugged, unsure how to answer. "I'm headed out to the police station. I'll be back later." He grabbed a key card off the small table near the kitchenette. "Is it okay if I take one of these?"

James turned down the volume on a news program and faced Wyatt. "Police station? You gonna report your friend?"

"What?" Wyatt hadn't even considered this idea. "No, I was just going to report my passport as lost, so I can get a new one."

"Oh, good." James snapped off the television. "I felt sort of sorry for Claudia. I wouldn't want anything bad to happen to her. Sounds like she's got enough problems as it is."

Claudia?

Wyatt furrowed his brow. "How did you know...?" His stomach dropped.

James looked flustered. "Fuck." He took a pistol out of an ankle holster and pointed it at him. He raised his voice, "Mel, we have a problem."

Wyatt's adrenaline spiked at the sight of the barrel aimed at his chest. "Who the hell are you?"

Melanie came out of the opposite bedroom, a glass of water in hand. "I'm not going back in his room, Jimmy. You got me once already. I'm not falling for that again." Then she caught sight of the scene. The gun. The two men in a standoff. "Shit. Put the gun down, Jimmy. For heaven's sake!"

"I fucked up," James said. "I can't believe I fucked up. He knows."

"I don't know anything. What in the hell is going on?

Melanie...?" Wyatt directed his attention to her. Wyatt didn't know who he'd befriended on the bus back in Mexico City, but the gun sure didn't ease his mind. Guns meant *bad* in his world. Nice, normal vacationing couples don't pull guns on complete strangers. Heck, tourists in Mexico don't have guns, period.

"Put it down, Jimmy, you're scaring the kid." Melanie's voice level lowered a few notches. She'd read the scene and wanted to play peacemaker.

Wyatt scanned through the possibilities. He wanted a few more minutes to choose the best route, but he might not have that time. Instinct would need to come into play here, and he didn't really trust his instinct enough. He never had. Acting impulsively could get him killed, or at the very least leave him trapped.

"Someone tell me what in the hell is going on." Wyatt's muscles tensed. A sense of dread filled him. "Are you cartel? Who are you?"

Melanie laughed.

Jimmy lowered the gun.

Wyatt couldn't relax. Not until he knew more. He wouldn't just chill out after having a gun pointed at him. He wasn't wired that way. But he did lower his hands.

Melanie pulled out a kitchen chair and sat facing Wyatt. "No, we are not cartel. Sit." She gestured at the empty chair across from her. "If you really are as innocent as you seem to be, Wyatt, everything will be fine."

"Innocent? What the hell are you talking about? Innocent of what?"

Melanie slid a billfold across the table. "Go ahead. Open it."

Wyatt tentatively picked it up. He shifted his gaze to James. The gun sat on the coffee table within easy reach. He opened it. "DEA. You're DEA?" The tenseness he'd held in his body faded. "Why didn't you just tell me?"

Melanie gave James a look. "Sorry about the whole tourist story. That was our cover. I hope you understand."

"Are you even married?"

James laughed. "Are you serious?"

Melanie gave her fake husband a hard stare. "We're partners. We've known each other a long time...pretty easy to pull it off. I know way too much about Jimmy."

Wait, he'd heard that name and that accent before—Jimmy.

The couple—the Steiners—who'd approached his desk in Mexico City. The man had a beard, the woman had been blonde. "I've met you before. At the embassy."

James put his gun back in its holster and held up his hands in mock surrender. "Guilty as charged."

"Did you know Selena almost was kidnapped off the streets? If I hadn't intervened..." Wyatt's blood pressure rose.

"Look, we had to let it all play out," James said. "You weren't part of the picture. When you showed up at the bus station, well, you kinda threw us for a loop."

"I don't understand. Why are you so interested in Selena —Claudia?"

"We can't really give you that kind of detail, Wyatt. I wish we could. But seems that James screwed it up...not sure how, but I guess it doesn't matter. You need to understand there's a larger game at play here. And since you seem to have had a connection to Claudia, we saw an opportunity to glean some information." Melanie crossed her arms. "Since all the cards are on the table, why don't we drop the pretenses and get right down to it, shall we?"

"What kind of information?" Even though he'd gotten a good look at the DEA badge with Melanie's name on it—Melanie Jaeger—he didn't know if they were telling him the truth or not. He'd been lied to so many times, he was having a hard time knowing what was real and what was not.

"Whatever you know about her," Melanie urged. She leaned

forward, her eyes aglow. "Anything. You never know what might be important."

Wyatt shifted in his chair and furrowed his brow. "So hold on a minute... You knew this whole time who she was, that the cartel was on our asses, and you left us hanging in the wind?"

"Again, we didn't know who you were or where you came from," Melanie explained in a soothing tone. "You know how many people Rios has on his team in this country? You'd be surprised." She flashed a knowing smile in James' direction.

"So this is about Rios. About the cartel...you think Claudia is somehow involved in all of that?" Wyatt had to forcibly calm his demeanor. Waves of emotion rolled through him from anger to worry to something he couldn't quite identify when he thought about Selena. "Well, I'm here to tell you she isn't." Even though she'd abandoned him on the side of the road, stolen his passport and disappeared, he couldn't help but defend her. Her fear back in Mexico City had been real. It had been a palpable thing that night in the discotheque. The fear he'd seen on her face. When he'd felt the need to calm her with a kiss.

"Let us be the ones who make that judgment call," James said.

"Why should I tell you anything?" Wyatt had his own concerns and Rios wasn't one of them anymore. He wanted to be on a bus headed back to his apartment where he had everything the way he liked it, where everything was normal and people didn't point guns at him. "I don't have an obligation to help you."

"No, you don't," Melanie soothed. "But you seem to care about Claudia. And I think that's all we want here—what's best for her. How we can help her. She's in serious danger."

"How did you even know who she was?" Wyatt stood. He gripped the room key card in his fist. He wanted out of here, but knew that gun could come out at any minute. "How did you even find us at that bus station?" Something didn't feel right. Had that been who Antonia had called at the embassy? The DEA? "Did you send those thugs after her?"

Raw fear filled him. Selena was in real danger. Alone. No one on her side. Even the DEA, supposedly the good guys thought Selena was in on something. This went far beyond some incidental theft of a passport. He latched onto Selena's look of fear. The reaction he'd had. Gut instinct had told him to kiss her, soothe her, make love to her. Instead of making a plan, he'd acted. He felt that same gut telling him he was in a lot of danger right here in this room. Planning or no planning, his instinct wanted him to move.

Melanie shot a glance at James. "Hey, calm down. We're here to help. You could be part of that, if you wanted. You don't want to see your friend get hurt, do you?"

Her words were tinged with warning. Friendliness gone. If James had a gun, so did she. Wyatt wanted time to think. Time to figure out how to get out of this mess. His heart picked up the pace. He broke out in a cold sweat. Then it dawned on him. "You've been following her ever since she left Arizona, haven't you?" His posture stiffened, and his voice grew shaky, "You knew her background. Knew who she was and used her. You used her to get at Rios."

James' eyes widened.

Wyatt had hit on the truth. "She doesn't know anything. She didn't even know she was born in Mexico until her mother got arrested. You threw her out there for bait, didn't you? That's sick, man. Fucking sick." His fear for Selena blossomed into a cold fire.

"We have our assignment. We didn't make the plan." Melanie attempted to reel him back in with an excuse.

"She doesn't know a goddamn thing." He curled his hand into a fist. He wished he could punch something. "She didn't even know who Rios was. I had to tell her."

"So you admit you knew her connection to Rios?" James stood with arms akimbo and feet planted.

"Shut the hell up. I mean, shut the fucking hell up." He paced in the small space between the table and the door, feeling like a caged animal. "Stop turning this around on me...on her. She didn't know anything. I saw her birth certificate, his name on it—the government knew too when they gave her some bogus offer she couldn't refuse. Was that even an attorney who gave her the advice to go back to Mexico?" When the two didn't answer, Wyatt knew he'd uncovered their plan. "You fucking lied to her." He forcefully pointed at James. "You forced her to go back. Sent her right into the arms of the cartel. I don't have any obligation to help you." Wyatt backed toward the door. "Let me out of here. I want to go."

"So you just happen to run into the long-lost daughter of Felix Rios? One of the most prominent leaders in the Mexican drug market?" James challenged with an ugly twist to his mouth. "Just stumbled across her and decided to help a random stranger?"

"Yes, yes, that's exactly what happened." Wyatt narrowed his eyes. "I wanted to help her."

"Why am I having trouble believing you, Wyatt?" James snorted.

"I don't know. I'm telling you the truth. I don't have anything to hide. Here." He took his wallet out and flung it at them. "You can check my ID, my credit cards, look me up online, whatever you have to do. I wanted to help. That's all."

James got up from the couch and picked up his wallet. He sorted through the contents. He held up Wyatt's driver's license for Melanie to see.

She glanced at it and then focused her attention back on Wyatt, "All right. The truth's out. Now you know. We know who you are. Maybe we can find a way to work together. Sounds like you care for Selena. We don't want to see her hurt either—"

"Right." Wyatt had a hard time believing that statement. Selena had disappeared on a bus and was never seen again. Where had she gone? Who had made sure to split them up? His chest hurt. The thoughts running through his head were not good.

"We want to find her just as much as you do," Melanie claimed.

Wyatt searched his mind for a solution. "How are we going to do that?"

"Well, what did she tell you? What do you know?" Melanie's gentle tone was in stark contrast to her partner's demeanor. "That's a good starting point."

"Nothing." He sifted through his memories. "We only met a couple of days ago."

"Sure seemed like you became pretty close to her in those two days. Think." Melanie took a small step in his direction, blocking Wyatt's view of James. "What did you talk about? What did she tell you about her family? Something must've been said."

"She had a bag of pictures, postcards—I don't know." All this talking was getting them nowhere. He needed to get away from these liars and think this through.

"Okay," Melanie soothed, "you said you saw her birth certificate. What kinds of pictures?"

Wyatt thought back to the bus ride to Puebla. The pile of things she'd sorted out on her lap and shared with him. "She said her dad died when she was little. That her mother had told her he'd died in a car wreck." He remembered how close to tears she'd been. The fantasy father her mother had built for her...it had been crushed with his crude comment about the name on her birth certificate. From sad story of true love and heartache to criminal mastermind all in one fell swoop. He couldn't imagine being in Selena's shoes. At least he knew who his parents were—an alcoholic dropout who went through men like water and a motorcycle mechanic with a bad meth habit who'd run out on them when he was six.

He steeled his mind against those thoughts. Selena needed him. She'd believed in him. She'd trusted him. She'd seen something in him that he wished he could see in himself, and he'd let her go. He'd let her disappear from his life and assumed the worst about her.

"Fuck." Wyatt's fist tightened again. The emotions building inside him had nowhere to go.

"Sit down, Wyatt," Melanie soothed. "I'll make a pot of coffee. We'll order some room service and talk this out. We'll find her. Don't worry."

"Ah, so you do remember me?" Miguel said with a smirk.

Selena's mind raced. "I don't have a brother."

Miguel's mouth flattened into a straight line. "You don't believe me?" He crossed his arms. "My father didn't let me forget I had a younger sister."

"My mother never said anything—"

"Pilar?" He scoffed. "That whore?"

"Excuse me?"

"That is right...whore. My father was a married man when they met." He grimaced, and his eyes hardened to flint. "Did not bother her one bit. And then she carried that bastard in her belly, flaunting it in front of my mother. It put her in an early grave." He spat on the ground.

"It's not true. You're lying."

He snapped, "I do not lie."

Selena sensed his barely controlled anger simmering under the surface. She had to tread carefully. "My mother lied to me my whole life. I thought my father—our father—was dead." She glanced at Yolanda and Patricia to gauge their reaction. Yolanda kept her eyes down and twisted a silver ring around her finger;

Patricia stood ramrod straight near the doorway and pursed her lips. "I didn't know my birth name was Claudia until I found my real birth certificate. I never knew you existed."

Miguel rubbed his chin. "I don't know why you'd think I'd believe the bastard daughter of a whore."

Selena gripped the pillow closer to her chest. "Why am I here?" She wished Yolanda would at least look at her. The only friendly face in the room.

"Felix Rios wants to see his daughter."

Selena wasn't sure she could trust Miguel. "He'd never come looking before—why now?"

"He's spent the last twenty years trying to find you and your traitor mother." He lowered his chin to look down at her.

"My mother's no traitor." Her heartbeat pounded in her ears. She maintained as even a tone as she could. "Maybe she wanted nothing to do with drugs and crime. Maybe she went to America to get away from him—from you, from all of it. I don't blame her."

"Your mother fled Mexico after she ratted out our father and put him in prison." He readjusted the semi-automatic rifle slung across his back.

A sudden coldness hit Selena's core.

"You think she was some *innocente* who wanted a better life for her child *en los Estados Unidos*? No, she was a rat who saved her own skin, and put Felix in jail for seven years. Seven long years. And I was left with nothing and no one, except my aunt, to care for me."

She had no answer for him. She'd known nothing about any of this. Her whole life she'd wondered what it would've been like to have a brother or sister, and now when she found out she had a brother, he despised her. Not exactly a warm family reunion.

"You thought you had gotten away from me in Mexico City." Miguel clicked his tongue as if scolding a naughty child. "Lucky for you a very accommodating bus driver let us know you were headed south out of town—rather than north. Very clever, sister." Miguel's words laced with venom.

"Too bad the police handed me over to the wrong people." Selena thought back to what Yolanda had told her about the *autodefensas*. "Guess someone paid more for the information. You were outbid." Her half-brother's tone caused her ire to rise.

Miguel's gaze snapped. "No one outbids Miguel Rios." He shot a glance at Yolanda who sucked in her breath.

"Well, you're lucky Yolanda and Patricia ran into us, or you might've had to tell Felix a different story."

Miguel snapped his fingers at Silvio, who'd been busy eating more rice. "*Nos vamos en quince minutos.*"

Silvio nodded, wiped his hands on his pants, and disappeared out the door.

"I promised my father I would bring you to him, and I will keep my promise." Miguel followed after Silvio. "I am not surprised your mother did not teach you Spanish. She was a fool. Maybe you aren't the daughter my father hoped for all these years."

Selena thought about the first time she'd seen him on the streets of Mexico City, gun in hand. That didn't seem like a son doing his father's bidding.

Her mother must've known she had a half-brother, but chosen not to tell her. She'd chosen not to tell her a lot of things about her background and her family, and that hurt. Selena had thought they'd been close. Why hadn't she trusted her with the truth? Even after she'd been arrested and her true identity had been revealed, why had she continued to keep Selena in the dark? It made no sense. Instead, her mother had left her to deal with the broken pieces on her own...a father who was very much alive, an affair, a marriage that never was, a half-brother. What else had she been hiding?

Selena had been bounced around like a ping pong ball. She'd thought she knew who she was, knew what her life would be, and now everything had been upended. She couldn't go back to the US and her old life, but she couldn't move forward either.

Did Felix Rios blame her as well for the time he'd spent in prison? Was her father really eager to finally meet his daughter after so many years or was he out to exact revenge? Based on Miguel's attitude, Selena leaned in the direction of revenge. But something didn't add up. Miguel came across as angry and bitter, but Yolanda, Silvio and Patricia—although hardened by their cartel lifestyle—had treated her quite well.

Would Felix Rios treat an enemy so gently?

Selena slipped on her shoes. Out of courtesy, she made the old woman's bed before she set her empty breakfast plate on the small table. She didn't have much choice but to continue forward and pray Felix Rios didn't blame her for her mother's betrayal.

SILVIO FLEW DOWN THE ROAD, BUMPING AND SLIDING IN THE mud. Potholes of all sizes combined with a crosshatch of ATV tracks to create an intimidating stretch of road. Instead of traveling between trucks as they had the day before, the Jeep had straggled behind since the beginning. First, they'd had a late start finding Silvio, who'd sneaked off to steal additional breakfast from one of the poor local women—a few tortillas cooking on the griddle while an old woman's back was turned. Then, the radios they used to communicate had been on the fritz. They'd had to barter for batteries for the handset in the Jeep. Meanwhile, Miguel and the anxious men who drove the trucks didn't want to wait. On a schedule of some kind, they were frustrated with the women and the younger driver and had sped down the road, not caring the smaller vehicle couldn't keep up. Arriving at their destination seemed more important to them than keeping track of Selena.

After a few hours alone on the empty jungle road, Patricia picked up the radio. *"Ramón, Ramón!"* She banged her hand against it and pressed the button. Not even static. The batteries they'd traded for had been duds.

Patricia let out a string of Spanish that Selena could only assume contained a few curse words.

She leaned over to Yolanda. "Is everything okay?"

Yolanda gave her a hard look and shushed her.

Patricia smacked Silvio on the arm. He wrenched the steering wheel too hard in one direction, and the Jeep bounced against a large rock.

Boom!

The Jeep turned to one side. Silvio pumped the brakes. The Jeep skidded to a halt. They had a flat.

"*Chíngate!*" Silvio cursed and thumped the steering wheel.

Patricia climbed out of the stranded Jeep and slammed the door.

The two had an argument, gesticulating wildly, pointing at the road, the tire, the rock, and everything in between.

While they quarreled, Yolanda got out and worked a jack under the frame. Yolanda lay in the mud, but she didn't seem to care.

WYATT TOLD THE BREWSTERS EVERYTHING HE REMEMBERED. If he didn't keep talking, he'd dwell on what might've happened to Selena. He didn't like where his mind took him.

They'd downed two pots of coffee and had eaten *chilaquiles* and *huevos rancheros* prepared by the small restaurant off the hotel lobby. At first it had been hard to eat, his stomach in knots, but the smell of the food had won him over. He gobbled down the hot eggs and salsa stacked on top of fresh-made corn tortillas.

James and Melanie quietly chatted in the living room, looking at their notes. Wyatt kept one eye on them and strained to hear the conversation. He didn't know if he could trust them. They'd screwed over Selena in Arizona, and they could do it again in order to get to what they wanted: Felix Rios.

Rios would be quite a capture for two DEA agents on an undercover op. Cartel bosses were well-protected. Although the federal government in Mexico pretended they were actively pursuing the cartels, the drugs and the people who ran them, after the capture and trial of El Chapo a few years' prior, it became clear many high up in the government had been bribed to look the other way.

The newest president seemed to be off to a better start. Forays had been made into cartel-led territories and the Mexican Army, which was considered the incorruptible force in Mexico, had been participating in more raids and successful operations against the cartels up north. The growth of the Rios Cartel in Quintana Roo had mostly been ignored since the violence, murders of innocents, and out-and-out defiance of law were hidden behind a sheen of legitimacy.

James' and Melanie's interest in pursuing Selena meant something had changed. Rios must pose more of a threat—maybe to the idyllic tourist destinations like Cozumel and Cancún, which brought in a large amount of foreign money, or maybe to the tenuous relationship between the police and the cartels. And for some reason, the DEA wanted to track down Rios. A notoriously hard-to-find man.

With his fleet of ships and mini-submarines, Felix Rios had been known the flee the country and head to Central or South America on a moment's notice, which put him out of reach of the Mexican Army. Rios had seemingly been allowed to operate his cartel without too much trouble. He'd run ships and subs from the coast of Colombia to the coast of southern Mexico for years. When meth had become the drug of choice, he used his prowess on the seas to find ways to get his products to Miami, New Orleans, and Corpus Christie. Using small boats and subs, he'd managed to evade the US Coast Guard for the most part. While all the other cartels were focused on the border crossing and the west coast, Rios had made quite the name for himself as the main supplier for meth, cocaine and marijuana on the Gulf Coast.

Yeah, Rios must've pissed someone off recently to get the notice of the DEA.

Wyatt finished off his coffee. "Okay, now that you heard everything I have, what's the plan? How are we going to find Selena?"

"We're working on it," James said.

Wyatt flashed back to the news they'd seen in the lobby of Selena's hotel. He swallowed hard. He had to get his mind off those pictures. "I need to know you have a plan. She could be in serious trouble."

"We know," Melanie soothed.

"Yeah, sure, but do you care?" Wyatt's voice rose a notch. "You used her and threw her away. If you can't find her, what does that do to you? Maybe embarrass you a little bit back at the office that you couldn't pull this off. Maybe you go back to small time crime in Wichita or wherever the hell you came from. No big deal if Selena gets thrown to the wolves. If you lose your one and only lead, who cares, right? Slap on the wrist for you."

"It's not like that, Wyatt." Her eyebrows drew together. "We're just as concerned as you—"

"Bullshit." Wyatt stood and tossed his hard plastic mug in the sink. "What the fuck is the goddamn plan? How are you going to guarantee me you can find her? Huh? What's the plan, *Brewsters?*" Wyatt emphasized their fake last name with a heavy dose of sarcasm.

❦ 20 ❦

Wyatt's phone buzzed against Selena's skin. She'd almost forgotten about it.

A signal!

Her heart raced. She slowed her breathing, not wanting to give anything away.

"I need to use the bathroom...*el baño*," she said to Patricia, interrupting the argument between her and Silvio. "Could I...?" She pointed at the jungle.

Patricia, still fuming, eyed her. "*El baño?*" She waved her away like an annoying gnat. "*Quédate circa.*"

Selena wrinkled her brow.

Patricia let out a breath. "*Circa. Circa.*" She looked to Silvio.

He shrugged.

In stumbling English, Patricia said, "No far." She wagged a finger at her and then gripped the rifle slung across her back. "*Entiendes?*"

Selena nodded and scooted out of the Jeep. She crunched through the underbrush and scouted out a hidden spot. Trees dipped and curved, reaching for the distant sky. Low growing palms had sprung up around the tree bases and tangled with other unidentifiable vines and shrubs. Moss covered stones tripped her up.

Patricia and Silvio dove back into the argument about the tire.

Selena crouched behind a palm, took out the phone and studied the screen. A phone message had arrived from an unknown number. She touched on the *play* button for the message and held it to her ear.

"Screw you, Selena."

For a fleeting moment her heart soared: *Wyatt*.

Even though it sounded as if he must've assumed the worst when the bus had taken off without him, he was her best chance to get out of this mess. She had to try.

She pressed dial. A weak ring echoed in her ear.

A sensation of being ultra-awake flowed through her. Adrenaline rushed to her fingertips, making her hands shake. No matter how mad Wyatt had been, he'd made an effort. He cared. Somewhere in that message, she knew he cared.

"Who is this?" a woman's voice answered.

Selena's stomach fluttered.

"I...I'm looking for Wyatt." Selena whispered. She didn't have time to process who the voice was on the other end of the line. "He called me from this phone. Wyatt Demko."

Patricia's and Silvio's prattling echoed into the woods. A rumble of voices and indistinct words.

"Did he now?" the woman said with an ominous tone. "Would you like to speak with him?"

"Yes, if I could." She slowed her speech and concentrated on her words. "Is he there with you?"

❧❦❧

Melanie raised an eyebrow and held the phone out to Wyatt. "You might be interested in taking this call."

As if in a trance, Wyatt walked toward the older woman seated on the couch. "Hello?"

"Wyatt," Selena said on the other end.

His heart raced, and his tongue froze.

"I don't have a lot of time." Selena unleashed a barrage. "The bus left without you... Someone paid off the police... They knew we were on that bus, Wyatt. They knew it."

"You have my passport." Wyatt couldn't think straight. All of his fears about what might have happened to Selena faded away. She was okay. She wasn't hurt or dead somewhere. The impossible task to track her down had turned into possible. She was okay, and they were going to find her.

"What?" Selena asked.

"My passport. You took it." Damn, he was really screwing this up. He was talking about the wrong things. Hearing her voice had thrown him off. Moments ago he had been so sure, so certain he had to find her. And now all he could talk about was the stupid passport.

"No, no I didn't. Your passport? Why would you think I had it...?"

"Shit, Selena, I'm sorry."

Chill the hell out, dude. You're going to scare her away.

Glancing over at Melanie and James, Wyatt knew he'd have to explain at some point how Selena had gotten the number. Melanie would likely be pissed she'd been used in that way.

Melanie scribbled quickly on a pad of paper and then held it up for him: *Find out where she is.*

"And you think I—" Selena's voice sounded small and far away.

"Selena, where are you?" He nodded at Melanie. "We can come get you."

"We?"

"I've got help."

"I don't know about that, Wyatt. There are people out

there... You think they are good guys, like the police, but they really aren't. I don't think we can trust anyone right now."

Doubt crept into Wyatt's mind about Melanie and James. He'd seen Melanie's badge, though, so she was legit DEA. Right?

Melanie tapped a pen against the question.

"Trust me, Selena. I wouldn't lie to you," Wyatt said with uncertainty. Selena stood within his grasp, but it could all go wrong very quickly if the Brewsters had lied to him. He chose his next words carefully. "These are good people." He eyed the DEA agents seated nearby. He had to keep the Brewsters believing he trusted them.

Selena let out a rush of breath. "I don't have a lot of time. They're gonna wonder why I haven't come back."

He was losing her. "Where are you?" Wyatt pressed a second time.

"I don't know." Her voice quaked. "The jungle. Hours away from the highway."

"Are you all right?" He had so many questions. Imagining her far away and alone, surrounded by scary, gun-toting cartel heavies distressed him. He glanced over at James, who stood with his arms crossed, his gaze intense. "Did they hurt you?"

"No... Well, I have a cut on my head from when the SUV rolled over."

"Oh my God, what?" He'd assumed the worst about her, and it tore him up inside.

"There was this gang... They took me off the bus, and then the cartel stopped them from kidnapping me. They killed them. Shot them all. Dead."

"Selena, you have to get away from them." He bit down on the inside of his cheek to control his emotions. Fear built up inside him like water rising behind a dam. "Please, tell me where you are."

Melanie wrote more notes. James checked his watch.

"HOLD ON." THE PHONE WAS RUNNING OUT OF BATTERY power. Quickly, she clicked over to the mapping program, saw the dot that represented her GPS location, and expanded the map. Green all around. She expanded it further—miles and miles away from any recognizable town or city. One more movement of her fingers, and she could see Cancun and Mérida on her map. Her dot sat slightly south and between the two.

Her heart sank.

"I don't know where I am—in the middle of the jungle. I don't know what to do." Her quick-thinking mind had turned into cement.

"Okay. Let's think this through," Wyatt encouraged.

Selena looked over her shoulder. Yolanda brushed off her hands and put the jack back in the Jeep. She didn't have much time.

"A village. We stayed in a village with a bunch of little huts up on stilts."

"There's a thousand of those, Selena. Are there any landmarks that you can see?" Wyatt urged. "Maybe you passed something?"

Selena scanned the jungle. "I don't know. I don't see anything." Her voice became thick with tears. She wished nothing more than for Wyatt to appear with his calm, cool exterior and his rational plans. Her mind filled with stray ideas. She couldn't focus on a single one. She needed him.

"Hey, hey, it's okay." Wyatt soothed. "I'll find you. It'll be okay. I promise. Did they say anything to you about where you were going?"

"No."

"Are you sure?" He paused. "Think for a minute. Even the smallest thing they said could be important."

"They said my father was waiting for me." She took a breath.

"I'm scared, Wyatt. I don't want to meet him. I don't want to have anything to do with him."

Patricia called out, "Claudia, *vámanos.*"

Her stomach churned.

"Wait, I think I have an idea." Returning to the map, she took a snapshot and texted it to Wyatt. "I sent you a pic of my location. Did you get it?"

Silence.

The phone had died. No more Wyatt.

The world fell out from underneath her. There was no escape. None.

❧ 21 ❧

"Dammit." Wyatt looked at the face of Melanie's cell phone. The connection with Selena had been lost.

"Did you get a location?" James paced the floor in front of the television.

Melanie held the pen in her hand with a grip so tight her knuckles were white.

"She's gone." He couldn't care less about helping the DEA right now. He'd screwed it up.

"What did she say?" Melanie pressed.

"Not a goddamn thing." Negative thoughts filled his mind. He wanted to turn up the water in the shower to scalding and wash away the failure. He threw the phone on the couch. "She's in the jungle somewhere. She could be anywhere. Everywhere. Nowhere." He strode to the window that overlooked the central plaza. People walked by a few stories below him. Couples held hands. Children strolled with their mothers. Vendors along the sidewalks sold their wares: blankets, gum, trinkets, tacos, tamales, hats, jewelry. The whole world buzzed beneath him and, in his head, his life had come to a complete stop. He wanted to beat on the glass, break it, shout out his frustration to the unsuspecting people below. He could never win. Never. He was a loser through and through. He wouldn't be able to escape that. No matter how hard he tried. No matter how much he wanted to.

What had his mother used to say? *You can take the kid out of the trailer park, but you can never take the trailer park out of the kid.* The stink of it followed him around wherever he went, making his life twice as hard, twice as awful, twice as ugly. Anything good that came his way was ruined. Always.

Melanie appeared at his side. "We'll find her. We have a few leads we're working on. Some kind of big event going on tonight... Rumor has it Rios might be there. Maybe that's where she's going."

Melanie's phone blinged.

James picked it up. "This might help." He smiled and turned the screen toward them. Selena had sent them a screenshot of her location.

Melanie grabbed it. "Looks like she's not too far from Chichén Itzá. This matches up with my source—a party at *las ruinas* somewhere."

Las ruinas.

Selena had those postcards in her bag. One was a picture of ruins. By the sea. He remembered it because the image had been an intriguing one. What was the name of it?

"How far is that from here?" His mind raced to formulate a new plan of action. A way forward. The pieces fell together in his mind.

"A couple hours," said James.

"Then, let's go." Wyatt headed to his bedroom and snatched his shirt off the shower curtain rod.

It could work.

"Hey." Melanie chased after him. "We can't just go running into this."

"Selena's all by herself out there." He compressed his lips.

"And you put her in that situation. I don't give a damn what you think."

She touched his arm. "From what I can tell, you're not the kind of guy who leaps into anything. Let's take a beat. Find out more details. Put together a plan."

Wyatt slowed.

"You wouldn't want her to get hurt by moving too fast." She stepped into his personal space. "These are dangerous people."

Wyatt let out a big breath. "Okay, what are you thinking?"

James stood in the doorway. "We need back up. Mexican Army. Let me make a few calls." He held his phone up to his ear and disappeared into the living room.

Wyatt jerked his head back.

The female agent crossed her arms and blocked his exit from the bathroom. "We got this. Stay put."

"She's out there alone, Melanie."

"I know."

"We can't screw this up."

"We won't." Melanie relaxed her pose.

"You've got to promise me." Wyatt thought of those dark eyes filled with fear in the discotheque. He had wanted to kiss it all away, make the fear disappear. He should've left Selena there to fend for herself, but something about her quick thinking, irritating, adorable self had drawn him back. He'd thought he wanted no commitments, no involvements, nothing serious. He'd only been hurt, disappointed, and humiliated in the past. But for some reason, he'd let her in. Maybe it had been the danger, the rush of adrenaline. It had put him off balance, and he'd opened the door to something more. Something he'd never allowed into his life. Ever. "She has to be all right."

"She will be." Melanie patted his arm reassuringly. "We've been looking for an opportunity like this for a long time. Rios is elusive—he's been known to use lookalikes before to fool the authorities.

And right now he's not expecting us. He thinks we're distracted by what's going on at the border, the influx of migrants. The onslaught of so many foreigners causes just the kind of chaos the cartels love to exploit. And with his competition ramping up their drug transports, Rios doesn't want to lose his foothold. He has a big shipment he needs to unload, and soon. Keeping the number of men he has on his payroll gets expensive. He can't afford to let the drugs sit for long."

"Mel, I need you." James called from the other room.

"We'll leave soon. I promise." Melanie gave a bright smile and joined her partner.

Wyatt stood in the bathroom, clutching his wrinkled, sweat-stained shirt and looked at himself in the mirror. He turned on the faucet, wet his fingers, and slicked them over his hair to force a cowlick back down. He hadn't shaved since the day he'd met Selena. He ran a hand over his chin. Even though he had a clean shirt on, he felt out of sorts. A mess inside reflected in the mess he saw on the outside.

The phone call had been reassuring, but the worry wouldn't subside. Until he knew they had freed her from the people who controlled her movements, he wouldn't be satisfied. And he couldn't trust the Brewsters to act in her best interests. They'd already shown themselves to be untrustworthy. The gun pointed at him only a short time earlier had proven that.

"Wyatt? You ready?" James poked his head in.

"Yeah." Wyatt tucked in his borrowed shirt even more tightly. "Let's do this."

The three of them exited the hotel room and left nothing behind but a tip for the maid.

They wouldn't be coming back.

W YATT DIDN'T HAVE MUCH TIME TO ACT.

The lobby, which had been empty and quiet when they'd arrived last night, bustled with activity. He scanned the area.

He had no idea how to get where he wanted to go, but his first order of business was breaking loose of the DEA agents. He had no intention of being another victim in their attempts to make a name for themselves and touted as heroes for taking down one of Mexico's biggest drug kingpins.

He trailed behind the couple who were focused on their mission. In fact, did they even need him any longer? They'd found out enough information to find Rios through Selena. For all he knew, they could abandon him in the jungle and leave him to rot. What loyalty did they have to him?

None.

A young, attractive tour guide, dressed in a navy blue golf shirt with *Mérida Tours* embroidered in white on the breast, clapped her hands and got the attention of a group of tourists milling in the lobby. "Ladies and gentlemen, if you are scheduled for the 10:45 bus tour of the Mayan Ruins, please follow me. Seats are unassigned. First come, first served."

The people in the lobby murmured and gathered around her.

Melanie and James circled the outside of the group to reach the exit out the main doors to the street.

Wyatt hung back. A brochure rack stood against the wall. He scooped up a brochure that matched the embroidery on the tour guide's shirt: *Mérida Tours*. He shoved it in his back pocket.

Soon, the Brewsters would be outside and wondering where he was. He only had moments to figure out his actions.

"We are the red-and-white bus out by the curb," the tour guide announced in clear, clipped English with a slight accent. "Please follow me." She lifted a fluorescent yellow flag. "This way, please, for the Mayan Ruins tour."

Wyatt scanned the lobby for another way out.

The tour guide led her group like obedient lambs, but instead of heading for the main doors, she took them down a hall.

Wyatt saw his chance and blended into the crowd.

Melanie and James exited to the street, none the wiser.

His heart beat a million miles a minute. Any second the DEA agents would figure out he wasn't behind them and come looking for him.

"This way," the tour guide said crisply.

Above a sign read: *Excursiones / Tours* with a gold arrow pointing to a different exit.

Wyatt pushed deeper into the group, stepping on the toes of one elderly woman who pulled a frown.

"Excuse me. I'm so sorry," Wyatt said. His gaze zeroed in on the doors behind him, and he barely watched where he was going.

"You need to step back, son," the woman's husband warned.

Melanie and James reappeared in the lobby, scanning the room.

Shit.

Wyatt pushed farther into the group, elbowing children, shoving to the front of the line. Complaints arose from the tourists around him.

The tour guide spoke in low tones to a stocky man wearing a red-and-white cap with the same *Mérida Tours* printed across it.

"How much, please?" Wyatt had his wallet in hand.

It would be only a matter of moments before the agents found him.

The tour guide gave him a startled look. "You need to book your tour at the concierge desk in the lobby."

He flashed several thousand pesos. The pink bank notes caught the driver's eye. "Please. I need to be on this tour." He shoved the bills into her hand.

The tour guide's mouth gaped like a fish.

The bus driver tipped his hat, smiled and said, *"Si, señor."* He poked the tour guide in the ribs.

The tour guide snapped her mouth shut and shoved the bills

into her bra. "I'm sure we have one more seat. Please." She held open the door.

The tour bus with tinted windows idled outside. The doors stood open.

Wyatt rushed up the steps and into the air-conditioned coolness.

A young boy waited at the head of the aisle with his hand out, "Ticket, please."

"I paid the guide."

Wyatt pushed past the boy and moved to the back.

The boy protested.

The tour guide entered the bus and shushed him.

Wyatt chose a seat with a view of the sidewalk.

The rest of the tour group entered the bus. He wished they would speed up the departure. He imagined the DEA agents entering the bus, forcing their way down the aisle, nabbing him by the collar and pulling him out.

He rubbed the back of his neck and sweat beaded on his brow.

The line of tourists slowly climbed up the steps and chose their seats. Most were older and took their time.

Wyatt kept his gaze on the door.

As the last ten people waited out on the sidewalk to take their seats, Melanie and James burst out of the hotel. James' face was bright red. Melanie had a pained expression.

James noticed the bus driver leaning against the building smoking a cigarette. James engaged the driver in conversation and pointed at the hotel.

Wyatt imagined smoke coming out of the agent's ears. He'd been fooled, and it was clear he didn't like it.

Wyatt hoped his bribe had been enough. His mouth ran dry.

The driver looked at James with a dull expression and shrugged. He dropped his half-smoked cigarette and put it out with the toe of his shoe.

The last of the tourists climbed onto the bus.

The tour guide called out to the driver in Spanish.

The driver scratched his nose and walked right past Melanie, who'd hung back while James had put the pressure on.

The driver climbed into his seat, pulled the door closed with a hiss, and winked at Wyatt in the rearview mirror.

James stamped his foot and looked intently at the darkened windows of the bus.

It pulled away from the curb.

Wyatt let out a huge breath, and a slow smile pulled at his lips.

James watched as the bus left.

Melanie grabbed James by the arm.

He shook it off.

They argued. James turned even redder.

"Welcome to Mérida Tours," said the tour guide who stood up front behind the driver. She used an intercom to get every-one's attention. "We are so happy to have you with us today on our half-day tour of Chichén Itzá."

❧ 22 ❧

Two-and-a-half hours later, the bus arrived in Chichén Itzá. The ruins buzzed with tourist activity. On the ride, Wyatt had learned all about the Mayans who'd built this place centuries ago. How they'd mysteriously disappeared and abandoned such amazing structures that had taken decades and generations to build.

As they turned into the parking lot, the largest structure at Chichén Itzá, *The Temple of Kukulcan*, rose above the trees that surrounded the ruins. The temple was a four-sided monolith massive stone steps on all around, Wyatt marveled at the ancient pyramid. As the bus approached, the crowds of tourists became more visible, covering the manicured lawns around the main structure like colorful ants.

He tuned out the tour guide as she explained recent history of the ruins, which sprawled over many acres, and the driver navigated to the bus parking area. Although Melanie and James had mentioned a party, he saw no evidence of that.

As the tour guide rambled on about rules and where to meet if they were separated during the tour, Wyatt pulled out the brochure he'd nabbed. Maybe there'd be a map.

The tourists around him exited the bus. The tour guide stood outside in the parking lot, holding her fluorescent flag.

Other tour buses arrived, pulling into the larger diagonal spots near the entrance. A wide set of steps at angles, which mimicked the steps of the pyramid, led up to a modern building with a blocky exterior flanked by palm trees. A large banner in front of the trees, with the famous pyramid in the center, read: *Chichén Itzá. Bienvenidos.*

Tourists in shorts, T-shirts and flip flops milled around, some heading up the stairs. Others waited in line under the shade of some leafier trees.

He followed the tourists outside into the oppressive heat of midday. Melanie and James had probably easily figured his tour bus destination. It might be only a matter of time before they showed up.

Wyatt blended into the middle of the tour group. He needed to find Selena first.

He flipped through the brochure. No details about Chichén Itzá unfortunately, but it explained additional tours to many other ruins in the area. He'd heard of some of them, but others were unknown to him.

On the last page, he recognized a name: TULÚM.

The hair rose on the back of his neck.

The postcard. Selena's postcard. The one with a love note on the back from Felix, written years before he'd become a notorious drug lord. Back then, he'd been merely a low-level drug dealer in love with a beautiful girl.

Tulúm's recognizable stone structure sat on the edge of the ocean and stood guard over vast blue waters.

Wyatt studied the entrance to Chichén Itzá. Too many tourists. Too much traffic. Too close to Mérida and prying eyes.

He flipped over the brochure. A map to all the pyramids in the Yucatán was on the back.

"Stay with the group," the Mérida Tours tour guide said in a singsong voice.

The group had moved on and left Wyatt exposed and alone at the bottom of the stairs.

The map showed Tulúm southeast of Chichén Itzá off a long stretch of highway that curved along the coast. Very few towns existed past Valladolid, which stood about twenty miles east of his current location.

He turned away from the tour group and searched the parking lot for a taxi. A few had lined up near the bus parking zone.

At that same exact moment, he caught sight Melanie and James. They exited a vehicle and were accompanied by a bald man with a familiar stocky build.

Shit.

The man who'd shot at him in Mexico City.

His heartbeat thrashed in his ears. The agents had mentioned a source for their intel about the party. If this was their source, they had no idea the whole thing was a set-up.

His stomach rolled.

Wyatt ducked behind a new tour group, skirted around them, made a beeline for the taxis, and prayed he had enough cash.

He approached the first cab in the line. He had mere moments before the agents and the hit-man crossed through the parking lot, and he would be seen.

Without even talking to the greasy-haired driver who leaned against his cab, Wyatt climbed into the back. The inside was as hot as a sauna.

The shocked driver scurried to get into the driver's seat.

"*Cuánta cuesta a Tulúm?*" Wyatt had learned when he'd first arrived in Mexico to ask for a price to avoid being ripped off.

"*Seis mil,*" said the driver. He was so short he sat on a folded-up blanket. His feet barely touched the pedals.

"Damn." He had only a few thousand pesos left in his wallet. He flashed his credit card.

The driver shook his head.

Wyatt showed him the bills he had. *"Cuán lejos?"*

"A Cobá."

Wyatt took out the map. Cobá stood a distance from Tulúm, but at least he'd be an hour closer. Better than nothing. He'd figure it out once he arrived. He nodded at the driver.

The man smiled and exposed a missing front tooth. He cranked on the car, and the air conditioning kicked into high gear.

Wyatt's borrowed shirt stuck to his sweaty back, the shower from earlier today a distant memory.

As the cab drove past the full parking lot, Wyatt slid down in his seat. The agents and their source purposefully strode toward the entrance, scanning in all directions. He didn't know if they were looking for him, for Selena or both, but a grin spread across his face as he left them behind.

Let them waste time trying to find Felix Rios. He'd be long gone to Tulúm before their man informed them they'd made a tactical error.

THE CAB DRIVER PULLED INTO COBÁ. ACCORDING TO THE Mérida Tours brochure, a lesser-known and less spectacular set of ruins lived here. As they entered the center of town, they passed a jungle-lined *cenote*—one of the endless water-filled limestone sinkholes in the Yucatán—with tufts of grasses dotted near the edge. White puffy clouds hung in a watery blue sky. The heat of the day had only grown since they'd left Chichén Itzá.

"Las ruinas?" said the driver.

Wyatt reviewed the map again. They were so close to Tulúm. He wished he had more cash.

"Por favor, llévame a Tulúm."

The driver glared at him in the rearview mirror.

"My watch." Wyatt took it off. "*Reloj. Puedes tenerlo.*" He pushed it at the driver.

Unimpressed with the cheap item, the driver pulled up to the curb. "*Véte.*"

"Please," Wyatt begged.

The driver turned off the engine and cranked down his window. The sticky, hot air of midday Cobá filled the cab. He tapped on the horn. People on the streets turned and stared.

"*Al banco?*" All he needed was a place to get more cash.

The driver shook his head.

He'd hit the end of the road. No more chances. No more help. Wyatt was on his own.

"*Véte.*" The driver turned and pointed at him. His nostrils flared.

Wyatt handed him what he owed and exited the cab.

The driver started up the taxi, made a U-turn in the middle of the road and zoomed back to the highway.

Wyatt was miles from Tulúm, out of cash and had no phone to guide him.

"Dammit."

❧

"WHERE ARE WE?" SELENA ASKED.

The Jeep curved around the coastline following the bumpy dirt road. Every now and then a flash of the ocean and a beach between clusters of palm trees appeared. A sign told them they were approaching Tulúm. Ancient ruins from the days of the Mayans. A tourist destination.

"We go to party. You like party, no?" Yolanda answered with a smile. "Your papa waits for you. You will like."

"A party?"

"Yes, he is *muy importante*. He celebrate great success. Drinks, music, food."

The palms disappeared and scrubbier vegetation appeared. The blue of the ocean stretched out, and waves crashed against the rocks and sand below. The huge blueness reached all the way to the horizon. Selena had never seen the ocean before, and it left her in awe. So much endless, endless water.

The sight quieted her thoughts. Made her forget. For the first time since the bus had driven away from the rest stop, she felt an inner peace settle over her.

Her mother had a few pictures of Selena on the beach when she was a toddler. She had always thought those pictures had been taken in Santa Monica or one of those beaches near LA. Her mother had explained they'd lived in California until her father had died and then they'd moved to Arizona. A single mother with a small child could get by on a lot less in Tucson than in pricey Los Angeles.

There hadn't been many photos of Selena when she was that little. Now she knew why...anything around that time, and she was in Mexico. Her mother had kept so much from her. She knew now the beach photos were from the Yucatán Peninsula. Possibly near this place. Her birth certificate had said she'd been born in this state, Quintana Roo.

She recalled her favorite picture. Her mother smiling in a red one-piece with a big beach hat on her head, bright lipstick on her mouth, huge sunglasses the size of saucers. A two-year-old Selena in a bright purple swim diaper and nothing else, wispy black hair like a halo around her head, squinty eyes from the bright sun.

Her father had probably been the one to take that photo. An odd thought just before she was about to meet the man.

She twisted her hair and spun it into a bun at the nape of her neck, and then let it go. Over and over and over. The breeze blew through the strands, and she imagined the tangles she'd have once the ride ended.

Twist. Twist. Twist.

They came around a bend. Ahead, a group of men in suit jackets and holding walkie-talkies blocked the road. They'd put up a white painted barrier with yellow-orange reflectors. A big sign read *Cerrado*.

Silvio stopped the Jeep.

Two men approached, handguns at the ready.

Selena sucked in her breath.

Patricia leaned over and said something in Spanish to them. She nodded at Selena. The younger man roved his gaze over her, peeked into the backseat. A quick once-over.

The younger man in a blue shirt waved at the group standing by the barrier. "*Adelante*," he said to Silvio and tapped on the hood of the Jeep.

The barrier was moved to the side. Silvio pushed on the gas.

Selena held back a cry. The fear she'd experienced in the taxi when Wyatt had saved her life returned. Her limbs shook.

The men with guns made her whimper. The peaceful feeling fled. At the end of this road she would meet her father. She watched as they ate the miles. For a moment she contemplated leaping from the moving vehicle.

Yolanda gently touched her arm.

Selena flinched. There was no escape. There was nowhere to flee.

"Soon you will meet your papa." Yolanda smiled.

Yes, thought Selena, as dread filled her. *Soon.*

$≋$ 2 3 $≋$

Wyatt pulled the maximum pesos allowed per day, three thousand, from the ATM he found around the corner from where the taxi dropped him off. Less than two-hundred dollars, but it should get him to where he needed to go. He shoved his wallet in his back pocket and scanned the busy street for a taxi.

Not a single one in sight. No tourists on the sidewalks either. He'd ended up on the wrong side of town.

He clenched his jaw and swore under his breath. His plan, his hastily put together plan, was falling apart.

He glanced at his watch. Almost three in the afternoon. He'd wasted too much time. He needed to get to Tulúm before the party began, before the raid, before Selena was caught in the crossfire.

The urgency to get to the ruins revved up inside him. He'd seen hitchhikers before in Mexico. Backpackers. European travelers. He approached the curb and stuck out his thumb. The only thing he had going for him was his American appearance, which meant money in a small town that relied on foreign tourists.

After only a few minutes, a beat-up Ford truck with a missing front bumper and faded green paint pulled up.

The driver, gray-haired, mustachioed and worn, eyed him through the open passenger's side window. "*Adónde?*"

"Tulúm?" Wyatt flashed the cash he had.

The old man's eyes lit up. An unexpected offer, perhaps? "Okay."

"*Gracias.*"

Wyatt climbed in and handed the driver the cash. The man tucked it into his shirt pocket, pulled away with a jolt of the accelerator, and took off for the highway.

Wyatt's stomach fluttered. All he knew was that there would be some sort of event. How many guests? How well-armed? How many guards?

After months of watching the news unfold in Mexico, Wyatt had some idea how the cartels operated. The drug lords were protected by layers of security. Low-level locals intimidated the small communities into ignoring or accepting the cartel moving drugs and women through in exchange for some sort of protection. Mid-level people handled the drug manufacturing, processes, movement and also took care of rival cartels. Police and local law enforcement were bribed to look the other way or threatened. The highest level of security was reserved for the drug kingpin himself. Sometimes he used body doubles to fool rivals or the authorities. He was treated like royalty. Any offense met with harsh punishment—most of the time death. Offenses could be as simple as looking at the drug lord's wife or girlfriend the wrong way and as dangerous as letting an assassin in too close.

Wyatt would arrive with no law enforcement training, no support, no weapons. He broke out in a cold sweat when the old man driving the truck made the turn westward down the coast toward Tulúm. He had no idea what he was doing. He'd made decisions purely based on emotions...his fears for Selena. The feelings he had for her. Not the way he should do things. He knew better.

He hit the dashboard with his palm.

The old man snorted his annoyance. "*Ten cuidado*, eh?" The man rubbed the dash with his wrinkled hand. "*No mucho más. Entiendes?*"

"*Lo siento.*" The last thing he needed was his ride dumping him on the side of the road.

"*El pueblo o la ruinas?*" The driver pointed at the sign ahead.

Twenty years ago, the Mexican government had pushed for more tourism development along the coastline near the Mayan ruins. Although the beautiful beaches and wild jungles had been very sparsely populated at the time, developers had dove in with enthusiasm creating new towns out of nothing to support the growing tourist trade. Across the Yucatán, ninety-two known Mayan ruins existed—a huge attraction for wealthy American tourists. To develop as much as possible became the mantra. Acres of mangrove were filled in to accommodate the exponential growth of hotels, motels, restaurants, shops and recreational activities to attract foreign dollars. The once empty, pristine beaches that lined the perfectly blue waters were filled with palapas, resorts, and exclusive hideaways to attract more and more visitors.

The town of Tulúm had been born to handle the ever-growing number of tourists who wanted to visit the spectacular ruins near the Caribbean. As it had been built mostly to support tourism, it operated more like a ghost town during the off-season. Not many foreigners during the rains of August.

The sign showed a difference of five kilometers.

"*Las ruinas, por favor,*" answered Wyatt. "*Si puede.*"

The man nodded and drove through the town. Along the highway, businesses dotted the way. Repair shops, gas stations, junky little store fronts that didn't indicate the high number of tourists who passed through this place on a given week.

Wyatt had expected at any moment to see the ocean. They were mere miles from it, as he'd seen on the map. But the low growth of jungle vegetation blocked the view of anything beyond the edge of the highway.

The road narrowed to two lanes. People, bicycles, cars, motorcycles all shared the road. The driver swore a few times when a bike swerved in front of him, but continued forward. Wyatt wondered how much longer the old man's patience and his interest in the pesos he had offered would last.

Wyatt unfolded the brochure, which was damp from sweat in his back pocket. He traced a finger from Cobá to the ruins of Tulúm.

So close.

His mind flashed to his finger doing the same down Selena's bare shoulder. Her perfect skin. Unmarred and beautiful. He wanted to touch her again and be assured she hadn't been harmed by his mistaken thinking. If she were, he didn't think he could forgive himself.

He crumpled the map.

The old man braked hard.

The traffic and people had disappeared. They'd stopped at two orange-and-white barricades that blocked the road. Men with guns, mean looks, large muscles stepped forward.

The old man put the truck into reverse, tucked an arm over the backseat, and backed up without a word.

Wyatt's stomach hardened rock solid.

Selena.

She was here. She was absolutely here.

"Stop!" Wyatt had to get out. He didn't care how many guards and armed men stood in his way. He had to get out of the truck and back on that road. Selena waited for him at the other end. He knew it.

The old man made a quick three-point turn.

Between the branches of trees and brush, Wyatt glimpsed the blue of the ocean, the yellow of the beach.

"Stop, please." Wyatt lost his Spanish vocabulary. His mind worked quickly on a plan. A possibility. Two steps shy of crazy, but he had to do it. Everything in him pushed him to this choice. He had to do it or he might never see Selena again.

The man drove on as if he didn't hear.

Wyatt grabbed the steering wheel.

The truck swerved in the gravel and bumped into the soft, sandy shoulder. The front end pitched into the brush.

The driver swore, his eyes round with fear, and elbowed Wyatt to force him to let go.

"I have to get out."

As soon as the truck came to a stop, Wyatt leaped out.

The man drove off, the door flung wide open, gravel spitting from behind its rear wheels.

Wyatt plunged down the embankment toward the beach. Branches slapped him in the face, scratching his cheek, his neck. He didn't care. He moved purely on instinct. Something he thought he lacked. But he had no time to analyze, no time to weigh options. He wasn't going to let a gang of goons with guns get in his way. He didn't goddamn care anymore. Selena had been the first woman in his adult life who hadn't disappointed him. The first woman who'd locked arms with him and put her whole life in his hands. The first woman he'd kissed who'd kissed back with meaning and feeling. He hadn't wanted to admit it, but she'd somehow filled a hole inside him that he didn't even realize he had.

The late afternoon sun sunk behind him. The glare off the distant ocean waves was magnificent. The scene took his breath away. The lush vegetation skirted the edge of an endless white sand beach that stretched for miles and miles. And there, beyond an outcropping of rocks, a sight he'd been thinking about since Chichén Itzá. The magical vision of a stone castle on the edge of the cliffs overlooking the crystal blue waters of the Caribbean—Tulúm.

Selena waited for him there.

Miles away.

But he would get to her. He would get past the guards and the cartel and the devil himself to get to Selena.

God, help him, he would.

AFTER THEY'D ARRIVED AND PARKED, PATRICIA LED THEM TO the line of people waiting to enter. Loud mariachi music echoed beyond a tall and ancient stone wall. The sun was setting, and torches lit the way from the makeshift parking lot full of Mercedes and BMWs, brand new full-size pickup trucks and a handful of rougher vehicles, like the Jeep they'd arrived in.

Three men stood at the head of the line, screening people as they entered through a narrow gate in the wall: checking pockets, scanning with a metal detecting wand, emptying purses onto a folding table. Women in short skirts and halter tops were accompanied by much older men in button up shirts, cowboy boots with pointed toes, straw cowboy hats.

When Selena and her group made it to the front of the line, a boy of no more than twelve took Selena's bag and emptied it on the table. Her clothes, pictures and papers spilled out. The boy picked up a few pictures, looked at them, flipped them over. He curled his lip. He shook out her clothes.

Then, the man with the wand, his eyes hidden behind mirrored sunglasses, ran it over her chest, arms, legs, back. He spun her around. She faced the line. A third man in a crisp, white shirt and ironed jeans patted her down. She squirmed under his searching hands. He felt across her bra and stopped. She knew he'd found the cell phone. Her stomach dropped.

Patricia said, *"Es la hija del Señor."*

"*Cáyate*." The man reached inside Selena's blouse.

Instinctively, Selena backed away from the intimacy.

The man in sunglasses closed in on her.

The boy warned, "*Cuidadosamente, señorita*." He reached for a gun on his hip.

"*Es la hija—Claudia Rios*," Patricia said with a sharp edge to her voice. "*Es Claudia*."

A hush came over the people in line. Selena felt all eyes on her. The gun stilled her. She let the man slip his hand inside her bra, over tender flesh, and remove the phone.

The man held it up for Yolanda, Silvio and Patricia to see.

Patricia closed her mouth into a straight line. She flashed angry eyes at Selena. She and her two helpers had never done such a search. Selena had had a phone this whole time, and they'd had no idea.

The touch of the man's hands felt like a violation. The discovery of the phone worried her. What the consequences might be she did not know.

He switched it on. The screen was dark. The battery had died hours ago. He flipped it over, slid open the back, and removed the SIM card.

The three repeated the security measures with her companions.

Selena waited for her bag.

The screeners scooped everything back inside. The one who had discovered the phone held onto it. "*Vámanos*." He gestured at the four of them to follow him through the narrow stone entrance that led into the ruins.

"Can I have my bag, please?" She tripped over the rough ground.

The boy ignored her and headed into the party beyond the security inspection zone.

"Yolanda," Selena implored the one person who might be able to help her. "Please. My things."

"No worry. You get it back." Yolanda had a smile on her face. "We never been invited to fiesta before." The girl passed through the stone opening after the guard.

Yolanda didn't care. Why would she? Selena had been her job for the past two days. Not a real friend. She didn't care what Selena wanted, as long as she delivered the daughter to her father as they promised.

Selena followed behind Yolanda. She emerged into an open space filled with people and music and lights. Twilight had begun to settle. A stage had been built near two large stone columns, another stone wall behind. A band of musicians in elaborate mariachi costumes played and sang. The sound system was much too loud.

A crowd of well-dressed partygoers milled around the stage. Most had beer bottles in hand. The women were everywhere handing out food, drinks, kisses. Whatever the men wanted, they would provide. This was clearly a party for the men of the cartel. The women were the servants. There to look pretty.

The uneven ground made up of stones embedded in dirt was particularly hard for the women to navigate with the spiked heels most of them wore. Selena had never been so happy for her practical shoes.

Clusters of partygoers filled every level of the incredible stone structure.

The realization she had ended up in the heart of one of the deadliest and more powerful cartels in Mexico suddenly hit home. Could she really be related to the man who ran it? Unbelievable.

How had her mother kept such a secret from her? They'd had led a very humble existence in Arizona. Living paycheck to paycheck, shopping at thrift stores. Taking the bus for a year after her mother's car died on the highway in a cloud of blue smoke. Making rice and beans last for weeks at a time.

Here, she passed by waiters in tuxedoes serving hors

d'oeurvres and champagne, women dripping with diamonds and pearls and wearing designer dresses, men in alligator boots.

Silvio grabbed a champagne glass. Patricia scolded him. He drank it anyway.

They passed by group after group after group. Each one fancier and drunker than the last. The music filled the whole space.

Selena wondered how they were able to pull off hosting a party at an archeological site. A tourist spot. A treasured piece of Mexico's past. Who did Felix Rios have to pay off to make that happen?

If she were here under different circumstances, maybe she'd enjoy herself. The stone structure had a gorgeous yet dilapidated quality—a feeling of history and permanence. The darkening sky and the torchlight all around created a mystical scene. Her soul shivered. She wished Wyatt were here. Even surrounded by crowds, she felt so alone.

The raucous music stopped.

The crowd quieted.

The crash of the waves on the shore distantly echoed.

A man stepped up to the mic. *"Bienvenidos, damas y caballeros. El Señor de los Mares llegará pronto."*

People cheered, and the rest of his speech disappeared into the roar.

A peace came over her. Back in the village her half-brother, Miguel, had made her believe perhaps her father held some grudge against her mother and, by extension, her. But nothing about the partygoers, the music or the atmosphere frightened her. It was not what she'd expected at all.

Her father was here somewhere—Felix Rios. She wondered why would he go to all this trouble to bring her here. Maybe he wanted her. Maybe he had worried about her. Despite his criminal background, could he have any feelings for a long-lost daughter of the woman who had betrayed him?

Their escort led them away from the crowd and around the massive stone walls and structures that made up the ruins.

Selena gave Yolanda an inquisitive look. "Where are we going?"

She had conflicting feelings about her father. She had a curiosity and a longing to know him, but an equally strong feeling of fear and distrust. In her mind's eye, she imagined the father she'd always wanted and thought she had lost. A champion for her. A man who would love her and be proud of her.

Selena never had a choice. Her mother had hidden her, changed her name, and denied her a relationship with her father. Despite his criminal status, he was still her father. Blood of his blood. Half of who she was came from him.

"It's okay," said Yolanda and linked arms with her, as if they were friends on the playground. "Your father wishes to meet you, but not here."

Patricia and Silvio flanked them on either side as the guard led the way.

They came around the corner of a smaller stone outbuilding. A huge pyramid several stories high climbed into the evening sky. Torches lit up the base. A set of very steep and wide steps led to the top. The view from there must be amazing as it looked out over the ocean. As they approached, the sound of crashing waves grew louder.

A breeze picked up and blew gently across her face, the smell of seaweed and brine filled her nose. She wished she had time to enjoy the beach and the glorious ocean. To take off her shoes, sift the sand through her toes and wade through the surf. Her stiffened muscles ached after hours in the Jeep bouncing over jungle roads.

"*Aquí.*" The guard had led them to another small stone building with a darkened doorway. He stepped to the side to let them pass.

Yolanda urged her forward. "Your father will come to you."

"When?" Selena peered inside. Candles lit the interior. Although she'd expected an empty archaeological site, someone had made the space into a comfortable room with a rug, two chairs and a small table between them.

Her stomach fluttered.

"Soon," Yolanda replied. "Do you want me to wait with you?"

Patricia crossed her arms and glanced toward the party where the food and drinks were plentiful. Silvio had already downed his glass of stolen champagne. He set it on one of the stone walls that ran along the front of the building.

"You go back to the party," Selena said. She took a hesitant step toward the entrance. "I'll be fine."

"*Adiós, Claudia,*" Yolanda said. "*Buena suerte, amiga.*" She turned and joined her small team.

"*Gracias.*" For a moment Selena felt as if she were parting ways with a good friend. She ached for Yolanda to stay, but she needed to meet her father on her own. Hear what he had to say. Ask why he'd brought her here. She had so many questions, and she didn't know how she would react to the answers.

Before Selena entered the building, she caught sight of Patricia approaching her half-brother, Miguel, who had appeared out of nowhere. He'd driven off and left them on their own in the jungle. He'd seemed so eager to make sure Selena got to the party, and then he had raced off and abandoned them.

Words were exchanged between the two, and Miguel handed her a wad of bills.

The trio headed back to the party. Their figures retreated past the pyramid with its line of torches and around the corner. Their shadows played on the stone walls. Miguel stood there unmoving. His face was obscured by the darkness and the fluttering light of the torches, so Selena couldn't tell if he looked at her or stared into the distance. She shivered.

Someone spoke into the mic. People cheered raucously. The music picked up.

Selena's nerves caught fire. She stood in the center of the room. On the table were several lit candles that sputtered every time the breeze blew in from the ocean. The scent of vanilla and smoke filled the air. Selena closed her eyes and breathed it in, hoping for calm. She played with her hair, twisting it into a knot at her nape and letting it go, over and over and over. Pacing the room, she couldn't sit still.

Distantly, she thought of Wyatt. The lost phone. Her only connection to him. She wondered where he was. What he'd think of her if he knew she was about to meet the most notorious drug lord in Mexico. He'd probably give her a wary glance and tell her all the facts about why this was a bad idea.

The guard outside limited her options. Would he hurt her if she tried to run? Could she escape? Maybe while everyone was busy at the party.

But she was tired of running. She trailed her hand across the back of one of the chairs. Where would she go? She'd be in the same exact position she'd been in when she arrived. No knowledge of anything. Why fight so hard when she couldn't win?

"Claudia, mi hija."

Selena started and turned to face the dark figure who stood in the doorway.

❦ 24 ❦

A middle-aged man with a goatee, wearing designer cowboy boots, crisp jeans and a western-styled shirt came toward her from the doorway, holding out his arms, and flanked by two muscular guards. "Finally, I see you after so many years," he said in accented English.

He embraced her warmly.

Selena stood dumbly. She wanted a moment to take it all in, but he enveloped her in strong, muscular arms. Although she knew who he was and had seen what he and his people were capable of, she found herself wanting the comfort she found there.

Their gazes met as they stepped apart. The same eyes. Hers. Miguel's. All the same. A deep sense of belonging came over her. It surprised her with its fierceness.

Her family.

He invited her to sit. Candlelight threw strange shadows on his face.

The two guards took positions by the door.

Instantly, the room felt crowded and too warm.

"I go by Selena," she corrected him softly.

Felix raised his brows. "Oh?"

"I thought you were dead." The words poured out without much thought.

Felix Rios regarded her for a moment. "Your mother told you I was dead?"

"Yes." Her stomach became upset. She'd been part of a lie without even knowing. More lies than one. "She said you died in a car accident many years ago. When I was a baby."

Felix Rios snapped his fingers and gestured to his body-guards. The two men left without a word. He waited until they left to speak. "And your mother? Where is she now?"

His eyes glittered in the dim light like a snake's.

"In jail." The admission embarrassed her.

"Hm," Felix murmured. His lips curled into a smile. "Never thought Pilar was the type to get herself into trouble. She always managed to find a way to avoid it." He put his hands together in a pleading gesture and spoke in a high-pitched tone, *"Fe, por favor*. No more with *las drogas."* He snorted.

The crude imitation of her mother struck her as unnecessarily nasty. "So, what really happened?" She had trouble swallowing and cleared her throat. "Miguel said you were never married to my mother..."

"A lie."

The strength of his answer startled her.

"Miguel is troubled. Many disappointments have turned him into an angry man."

"My mother never told me I had a brother."

"No, I suppose she would not have." He gave a grim twist to his mouth.

Her father seemed unwilling to expand on any of his answers and provide clarity. She changed the subject, "How did I end up in Arizona and you end up..." Selena didn't want to say the words —how had he ended up as a cartel boss.

He waved a hand. "We can discuss this later."

A hardness existed inside the man. A warm exterior covered something more sinister. The way he commanded the room. The strength of his voice. The attitude toward his own son, his own flesh and blood. Felix Rios was used to getting his way.

"I have something special planned. For you." He stood and offered a hand.

"For me?" The little girl inside her wanted to trust him. Her mother had loved her, but she'd never felt the love of a father for his daughter.

"Yes. Come." He led her out of the small building.

Miguel had disappeared.

A woman—about her mother's age, with a beautiful mound of prematurely white hair intricately piled on her head and wearing bright red lipstick—waited for them with the two body-guards on the grass carpet that covered the entire site. "*Dios mio! Fe, quien es?*"

"This, Gabriela"—he urged Selena forward into the torch-light—"is my daughter. *Tu sobrina.*"

"Claudia?" The woman cocked her head and scanned Selena from head to toe. "*Se parece a Pilar.*" She frowned a bit at the declaration.

"*Piensas?*" Felix asked. He addressed Selena in English, "This is your Tia Gabriela. My brother's wife. She will help you. Go with her now."

"And the surprise?" Selena's head was spinning.

He smiled a bright, wide smile. "No worries, *mi hija. La sorpresa llegaré.*" He held his forefinger and thumb close together. "*Casi-casi.*"

The bodyguards flanked him as he left her with Gabriela. Before he walked away, she leaned into her brother-in-law, whis-pered in his ear, and handed him a cell phone. Felix looked at the phone as she whispered—his gaze landing squarely on Selena.

Wyatt's phone.

The hair lifted on the back of Selena's neck.

Gabriela held his upper arm and nodded. A look passed between them.

"Come," Gabriela said to Selena, "let's get you dressed for the party."

Behind the main walls of the Tulúm ruins stood a wild coastal tumble of trees and shrubbery. Thick, almost impassable.

Tia Gabriela led Selena right to the edge of the dense greenery. With the sun almost gone behind the trees, Selena shivered. It made no sense. Why were they headed away from the party?

"Felix wanted me to pick out a dress for you. Something special and fitting for the daughter of *El Señor de los Mares.*" The woman broke through the tree line, and a narrow dirt path appeared, barely visible in the gloom.

"And the dress is back here?" The doubt in Selena's voice must have been obvious.

"Your father is placing his trust in you. He has many secrets, and nobody knows them all. I am to share some of his secrets with you."

"And why would you know any of his secrets?"

"Felix trusts almost no one. But I was the one who took care of his *hijo* while he was in prison." She said the last word with a snap. "My husband had died, so I raised Miguel like my own son. That bestowed a certain amount of trust on me."

After the two women walked a short distance, the trees opened into a clearing. A small wall tent had been erected there. A strange place for one.

The music grew more and more distant. Selena forced her feet to move forward even though everything in her was telling her to run. Everyone she'd met so far who was supposed to be family gave off sinister waves. Her brother, father, and now her aunt all had a hard tinge to their words, their actions. Any warmth seemed faked. Again, Selena was left wondering exactly why she'd been brought here. Why had she been chased across Mexico, had guns pointed at her, had men drag her through the jungle only to now tell her they were going to dress her up for a party. It made no sense.

Her mind turned toward the only solid thing she'd been able to depend upon: Wyatt. Although she'd misjudged him when the bus had been hijacked, she realized now she'd been wrong about him. About his motives. About his feelings. When she'd heard his voice on the phone, it had brought her relief and a small amount of joy. She'd felt hope and lightness and possibility.

She wished he were here now.

But Wyatt was not coming, and she would have to figure this out on her own. Whom could she trust? Yolanda? Patricia? It seemed as if her very angry brother might have had something to do with how she'd ended up here. The bus on the highway. Had that been his doing? He'd shot at them in Mexico City. He'd barely concealed his anger and bitterness from her in the hut in the village.

And now she felt the same vibe rising off of Gabriela. Resentment. Hatred. Seething anger.

"Yes, Miguel told me you cared for him while his father was in prison." Selena hoped that her praise would soften Gabriela's feelings toward her.

"He had no one else." They stopped at the entrance to the tent. "Your mother made sure of that."

"I don't know what you mean."

Gabriela confronted Selena. "Pilar had a hand in the death of Miguel's mother. She died of a broken heart. I saw it with my own eyes." She swept her hand up her elaborate hairstyle to smooth any stray strands into place. "Your mother was no angel, Claudia. You can get that out of your head right now. She abandoned Felix. She put him in prison to save herself, fled to America and disappeared. She didn't care if Felix ever came out alive. She was a cold, unfeeling bitch. I'm curious what kind of daughter she raised."

Selena widened her eyes. "I had nothing to do with any of this, if it's true." She raced through the memories of her mother: hard working, loving, sweet-natured, kind. She couldn't imagine the woman Gabriela was describing.

"Felix learned to be more cautious after your mother's treachery. We don't let anyone outside the family get close." Gabriela paused and a raised a brow. "We aren't quite sure what to do with you yet, but better you are in our hands than the hands of our enemies."

Selena felt dizzy. She had no words.

Gabriela's demeanor changed in a split second from angry to pleasant. "Let's set this aside, shall we? Your father wanted you to be dressed properly for the occasion." She scanned Selena's bedraggled appearance from head to toe. "And I want to follow his wishes. Come." She held open the tent flap.

They entered.

Inside was a rack of dresses and boxes of shoes with designer names on them. The ground had been covered with a tarp. Two wooden chairs sat in a corner.

Strange.

Gabriela flicked through the choices. Blue. Black. Green. Floral. "This looks like it might fit you." She held up a red dress with a bodice covered in sequins and a short, flouncy skirt. "Put it on."

She handed it to Selena.

Selena looked for a place to change.

Gabriela smirked. "We are both women. There is nothing to be ashamed of."

Selena's face heated. She clutched the fancy dress in frozen hands.

"Your father is waiting for you. I don't think you want him to come looking for us. Do you?" Gabriela turned to the boxes of shoes. "Size six?"

While Gabriela's back was turned, Selena whipped off her T-shirt. She wished there was a shower here so she could rinse off the sweat and dirt. Her hair felt limp and greasy. Not exactly party-ready. Then, she slipped the dress over her head.

"Good. Good." Gabriela eyed her niece. "It fits well. Your father will be pleased. Only the best for his daughter."

Selena stepped out of her jeans and smoothed down the skirt. There was no mirror for her to see herself. She touched her hair.

"I will fix that for you. Sit." Gabriela pointed at the chairs. "And try these on." She handed her a box of silver stilettos.

Selena imagined walking back to the party in such shoes. She wondered how she'd avoid breaking an ankle.

She took the box and sat in a chair.

Gabriela positioned herself behind. She ran her fingers through Selena's hair and worked out the tangles. "Braids would work best, I think."

Selena smoothed the flouncy skirt and kicked off her flats she'd been wearing since Mexico City.

Gabriela braided two individual braids on either side of Selena's head. "Your mother was a beautiful woman."

Selena listened, unsure of where her long-lost aunt was headed.

"Your father was crushed when she betrayed him. Do you know how long we've looked for her—for you?"

"No."

"Many years." Her aunt pulled gently to tighten a braid. "I did not think Pilar could be so clever."

"I never knew any of it. I swear."

Gabriela stilled her hands. "Miguel said there was a likeness between the two of you." She leaned forward, her breath hot in Selena's ear, "Nothing about you is alike. Nothing."

Gabriela tightened her grip on Selena's hair, pulling painfully at her scalp.

"That hurts."

"I am almost finished," her aunt spat out. She crisscrossed the braids over the top of Selena's head and forced several bobby-pins in to secure them.

The last pin pricked. Selena jerked out of the chair. "Enough. Are we supposed to go back to the party now?" She slipped into the silver heels.

Gabriela touched her throat. Her hands shook slightly. "Pilar..."

Selena touched the side of her head. One braid had been plaited more tightly than the other. "Can we go?"

A few beats passed. Her aunt pursed her lips. "Felix trusts me. I know him well. Maybe now he will see with clearer eyes." She whisked away the dress hanger and the empty shoe box. "She was nothing more than another pretty girl in a red dress," she murmured.

Selena followed Gabriela out of the tent. Distant music echoed through the dense trees. From their position in the dark of the jungle, the spotlights and torches created an eerie glow above the walled ruins.

Selena's spiked heels sank into the dirt. The oddness of wearing party attire in the wilds near the ocean crossed her mind.

Gabriela led her back to the ruins and through another stone entrance.

Miguel and one of Felix's men were in the distance, talking.

"*Miguelito*," Gabriela called out in a bright voice. She held out her arms to her nephew.

Miguel gave his aunt a quick embrace and kissed her on the cheek. "*Muy hermosa, tia mia.*"

Selena couldn't help but notice the warm affection between the two. Almost like mother and son. Clearly, Gabriela had stepped in while Miguel's father was in prison and treated him as her own child. Selena wondered if the older woman ever had children of her own. Her attitude toward Miguel revealed maybe not.

"Come." Miguel directed to them both with a sweep of his hand. He barely gave Selena a glance. "*El Señor* awaits."

Tia Gabriela took Miguel's proffered arm with a warm smile.

Selena trailed behind in her uncomfortably high heels. She hadn't worn shoes like these since senior prom when she'd thought she was the height of maturity. Three painful blisters and pinched toes later, she'd realized how stupid heels could be.

The music grew louder, the crowd rowdier as they came around the bend. Selena was shocked to see men on horseback. Very drunk men holding wine bottles and wearing spurs. Hooting and hollering, one held a pistol in the air and fired it into the darkened sky.

Selena started at the unexpected noise and nearly stumbled as a heel turned under her in the soft grass. She longed for her practical flats.

One of the men in the crowd grabbed her elbow and helped her find her feet.

"*Señorita Claudia,*" he said with a bit of wonder.

She nodded and thanked him for the assistance.

The crowd parted as she approached the stage.

Gabriela frowned at the attention Felix Rios's daughter caused.

Miguel scowled.

On the stage stood the drug lord. He'd joined the mariachi band on and had grabbed a mic. "*Caballeros y damas! Esta noche es una noche especial. Te presento a mi hija—Claudia Rios.*"

Time froze. Selena stood in the middle of a hushed crowd of finely dressed young women and men in fancy western wear. Horses stomped their feet impatiently on the ground. In the distance, waves crashed against the shore.

"*Querida, ven aquí.*" Felix stood back from the microphone and bid her forward.

"Come, sister, my father asks for you." Miguel grabbed her by the hand and roughly pulled her toward the stage.

Gabriela, head held high, stood near the edge of the crowd, a sly smile on her face.

Selena ordered herself to calm down. Relax. Do what they wanted her to do. She had nowhere to run to. No escape. To act irrationally could be deadly. None of her *family* appeared happy to see her. She couldn't quite grasp the reason why they'd wanted her to dress up and play a part, if they despised her so.

Was it jealousy? Could Miguel and Gabriela be jealous of her father's interest in tracking her down? Had she been the child they'd wished stayed lost?

Miguel pushed her toward the stone steps that led to the stage they'd created amidst the ruins. Her father held out his hand and helped her up the final one. Selena stepped into the bright spotlights.

Felix stiffened. He looked into the crowd and met Gabriela's gaze. She gave him a nod.

The exchange made Selena catch her breath. Something was horridly wrong here. The smiles, the pleasantries, the expensive dress and designer shoes. She felt as if she were a puppet on a string, a character playing a role in a play she knew nothing about. Although deep down she wanted to believe her father had come looking for her out of love, out of some sense of obligation, the conversation with Gabriela made her think differently.

Wyatt would think it through. Take in all the evidence and decide how to move forward. God, how she wished he were here. He would know what to do.

Selena tamped down the part of her that wanted the love and acceptance of a father she'd never had in her life. It would be so easy to grab onto it and never let it go. Forget about the hurts of the past and leave behind the lies and walk into a ready-made family in Mexico.

In some ways it would be the easier choice, as bizarre as that seemed. Officially, she was Mexican by birth. She had every right to remain in this country. She could dump her worries and concerns about her visa problems and forget about her life in America.

She fought back her uneasiness and smiled broadly at the crowd. She was the daughter of Felix Rios, *El Señor de los Mares*. People respected him, feared him, obeyed him. Maybe this had been her rightful place all along. She put out of her mind the strange things Gabriela had said in the tent, the internal sense of forboding, and relied on her father's words not to worry.

"*Claudia Rios, bienvenidos a México!*" her father said into the mic.

The crowd cheered and clapped.

"*Y bienvenidos a la familia Rios!*" Felix kissed her on the cheek, and the mariachi band began to play.

"Come, dance with me," said her father after the applause had died.

"Dance?" She questioned her ability to dance on a stage in front of a crowd of strangers in her stilettos.

"You can dance, no?" Felix pinched his lips together. "Or did your mother forget to teach you that as well?"

Selena didn't want to anger him. If he wanted to dance with her in front of his crowd of armed men, she'd dance. "Yes, let's."

He nodded at the mariachi band, who played a less raucous tune. He bowed and held her at arm's length for the crowd to admire. A smattering of claps erupted from the crowd. Women whispered behind their hands. Selena wasn't used to being the center of attention. She'd been nobody special back in Tucson. So strange to be here, in the midst of so many people, as if she were some sort of royalty in her fancy red dress and high heels.

Felix pulled her in and held her with a light touch. A respectable distance for father and daughter. Her father had an unreadable expression on his face. From across the courtyard, she spotted disapproving looks from her aunt and half-brother.

The rest of the partygoers stepped onto the dance floor with their dates. One by one they filled the space, and Selena's view of Miguel and Gabriela disappeared.

Felix spoke to her in a low voice. "Who braided your hair this way?"

Selena touched her head self-consciously. "Do you not like it?"

"I did not say that."

"Tia Gabriela."

Her father made a grunting noise. "When I saw you come to the stage, I thought I was seeing your mother in front of me. Gabriela likes to play her tricks."

Selena remembered the photo. The one she'd shared with Wyatt on the bus—a teenage Maria Hernandez in braids of a similar style wearing a red dress. "I didn't even realize."

"*No te preocupes*." Felix swirled her around. "I suppose it only makes me believe one-hundred percent that you are Pilar's daughter. You are my child."

"Why am I here?" Selena asked. "Why did you have to do this?"

"I am a dangerous man. Many people are interested in getting to me. When Miguel told me he found you in Mexico City through one of his contacts, I knew if he didn't pick you up you, they would."

"They?"

"My enemies. Whoever you think them to be." He gave a half shrug. "They all have a reason to use my daughter against me, and I wasn't about to let them do it."

Selena glanced at the crowd around them. "Do you have enemies here I should know about?"

A muscle twitched at the corner of his eye. "Perhaps." Felix led her off the dance floor. "Something came into my possession this evening, and I'd like to speak to you about it. Come with me." They melted into the crowd.

Gabriela and Miguel stood in the flickering torchlight and watched.

⁂

"I FIRST WANT TO SHARE SOMETHING WITH YOU," FELIX RIOS purred as he led her away from the music and noise.

"Oh?" Selena brows drew in.

"Something your mother never would've have believed." He captured her by the shoulders and squeezed. "A life that she couldn't envision and only could foresee the worst."

He paused then and scanned her face. Selena thought he might say something else, but instead he offered her an arm.

They walked around the stone structures. Elaborate construction. Amazing details. Even in the dim lighting, the craftsmanship and skill displayed was awe-inspiring.

"Did you know this was one of the last cities occupied by the Mayans?"

"I really know very little about the history of Mexico."

Felix clicked his tongue in disappointment. "Your mother didn't teach you Spanish and never told you the history of your birthplace?"

"She wanted me to be an American."

"Yes, I suppose she did."

The moon, low on the horizon, glowed brightly in a clear night sky. The breeze from the ocean blew more strongly than earlier in the evening. Selena pressed her hands against the gossamer netting of her skirt to keep it from flying away.

"I wanted to have the fiesta here because of its importance in Mayan trade routes—both by land and by sea. I also have trade routes by sea. I feel a deep connection to this place."

Selena noted how he made an attempt to normalize his business by connecting it to legitimate trade.

"The Mayans built this as a fort to defend against invaders. Tonight, I will defend our position against invaders as well. Those who wish to do us harm. To destroy what I've built all these years."

Selena wished she knew more about why her father had gone to prison. Had her mother been involved in his illegal activities? Had she truly ratted him out to the authorities as Miguel had said?

They approached the largest structure. "This is called *El Castillo*. Beyond the wall is the Temple of the God of Wind."

"Impressive." The steep, wide steps reached to the top. Selena wondered what *El Castillo* had looked like before the ravages of time. She touched the stone. Solid, permanent, real.

"*Venga*, Claudia." He held out his hand to her.

She accepted it. Rough hand in hers. Warmth. Security. A million promises in a simple touch. How much she wished for her father to be a different man—someone similar to the person her mother had described instead of a dangerous criminal. Conflicting emotions rippled through her.

Felix Rios, *El Señor de los Mares*, led her up the precipitous stone steps of the main structure in the middle of the ruins of Tulúm. In the fancy heels she'd been given, she trod carefully to avoid stumbling.

They ascended to the top and, beyond the ancient wall, stretched the sea. A rocky cliff lay below them. Anchored offshore, a large sailboat floated—its railing decorated with strings of lights. The moonlight lit up the white hull with a breathtaking glow. White-capped waves lapped against it.

"Oh." The word came out in a hushed voice.

"She's beautiful, no?"

Selena had never been on a sailboat or any boat. She'd lived most of her life in the desert. The sight mesmerized her. How lovely it would be to climb aboard, sail the blue waters of the Caribbean, and put all her worries behind her. She could forget about her visa problems, her mother in jail, the last, nightmarish three days.

"This could be your life, if you wanted it," said her father. "Everything could be yours."

Selena's heart flip flopped. She didn't know how to answer. He'd offered her the very fantasy she'd been imagining. But that was crazy. To live as a drug kingpin's daughter?

"I'm not sure," Selena said. Hearing his offer switched something on inside her. She was torn between what she knew was right and what she'd longed for her whole life—a father's love. "This is all a lot to handle. I'm not interested in being a part of... your work."

"I'm sorry to hear that. I wanted to believe my daughter had returned to me. That you were sorry for leaving me. That you came seeking forgiveness." His eyes narrowed. "I needed to see you, ask you for myself."

"I never intended to come here. I was forced to." She stared out at the sailboat bobbing in the water. "And finding out you were alive...I'm still trying to wrap my head around it."

"Miguel warned me when he found you. He warned me to let him handle it because you were too much of a risk," her father said. He gripped her hand tightly. "Now I know why you came to Mexico, *mi hija*."

Selena sensed a shift in his demeanor. A cold shift that chilled her.

"Miguel told me: You are helping the DEA. I did not want to believe him, but he showed me indisputable proof."

Her stomach dropped. "The DEA? Proof? I don't know what you are talking about." Selena wondered where Miguel had thought up such a crazy idea and when he'd shared this with Felix. "When they arrested my mother they told me I had to leave the country. I was scared. I trusted them when they told me I could get a visa here and go back home."

Felix laughed darkly. "No one is that naive. You think I'm

going to believe your little story?" He pulled a cell phone out of his pocket—Wyatt's cell phone that Gabriela had handed to him earlier. "The guards found this in your things, and Miguel had suspicions. He recharged it and found some very damning evidence. You had a direct line to the DEA. You sent them a map."

Selena's posture stiffened. Wyatt was DEA? "I—I didn't know. He worked at the embassy... He helped me get away." Her mind scrambled, but she formed a single question to take back control, "Did you know Miguel botched it?"

His eyebrows shot up.

She'd actually surprised him, so she took advantage of the momentary weakness. "The police handed me over to the *autodefenses* on the road to Mérida. Does that seem like something a capable son would do? Allow an enemy to get a hold of your daughter?"

In moments he'd processed the shock and hardened his features once again.

Felix held up the device. "Do you deny this is your phone?" His voice had a serious undertone. He touched her cheek. "So much like your mother. Did she tell you to come back? Did she use you to get herself a better deal? A way to get out of prison?"

Selena pulled away. "My mother lied to me my entire life. I knew nothing about you until your son tried to kidnap me off the street."

"You may be my daughter by blood, but you are the child of Pilar who betrayed me and took my family away. Gabriela and Miguel warned me not to bring you here. They thought it all seemed too easy. They were right." His face contorted into a mask of evil. "When I heard Pilar had disappeared after my arrest and had taken you with her, I didn't want to believe it. My child. How could she do that to me? I wanted to believe she'd left to protect you from my rivals and would return when things were safe. But years went by, and I never heard from her again. She'd stolen you away."

"I don't know what you want me to say. I was a little girl," Selena said. "I didn't know any of this. I was a little girl who thought her father had died. I've done nothing wrong."

"I wanted to bring you here for a reunion. A second chance for me to be a father to my only daughter." Felix's skin grew mottled, and his nostrils flared. "But now I know for you it was only about leading the wolves to my door."

Selena shrank back. The only escape from the dangerous drug lord lay many feet below. The sea breeze softly caressed her naked shoulders in stark contrast to her father's hard glare.

Felix Rios dropped Wyatt's cell phone on the stone and crushed it under his boot. "You exposed me with your sloppiness. *Estúpida!*"

A flame of anger sparked inside her. Nobody had the right to call her that. Her brain came to life. Her quick-thinking ways sprung to the forefront of everything.

She searched for a route of escape. Her father might, at any moment, send her plummeting down the stone steps. His hatred was that palpable. She stepped back a few more feet.

"But thank God for Gabriela and Miguel. They opened my eyes."

She calculated several things at once: the distance from the side of the wall to the next level below, the dash she'd need to make through a small courtyard, and then a leap to the ground below... Maybe a ten- or fifteen-foot drop.

He stalked toward her. "Just like your mother, you are not the innocent girl you pretend to be."

She frowned.

He crossed his arms and took a wide stance. "Miguel is right. I don't need a traitorous daughter who would destroy my life's work."

In a flash, he grabbed hold of her upper arm. He forced her

to face the ocean. "That sailboat? The one you so foolishly thought I was offering to you? You are here for one reason alone —so that I can destroy my enemies once and for all, and you are going to watch. A punishment for your foolishness."

Selena gasped. "No." She leaned away from him.

"After tonight, they will think twice about fucking with *El Señor de los Mares*." He shoved her.

She stumbled on her stilettos and landed hard on her knees, inches from the edge of the steep stairway. A cry of pain escaped from her lips.

"Yes, Miguel created the perfect tool to use against them. *Inocente* Selena." He ground out her name between his teeth. "Even now they are coming here thinking they have surprised me, caught me unawares. But Miguel made sure that wouldn't happen. The leak about the party. That was him. Your boyfriend is headed my way with his DEA friends, and we will be ready for them. Your mother couldn't get the best of me twice." He spat on the stone slab beneath his feet. "I'm disgusted that you are my daughter."

She grew numb. Wyatt was in danger, and she'd been the one to lure him to her.

"All those are party guests down there?" He laughed. "Those are my men, armed to the teeth. Ready to protect their *Señor*."

Hot tears pricked at the corner of her eyes. She didn't deserve such scorn, such hatred. She quietly slipped out of her heels in preparation for her escape.

"Nothing to say now? You have become dumb, like your mother. Your helpless, pathetic mother who ran away. Only a weakling hides from his enemies."

Selena felt a bloom of hot anger grow inside. An anger she'd never felt in her life. Everything had been taken from her. Her mother, her life, Wyatt, and now the father she'd long idolized. The man she thought was dead and had loved her turned out to be a warped man. "You think your son is so loyal to you?" she whispered from under her veil of hair as she knelt on the steps. "You think you can trust him with your life tonight?"

Felix grabbed her by the hair and hauled her up.

Selena yelped in pain.

He tilted her head back and stared into her eyes. "How dare you? I could snap your neck, and nobody would even know."

"You know I'm right. You've wondered before, haven't you?" She glared back at him, unafraid. Selena knew she'd hit on a soft spot. The all-powerful Felix Rios was not as tough as he wanted her to believe. "The *autodefenses*. Was that really a mistake? Or did Miguel tip them off to give them leverage against you? Maybe he wants your empire for himself."

"You lie!" He twisted her hair even tighter in his hands.

Her scalp burned. "Miguel cannot be trusted. He tried to lose us in the jungle. Raced ahead. Left us behind to rot with a broken-down Jeep and a flat tire in the middle of nowhere. He didn't care about your plan. He only cared about himself. Ask Patricia. She'll tell you."

For a second time, he shoved her away from him. This time, with her high heels discarded, she caught herself by holding onto the low stone wall behind her. "Miguel and Gabriela. The two of them. I saw them talking. Plotting near the stage. How much do you trust your sister-in-law?"

"Gabriela has always—always—been on my side," Felix raged. "When your mother sent me to prison, Gabriela took care of *Miguelito*. She was like a mother to him. And she was there when I got out. She had kept my business going all those years..."

But Selena knew her words had disturbed him. His forehead wrinkled, and he rubbed his jaw. "How do you know my mother was the one to turn you in?" She didn't know if this was possible, but went on gut instinct. Anything to create doubt. Anything to give her time to get away from this madman. If Wyatt was on his way, she had to warn him about the trap he was walking into.

Felix Rios cried out in anger and frustration. *"Cállate!"* He lunged at her. "You are a liar."

Selena scrambled onto the wall and peered over the edge. A courtyard lay below. She hesitated. It was far. Too far. She'd likely break a leg.

"Demasiado tarde, hermana." Miguel locked a hand down on her forearm. A wicked smile flashed.

Where did he come from?

"Gracias, Miguel," said her father. He rebuttoned his suit jacket, which had come loose in their scramble. *"Debo volver a la fiesta. Sabes que hacer."* He swept his hands down the front of his clothes as if to rid them of contamination.

Selena's hesitation had cost her the chance to escape.

"Come. My father has the perfect spot for you to wait for him." Miguel twisted her arm painfully. "You will not put up a fuss now, will you?" He revealed a revolver in a holster at his side.

Selena, seeing only dead ends in every direction, followed him down. She sent up a silent prayer for Wyatt and hoped he would be smart enough to stay away. Far away from her, from Tulúm, from the trap waiting for him.

❧ 26 ☙

iguel held her upper arm like a vise and marched her to a wooden staircase that led from the bottom of *El Castillo* to the beach below.

"I hated you," he spat out between his teeth.

The stairs were cool beneath her feet. "You never even met me until this morning." She fantasized about pushing him over the railing to the rocks below.

"You ruined my life."

The music from the party grew quieter here, masked by the noise of the surf. The wind had picked up and, in the moonlight, white caps were visible in the distance.

"I did no such thing." Selena had managed to seed some doubt in her father's head. She'd seen it in his demeanor. If it had worked with him, why not with Miguel? "I was a baby when my mother took me out of Mexico. I had no idea what she'd done. Besides, how are you so certain she was the one who turned your father into the authorities?"

"Who else could it be?" Miguel pulled her roughly down the next set of stairs to the landing halfway down the cliff-side. "Pilar knew everything about his business. Everything."

"So did Gabriela." The wind picked up and blew her skirt around her legs.

He quickly twisted her arm behind her back. "Fuck you."

Selena gasped at the pain. "Who took care of the business while your father was in prison? Gabriela." He twisted it harder. She swallowed. "Who would have something to gain if he was out of the picture? Gabriela. She never had children of her own. She acts as if you are her own child."

He put his face inches from hers. Their twin gazes met. "I am her son now."

"I'm sure she was surprised as anyone when Felix made it out of prison alive." She shoved her fear to the back of her mind. "A dangerous place, I'd think."

He stood motionless on the landing.

"I've read the stories. Mexican prisons are notorious for their deadliness. Stabbings, corruption, bribery, murder. All of it. And Felix managed to survive how many years in such a place?"

"Seven years." Miguel relaxed his grip on her arm.

"Seven years. Wow." Selena let out a ragged breath as the pain receded. "Someone would have to be truly evil to want your father to risk death for a few drug deals."

"Yes, your mother." He let her go and shoved her toward the next set of steps that ended at the beach.

Selena massaged her sore arm. "Who had the most to gain if your father was arrested? That's what I'd be wondering." She took the steps slowly, deliberately. "My mother got nothing out of it as far as I can tell. We were poor, very poor. We struggled. She worked as a waitress all those years. While Tia Gabriela grew rich off of your father's business…"

"You lie. I will not listen to this shit. You think you can show up here and step into the role of daughter when you did nothing to help him?" They reached the sand, and he loomed over her. He stood almost a foot taller than she, lean and muscular. Dangerous. "This is my legacy. My future. My family. You are nothing. You are less than nothing. An ignorant girl who stepped off that plane in Mexico City completely unaware. Useless."

The cool of the sand felt good between her toes. She had no idea what Miguel was going to do with her, but she would make goddamn sure she didn't go down like a coward. "And yet Felix wanted you to bring me to him. Why do you think that is? Why would he prefer a daughter he never knew over his only son?"

"He never loved you." He picked up a gas can that sat under the landing in the shadows.

"Why did he bring me here, Miguel?" Her breathing picked up at the sight of the can. Images of burning bodies flashed through her mind.

"To exact his revenge."

"So, I'm a pawn in some game?" she asked.

Miguel pushed her forward to the waterline.

Selena moved in the direction he wanted. "When Gabriela looks at me, when you look at me, I feel hatred. I've done nothing to either of you. I was dragged into this mess. You are the one that followed me, tracked me down, forced me here against my will. Why?"

"My father wanted to find out the truth. And he did. I made sure of that."

As they made their way down the beach, Selena spied an inflatable boat on the sand beyond the high tide line. "And you? Why were you willing to play along? I seem to be getting in your way."

"I do as my father tells me to do." He set down the gas can next to the watercraft—a Zodiac.

Selena's mouth grew dry. The gas had been for the outboard motor. "Is that true? Or are you doing what Gabriela asked you to do?"

Miguel said nothing. He rolled away a large stone that held down the Zodiac's line to keep it from drifting in the tide.

Selena kicked at the sand in frustration. "I'm sick and tired of being used. I want no part of your family, this business. Don't you understand that?"

"Get in." Miguel urged. "My father wants you to wait for him on the sailboat."

"To watch people die? I don't understand."

"Get. In." He grabbed her by the arm and flung her into the boat.

Selena caught herself on the bowline that ran around the edge of the craft and twisted her knee. She scrambled to get out. She didn't trust her half-brother. They'd be far away from the party, the crowd of people, her father. Any number of things could occur in the ocean on a boat with no one but the two of them.

Miguel grabbed her skirt and yanked.

Selena sat hard on the sand. In anger and fear, she seized his foot and pulled.

He tripped and fell with a grunt.

Selena scrambled to her feet, her knee burning, and ran down the beach. In the distance she saw a figure and ran toward it. She didn't know if she could reach this person, but she would try. "Help me!" she screamed. The wind and waves carried away her voice. She knew her half-brother could catch up to her at any minute. Plus, he was armed. Would he go so far as to shoot her in the back?

Fear pushed her forward. She stumbled over the loose sand, until she found herself closer to the surf. The wet sand beneath her feet made for easier running. "Help, please!" She waved her hand at the figure, now closer. Now visible. Now recognizable.

Her whole body shook. Tears streaked across her face. Relief filled her as she fell into his arms. "Wyatt. Wyatt, help me."

❦ 27 ❦

From afar, Wyatt spied the ruins of Tulúm lit up with torches and spotlights. He slowed down and bowed his head to catch his breath. After the sun had set, he'd followed the distant lights for miles, hiding from the guards who'd roamed the road above.

Exhaling, he looked up to scan the ancient walls and the surroundings for guards, guns, obstacles. Alone and unarmed, he fought off negative thoughts that threatened to immobilize him. The night of the fire came back in a rush. How worthless, weak and incapable he had been. His mother had berated him and even then, he'd failed. What chance did he have against an entire cartel?

A figure, etched by moonlight, appeared on the beach.

"Help me!"

Wyatt knew the voice. He knew it.

A jolt went through him. He leaped forward.

Selena.

"Help, please!"

He caught her in his arms. She collapsed into them.

Warmth radiated throughout his body. His mind skipped into the present. The dark past faded.

"Wyatt." Selena shook all over. "Wyatt help me."

"Are you all right?" Wyatt asked. He tipped up her chin and scanned her face. "I didn't know if you'd be here. They said there was a party at Chichén Itzá, that your father had you. The DEA is coming."

Selena wrapped her arms around his neck and kissed him. Full, fast and hard. "Miguel... He's right behind me."

The kiss shocked Wyatt into silence.

She grabbed his hand and tugged him into a run. Back up the beach in the direction he'd come from. "Come on!"

Wyatt turned over in his mind the distance he'd covered, the guards patrolling the road. Selena wore a party dress and bare feet. What now?

Flashlights played on the sand several hundred yards distant. Felix's men must've heard the cries for help.

Wyatt's heart skipped a beat. "We can't go that way." The only direction they could run would be back toward Tulúm and the cartel.

He scanned the beach beside the ruins ready to flee.

"But he's got a gun."

"He hasn't moved." Wyatt pointed. "What did you do to him?"

"I just...I only tripped him up." Selena took in the distant scene.

The Zodiac, loosed from its mooring, drifted in and out with the surf. A body lay on the sand, unmoving.

"Well, he must've fallen pretty hard." Wyatt contemplated their best hope to reach safety.

"The party is a trap," Selena explained. "We've have to go. We need to tell the DEA."

"You know about the DEA?" He cocked his head.

"Where are they, Wyatt?" she pressed. "He's going to kill everyone."

"I don't know." He scanned the beach around them, seeming to focus on nothing. "We got separated."

The men on the beach rapidly closed the distance.

SELENA DUG DEEP FOR IDEAS. THEY HAD NO BACK UP, NO CAR, no phone, no nothing to call for help or get away. Armed cartel men were mere yards from their location.

"The boat." She turned and headed back down the beach. "Before he wakes up. It's our only chance out of here. Come on."

"You know, I thought I wouldn't miss this," said Wyatt. "But I was wrong."

"Miss what?" Selena limped across the wet packed sand in bare feet.

"You," he said matching her much shorter, more awkward stride.

She held his hand, and they backtracked down the beach. A tingling warmth filled her limbs. She never wanted to let go.

₭ 28 ₰

As they cautiously approached the scene, Wyatt set off after the drifting Zodiac. Selena crept closer to the still body of her half-brother. He lay awkwardly on the sand. She expected him to regain consciousness at any minute, and she wanted to make sure he was disarmed before that happened.

She inched closed and leaned over him for a better look. Her nursing skills kicking in. ABC—airway, breathing, circulation. Basic first aid concepts filling her mind.

His eyes stood wide open. A splash of blood visible across the large rock that had served as the anchor.

Oh God.

"Wyatt?" She backed away.

"I got it!" Wyatt, up to his knees in the surf, held the rope that connected to the boat, which had almost drifted away.

Selena glanced at the ruins. She expected to see Felix Rios at any moment, gun drawn and pointed at her. "Wyatt, we have a problem."

Wyatt joined her on the sand, his wet khakis clinging to his calves. He dragged the watercraft behind him. "Is he dead?"

She nodded.

"Shit."

"I didn't mean to." She mentally ordered herself to calm down. "I tripped him, and I guess he fell on it." She pointed at the offending rock.

"Who is it?"

"My brother," Selena whispered in disbelief. She couldn't take her eyes off the blood pooled in the sand around his head. The sea breeze played with a few strands of hair that had been missed by the pomade he wore.

"Oh, I'm sorry." He ran a hand over his face. "I didn't know you had a brother."

"I didn't either. Not until today." Her voice drifted off

"Ah." Wyatt knelt by the body, checking pockets. He tucked Miguel's gun in his waistband and recovered a cell phone and wallet. "These might come in handy."

Wyatt set upon the barely cold body of Miguel. His ability to be calm and thoughtful in the midst of horror startled her. He shoved his finds into his own pockets.

"Come on." He placed his hands on his hips. "Let's go."

"We can't leave him here." A weighted down feeling overtook her.

"Yes, we can." He grabbed her hand. "You hardly knew him. It's okay."

"No, it's not that. Those men coming down the beach..." A heightened watchfulness invaded her mind. "If they find the body, I don't know what Felix might do."

Wyatt instantly understood. "Let's get him into the Zodiac. We can dump him in the water."

Selena wished she could be anywhere else in the world. She took a deep breath. "Okay."

"It'll be all right." Wyatt picked up on her uncertainty. "I'll take him by the shoulders, you do the feet end. We can drag him to it, and then roll him in. It'll work."

Wyatt grabbed his end. Miguel's head lolled to one side. Selena's stomach roiled.

"Focus on his shoes," Wyatt encouraged. "You've got this. Almost there."

She had no idea how hard it was to carry dead weight. At barely five-foot-two and a little over a hundred pounds, Selena struggled in the sand. Wyatt did most of the work.

A booming voice carried from the loudspeakers. "*Nuestras invitadas estarán aquí pronto. Prepárense, caballeros!*"

Selena recognized it as Felix.

"We don't have much time," Wyatt said.

Selena didn't ask him to translate. She grunted and took several difficult steps forward. Her ankle burned at the extra weight.

Wyatt reached the Zodiac first and hauled the front end of Miguel into the watercraft.

Selena worked hard to shove his feet over the side. Wyatt grabbed around the dead man's knees and helped lift the rest of the body inside.

She shuddered at the thought of sitting next to Miguel's still-warm body in the cramped boat.

Wyatt grabbed the rope and pulled it back toward the surf. "Come on!" With the extra weight, it took a lot more effort to move it across the sand.

Selena limped behind.

Wyatt dragged the craft into the shallow water. The waves caught it and lifted it a few inches. Wyatt again stood to his knees in the ocean. "Get in."

He grabbed the rope that ringed the outside and stilled it for her.

Selena rushed forward. The warm tropical waters of the ocean felt good between her sandy toes. She'd never been on a boat in her life, except a raft in the community pool. She threw a leg over the side. Her barefoot touched Miguel. She shuddered.

Pushing off from the ground with her other foot, she propelled herself into the watercraft. She tumbled and landed on top of Miguel's body, scrambling in horror. The Zodiac bumped along the sandy bottom with her extra weight.

Wyatt waded deeper.

A single gunshot rang out.

"Hurry, Wyatt!" She could see the flashlights closing in on their location.

The tide worked against Wyatt, pushing the watercraft back toward the shore with each wave. Soon, he stood chest deep. A large wave rolled toward him and blasted seawater in his face. He sputtered. "We have to get out past the breakers."

"Can you get in?" Selena sat near the bow. She wanted to help, but her arms were too short. The deep water would make it difficult for Wyatt to climb in.

The sailboat loomed in the distance. The lights along its rail lit up the water's surface.

Wyatt grabbed hold of the rope around the edge and hauled himself out of the water.

Selena marveled at his strength. She grabbed his soaked shirt and leaned back, using her weight to help him over the side. As Wyatt tumbled in, so did a good amount of seawater.

Several more gunshots fired. And then more. Pauses of silence followed by the rat-a-tat of rifle fire. A few loud cries.

"We've got to start the motor." Wyatt, barefoot and dripping water, stumbled over Miguel's body to reach the rear of the craft. A small outboard motor was mounted to the back. He pulled out the choke, braced his foot on the side, and yanked the cord. The motor sputtered to life.

As the boat leaped forward in the strong current, Selena stumbled. Sitting down hard on one of the seat planks, she met the dead-eyed gaze of her half-brother and looked quickly away.

Wyatt latched onto the steering handle, ignored the gun fight on shore, and fixed his gaze on the deeper water beyond. He wiped saltwater out of his eyes and fixated on the task.

The ocean was rougher than she'd anticipated. The waves tossed the small inflatable craft, even though it was equipped with a powerful outboard. They bounced in the air and landed hard. Selena's teeth bit down on her tongue in one unexpected drop. Her stomach roiled. She had nothing to focus her gaze on but the lights from the ruins and the occasional explosions from rifle fire.

Wyatt steered them to the east and veered away from the sailboat.

On the shore, the men had caught up to the place where the Zodiac had once been beached. The played their lights on the dark ocean waves, but Selena and Wyatt were too far to be seen, and the gunfire and crash of the water against the shore, covered up the rumble of the engine.

It could be dangerous to be within visual range of anyone who might be aboard Felix's boat.

"The water's too rough. I'm not sure we'll be steady enough to dump him." Wyatt gestured at the body between them.

"We've got to get out of here, Wyatt." Selena scanned the deck of the sailboat as they buzzed past, worried someone might appear at any moment and realize what had happened. Felix's men were expecting Miguel to arrive with her aboard.

Wyatt headed the small craft straight into the rolling waves to break them against the bow. "That's about the best I can do."

Selena froze, scared to let go of the seat.

Wyatt left the engine running and tied off the handle with the mooring rope, so it would continue its course. "Come on," he urged. "We have to get rid of him now."

Selena scrambled to her feet and grabbed hold of Miguel's legs. The roll of the waves frightened her. She used all her strength to steady herself.

Wyatt grabbed under his arms. They both hauled him toward

the water. The uneven weight distribution caused the craft to dip. Selena and Wyatt both stumbled toward the water, carrying Miguel with them.

Selena lost her footing, screamed, and fell out of the boat, landing in the rough ocean along with Miguel's body and Wyatt.

She waited for someone on the sailboat to see them and shots to come their way.

Nothing.

The sailboat floated silently. Waves slapped against its hull.

"The boat." Wyatt sputtered as the watercraft buzzed away, its engine still running. "Oh, shit, I lost the gun."

Selena tread water with a manic energy. As the Zodiac disappeared, her heart sank. She kicked at her skirts, and her feet hit the dead weight of Miguel. She didn't have time for disgust. She pushed against him with her bare feet and jettisoned away.

Her half-brother's body drifted with the current, swallowed up in the dark ocean.

Selena had learned basic survival swimming as a child, but had never been in deep water before. Only in swimming pools at a friend's house or at the YMCA in Tucson. The dark depths beneath terrified her. She imagined sharks and stinging jellyfish and other creatures watching her.

"Selena," Wyatt soothed. "We need to head for shore."

"I can't do it." Sea spray hit her face. She didn't want to drown. "It's too far away." The ruins were barely visible. Her heart thudded dully in her chest. Impossible.

"You can do this." Wyatt swam up to her. "One kick at a time. We're drifting out to sea. We have to move."

Wyatt's words helped her beat back the panic. She had to forget about her fear and focus on what she needed to do to survive.

Selena stroked with her arms and kicked hard. Wyatt swam beside her. He had an even, strong stroke. Trusting he wouldn't abandon her, Selena found the inner strength to paddle and kick.

"That's it," Wyatt said between pants.

She ignored the sounds of distant gunfire, the eerie quiet of the ocean at night, and focused on her body. Each stroke brought her closer and closer to land, to shore, to rescue, to escape.

Selena's lips trembled, and her breathing came out in erratic bursts.

Not everyone could handle deep water. Wyatt had to come up with a different plan. She'd never make it to shore.

He calculated their options.

"This way." He swam for the sailboat. Selena's stroke grew weaker, her chin dipped below the water line.

He pushed aside his worries about Rios' men being on board. He had no choice. His gut tightened at the thought of her drowning right in front of him. "You can do it."

He swam for the diving platform at the stern of the forty-foot sailboat and scanned the deck for signs of life. He reached out for Selena. They'd have to be quiet. Each stroke weaker than the last. He focused on her dark, dark eyes, which were round with fear and wet with unshed tears.

He peeked over the edge. No one on deck. Quickly, he untied a life ring and threw it in her direction, holding onto the rope. "Grab on to it," he urged in a whisper, not yet convinced they were alone. "Let me pull you in."

Selena slung an arm over the ring.

He pulled her in and helped her onto the diving platform. At any moment, he expected discovery.

She shivered, in shock, and huddled on the wet fiberglass.

Wyatt knelt and pulled her close, his chin on top of her head. "You're okay, Selena. You're okay."

Selena burst into tears.

"I've got you." Her petite body shivered under his hands. Although the water had been warm, the wind cooled them both.

A BALD HEAD EMERGED FROM THE CABIN BELOW.

Wyatt froze. He didn't know what to do. They were trapped on the dive platform with nowhere to go.

Before he could make up his mind, the man, in jeans and a button-down shirt, pointed a rifle at him. *"No te muevas."* He yelled over his shoulder, *"Enrique!"*

Shit, there were two of them.

Wyatt calculated the odds. Not good. What chance did they have against two armed men on a sailboat with no way to escape?

Wyatt put up his hands and nodded at Selena to do the same. He stood, water dripping from his clothes. She obeyed. Instinctively, he put his body between the man and Selena.

The second man, Enrique, with long hair and a mustache, appeared with a radio and a rifle of his own.

The men exchanged looks of surprise.

Selena stepped from behind Wyatt's protection. "We were at the party. *La fiesta.*" She pointed toward Tulúm, its lights visible in the gathering dark.

Distant gun fire interrupted her explanation.

Enrique didn't like that. He gripped his rifle more firmly and spoke into the radio. *"Soy yo. Qué está pasando?"*

His buddy narrowed his eyes and kept his rifle trained on them.

Wyatt swallowed. He couldn't believe Selena was trying to talk her way out of this one.

"I'm Claudia Rios, Felix's daughter. We were supposed to wait for him here...on the boat? Didn't he tell you we were coming?" She touched Wyatt's arm. "He's my bodyguard. We had a problem with the Zodiac. Had to swim for it."

Enrique stared at Selena as if she had two heads. He attempted to get someone on the radio for a second time. "*Eh, mamón! Qué está pasando allá?*"

Only static echoed.

Enrique shrugged. "*Qué hacemos con ellos, compañero?*" Casually, he slung his rifle on his back and set the radio on the command console.

The two men chatted back and forth about what to do. Wyatt stood rigidly, hands held high. He couldn't say the same for Selena. She watched the men instead.

"Hey, can I get a towel here?" Selena stepped onto the deck with her head high. "I'm soaking wet."

"*Paso atrás!*" the bald man commanded.

"I don't know any Spanish. I'm sorry." She lifted a shoulder. "Do you speak English, Enrique?" She said the words very slowly, as if he might understand them better. "English?"

The bald man took a step forward.

Wyatt's insides clenched. He braced to make a jump.

The radio crackled to life. "*Simón. Simón.*" A woman's voice. "*Respóndeme.*"

Selena gasped.

The bald man whipped out a command to Enrique, "*Respóndele!*"

Enrique picked up the radio and answered the woman on the other end. They talked back and forth for several minutes. In the background, gun shots exploded, but the woman remained calm and steady.

"*Miguel?*" the woman asked. "*Y la chica?*"

"No Miguel."

Wyatt knew they didn't have long before the truth came out. He scanned the deck for any kind of weapon and hoped for a distraction.

"Miguel is on the beach," Selena explained. "We left him on the beach. He told us to take the boat." Her hands trembled, her fear too obvious.

"Dónde está Miguel?" the woman demanded.

A loud *chop, chop, chop* could be heard in the distance. Bright lights in the sky. A helicopter approached.

Simón turned to look.

Wyatt leaped onto the deck, grabbed a fire extinguisher recessed into a panel near the captain's seat, and slipped on the wet boards. He knocked Selena off her feet, and she hit the rail hard with her head.

Enrique dropped the radio and reached for his rifle.

Wyatt, flat on his back on the deck, swung the fire extinguisher by the hose.

Smack!

It made contact with Enrique's knee.

The man, crying out in pain, fell hard.

Simón spun at the noise.

Wyatt scrambled for cover behind the captain's chair.

Simón let out a burst of gunfire, which scattered across the deck. He missed injured Selena by inches and, instead, hit Enrique in the face.

Enrique, blinded and in pain, took a few steps in the wrong direction and fell onto the diving platform and then slipped into the ocean.

Wyatt swung the fire extinguisher for a second time, making contact with Simón's head.

The cartel man dropped to the deck. A massive pool of blood formed like a halo around his head. He wouldn't be getting up again.

. . .

SELENA'S MIND BLANKED. MIGUEL'S BODY, THE BOAT, THE water, the swim in the dark and now one dead man taken out by Wyatt in a most brutal fashion. Her senses were overwhelmed.

Their escape plan had fallen apart. The Zodiac could've carried them far away from the cartel men, the shooting, the whole thing. They could've followed the shoreline for miles in either direction until they found a safe place to land.

She glanced at Wyatt, who was busy with the sailboat controls. He'd risked everything by chasing after her. And now he'd killed someone. She couldn't ask him to do any more. This was her problem to solve. Her life to fix. Her world that had come crashing down around her. It wouldn't be fair to drag him further in.

She had to live in the moment. Not acknowledge the past or the future. Make decisions that made sense and didn't risk anyone's life...except her own. If she focused too closely on the dead body at her feet, she'd fall apart, and Wyatt would feel obligated to step in once more.

First, she'd have to find a way to reach the shore. Tia Gabriela knew she was there. Knew Miguel, for some reason, was not with her. Gabriela would come looking...and soon. Selena needed her paperwork. She'd need her birth certificate at the very least. And that important document was back in the tent, in the woods. She glanced toward the land. The short strip of jungle where she'd been taken to change. Her documents were all there. Any family connections she might have in Mexico on her mother's side, also in the bag. Addresses. Names. People to search for. She had options. She didn't need to let Wyatt run the show.

Innocent, brave Wyatt who'd been so unlucky to meet her on the street. Unlucky to follow her. Unlucky to kiss her. Unlucky to want something more.

She had to break that connection for his own good. She had to plow forward without him. No matter how scared she might be, it was her mess to fix. Her life to straighten out. And if she didn't succeed, then so be it.

WYATT FIDDLED WITH THE SAILBOAT CONTROLS. HE KNEW nothing about sailboats, but he did know they had motors in case the wind died down. Surely, he could figure something out. Adrenaline pumped through his body after the battle he'd had with the cartel men. He couldn't stop to process what he'd done: he'd killed a man. He buried his emotions under the more important action—finding a way out of their mess.

He flipped switches: *bilge, blower, lights nav, acc.* He didn't know what he was looking at. And how to haul up the anchor?

His mind was at a loss. He felt the pressure to get it right, to figure it out. To save them both from the cartel, the DEA, the Mexican Army. The woman on the radio had sounded pissed when she'd heard Selena had arrived without Miguel. Who knows when she or her crew from the cartel might arrive to find their men dead? It could be any minute. They had to go.

He wracked his brain for a solution. If they couldn't sail away, what else could they do?

He pounded his fist on the instrument panel. "Fuck."

A failure. Again.

He looked up at the shore. Not too far off. Sure, it wouldn't be a walk in the park even for someone who could swim well, but it was possible. He calculated the distance. Two-hundred yards. Maybe more. They'd have to swim for it.

Selena might have trouble. But she could make it.

He'd make sure of that.

"I HAVE TO GO BACK." SELENA SAID.

"Yeah, I think we do." Wyatt studied the panel of buttons and switches next to the big steering wheel. "I don't know how to run this thing."

"No, just me."

His thoughts grew fuzzy. He couldn't comprehend what she'd said. "You can't swim." He turned back to the panel. "I can figure this out. Really. Just give me a minute.

"I'm tired of running, Wyatt. Running from my problems. I have to face them. And they aren't your problems."

"I'm not going to let you leave this boat." The echo of gunfire erupted in the background. "Go back there by yourself. Are you crazy?"

"This isn't your choice to make. It's mine. And I am saying I don't want you to come with me. I don't want you to chase after me. I have to do this myself."

"But you can't—"

"Yes, I can. I decided to leave the United States. It was my decision...you shouldn't have to suffer the consequences because of that. Those men almost killed you. I couldn't live with it if you got hurt. I need to fix this on my own. Alone."

"There's something I have to tell you, Selena." Wyatt had difficulty swallowing. He couldn't let her disappear without telling her the truth about her situation. "Something you don't know."

"Stop it, Wyatt. Stop inserting yourself into my problem."

"But—"

"Please," she begged. "If I run away with you, if we sail this boat away, how does that solve anything? You know what I'm saying is true. We have no plan."

Wyatt hesitated. He had no answer for her. Everything in him wanted to stay close to her, make sure she was safe, make sure everything was okay. He bit the inside of his cheek. He'd fled the meticulous plans he'd made for his life. He'd obliterated his past and transformed into a more disciplined Wyatt. But meeting her made him want to risk it all. "Selena—"

"I can't stay here," Selena whispered. "Tia Gabriela knows something is wrong. She'll send someone."

"You need to rest." Wyatt clung desperately to the idea they'd stay together as long as they could. Until fate or the authorities intervened. He wasn't going to let her slip away so easily. "The only way out of here is to get back in the water, and I don't think you're ready for that.

The helicopter circled over the ruins. Its bright lights scanned the stone walls and structures, searching for cartel men.

"Do you really think the good guys are losing?" Wyatt willed her to change her mind.

A bright streak appeared in the night sky. It snaked toward the helicopter.

Both of them watched, mesmerized by the war-like actions playing out in front of them.

The rocket found its target.

The helicopter exploded in mid-air. The propeller spun off into the dark jungle and pieces of the fuselage rained down on the ruins and the beach below.

❧ 30 ❧

yatt's heart sank.

Although he knew the cartels had some serious weaponry, he hadn't expected it here in the sleepy beach town of Tulúm. The destruction of the helicopter meant Felix Rios might be the victor in this fight. He tightened his grip on the wheel, wishing he could whisk them away from the hell that was happening on shore.

"Wyatt, I have to go." She stared at the destruction, and her voice trembled. "I don't think I have much time."

He couldn't imagine parting ways while chaos swirled around them and danger lurked around every corner. But maybe her feelings had been fleeting, turning from white hot passion to cool in a flash. He'd experienced a quick reversal of feelings many times before, so he shouldn't have been surprised. A kiss on the cheek turning into a slap. A hug turning into a chokehold. But she'd shown nothing but compassion and caring toward him. Even when he'd accused her of wrongdoing, she'd forgiven him almost instantly. Held no grudge against him for it. He'd convinced himself she was different. That he could trust her.

He wanted to give her complete honesty. It might be his only hope to win her back. To keep her close to him. To continue fighting for her. He drew in a deep breath and released it. "Back on the bus, when I gave you those notes about applying for your visa?"

She tilted her head. The topic must seem out of place with the crisis playing out around them.

He took a breath. "I remembered something from my training..." He wanted to flee and plunge himself into the ocean to avoid the negative response he expected from her. "And I think you should know the truth."

Selena drew away. "The truth about what?" She blinked rapidly. "What didn't you tell me?"

He couldn't meet her gaze. "Because you were in the US illegally and voluntarily left, you'll have a penalty put on you."

Her brow wrinkled. "A penalty?"

"A punishment for going about it the wrong way."

"But I didn't know. My mother was the one—"

"I don't make the rules, Selena. I know it seems wrong and unfair. I wish they'd been honest with you when you decided to come back to Mexico. They lied to you back in the States because of who you were...Rios's daughter."

Selena stepped away from him. "You mean your friends, the DEA agents..."

"They weren't my friends."

"You were with them when I called you. Felix told me as much."

"Look, Selena, I want to let you know what you're facing. I don't want you angry with me over it. Please."

"Fine. What's the penalty?"

"Ten years.

"What do you mean ten years?"

"You can't apply for a visa to go back to the States for ten years."

She collapsed into the captain's chair. "Ten years?" Her trembling fingers touched parted lips. "What am I going to do, Wyatt?"

He leaned over her. Her lashes wet with unshed tears. "You are going to let me help you." He kissed her forehead, her cheeks, her nose.

She searched his face and slowly nodded. "Okay."

Wyatt shook out the seawater from his hair and whipped off his soaked shirt. "There has to be a life raft or life-jackets or something on this boat we can use."

One of Selena's braids had come loose and hung down like the tail of a drowning mouse.

She looked so bedraggled and adorable at that moment, he wanted to sweep her off her feet and kiss her. But fears for her safety forced him to make a different choice

They descended into the belly of the sailboat. Wyatt fumbled for a switch. They found themselves in a well-appointed galley with gleaming black granite countertops, leather banks of seats around a dining table and alongside one wall. A massive orchid plant stood on the table next to a gift basket filled with a bottle of wine, fruits, and chocolates.

Wyatt opened cabinet after cabinet, looking for towels, life-jackets, anything they could use. Everywhere he looked he only found pots and pans, canned goods, utensils and, in one tall cabinet near a small refrigerator, a Vitamix blender and a full complement of liquor and spirits.

Selena stood frozen in the middle of the galley. She left a puddle of water on the pristine hard wood deck beneath her bare feet. "We can't stay here."

"I know." Wyatt slammed one cabinet closed, kneeled and pawed through a stack of paper plates, paper towels, dish soap and sponges. "You can't swim the rest of the way. There has to be something in here that can help us." He focused on the task at hand.

"Maybe in the bedroom?" Selena snapped him out of his closed loop thinking.

"Yes, the bedroom." He rushed past the table and into the darkened cabin in the bow of the boat.

He snapped on the light and rifled through drawers.

Selena understood and opened a small closet and pawed through the contents.

"They've got to have life jackets in here somewhere."

"I'd hope even drug lords pay attention to boating rules," Selena quipped.

They both scoured the bedroom, pulling open drawers and closets they'd left untouched.

Selena knelt down. "Hey, there's storage under the bed." She slid open a cabinet door. "Holy hell." She sat back on her heels.

Plastic-wrapped bricks spilled out. Dozens and dozens of them. In awe, she picked one up. A white powder dusted the exterior.

"Shit." Wyatt joined her on the floor. "I guess I didn't think he'd hide drugs on his own sailboat."

"He's arrogant." Selena hefted the brick and judged its weight. "I have a feeling he liked the idea of duping the DEA so much that he wanted to stick it to them. Like twisting the knife, I suppose."

"Put it back." Wyatt's voice deepened a notch.

Selena set it down with the others. "We need to get out of here." The reality of what she'd ended up in the middle of settled on her like a dark weight. The sailboat, the drugs, Miguel, the men Wyatt had killed. Tia Gabriela knew where they were and that Miguel was missing. She'd be livid. "That woman on the radio, she is my aunt—Tia Gabriela. She hates me, hates my mother. She won't let us go."

"Maybe she will, if she thinks there's no one to chase after." He set his jaw.

In the dark cabinet Selena spotted something orange. "Look." She shoved the plastic-wrapped drugs out of the way. "Life jackets."

"Head up top," Wyatt said in a monotone. "I'll meet you up there in a minute."

"What?" Selena didn't understand. They'd found what they needed—what else was there to do but abandon the sailboat and make another attempt to get to shore?

"I've got to do something."

"What do you mean?"

"Just go up top and wait for me. I'll be right behind you."

WYATT DIDN'T HAVE TIME TO CONVINCE SELENA. HE HANDED her two lifejackets and led her to the steps. "Wait for me topside. Please," he begged. The helicopter being taken down had shaken him. The fight appeared to be going the cartel's way. He had to create a smoke screen, a way to escape before it was too late. If he didn't do it now, Rios and Gabriela would come after Selena.

He crouched by the kitchen cabinet and exposed the fully stocked bar inside that he'd seen earlier and picked the bottle he knew would work best. The plan didn't need much thought. He knew what to do.

Wyatt's mind took him through the steps. He walked around the cabin and sloshed Everclear everywhere. On the floor, the walls, the curtains at the portholes, the bed and even the packages of drugs in the open cabinet beneath. All of it doused in the flammable liquid.

Selena paused partway up the stairs. He was distantly aware of her presence. Inside, a raw power grew. A new feeling he'd never had before. His life had been filled with guilt and shame because of his background. His mother, a drunk. His father a junkie lowlife. He remembered nothing good from his childhood, nothing happy about his family life. Instead, his past haunted him. An indescribable darkness had followed him. He couldn't escape it. So he drew on that dark part of him, the memory of the one night he'd wanted to forget.

The demons he tried so hard to shake with the respectable job, the controlled lifestyle, the routines he'd built...and now he'd walked right into the most impossible mess of his life. He thought he would've been afraid and would've felt the same fears he'd had as that little child, forced to participate in something horrible, but inside power roared. A fearlessness he never knew he had.

The Everclear soaked everything. The sharp smell of it played in his nostrils. He dumped the last of the bottle.

Selena had disappeared.

He'd scared her off. The wild actions of a madman perhaps. The intense focus on destruction maybe too much for her. He was going to screw up with her anyway, so why not when he acted the most real he'd been in years. This was his true self. The trailer trash kid who wore the same unwashed clothes to school every day because his mother had been drunk out of her mind and they'd been out of laundry detergent for weeks. The kid who ate a can of baked beans for breakfast and washed it down with a warm beer left on the counter. The kid who'd gotten his GED at sixteen to get the hell out of there and somehow managed to get himself a job and a place to stay.

That was the man Selena had seen and had fled from. But at least he'd been honest for once. He'd let her see the side of him he always knew was there. Destructive. Angry. Dangerous.

"Here." Selena had climbed back down into the galley, a pack of matches in hand. "Need a light?"

Warmth flooded his body. Wyatt smiled. A full, real smile.

She hadn't run away. She hadn't fled him in fear. "God, I love you."

He approached her, took the matches, entered the bedroom, and lit the bed on fire. The Everclear caught fire slowly, following the trail Wyatt had left from the bedroom to the galley, eating up anything in its path, devouring the drug stockpile. The delivery Felix Rios had planned to smuggle to the United States went up in flames. Raging, hot, orange flames. And instead of the horrible guilt that had eaten him up many years ago as his mother had burned up his father's belongings, he felt right inside. Good. Heroic.

"Let's get out of here." Selena headed for the ladder.

Wyatt waited thirty seconds. The flames grew more intense. He wanted to make sure the fire would continue long after they'd swam to shore. He wanted to know that Felix Rios would be trapped, nowhere to go, and that he had made it happen.

31

The helicopter had landed to the south of the ruins, blocking the road and escape for the cartel. Selena and Wyatt had a clear view of the whole scene as they paddled toward shore. Shadows played across the stone walls as people fled in all directions.

Selena reflected on what Wyatt had shared with her...she'd have to spend ten years in Mexico before she was allowed to apply for a visa. Her simplistic dreams had been shattered at that moment. Ten years seemed like forever. Her whole life and all of her plans snuffed out in a matter of minutes.

"Let's shoot for as far down the beach as we can manage," Wyatt said.

In the dark, she could only see the outline of his head and shoulders in the moonlight. She forced her mind to focus on the shore and the lights rather than let her thoughts dwell on what her future held. "Okay." She lay on her left side and kicked in the direction he'd suggested—as far away from the chaos as possible and closer to the jungle.

After thirty minutes of nonstop swimming, the waves carried them to the beach.

The sailboat had been a respite from reality. Back in the thick of things, the battle had grown out of control.

They emerged from the water, bedraggled, tired and completely exposed to the violence happening mere yards away.

"Now what?" Selena said breathing heavily. Her legs trembled under her. She wished she could shed the uncomfortable dress that made her stand out like a stop sign.

A flood of well-dressed partygoers emptied out from the ruins onto the beach about a hundred yards away. Women ran toward the parking lot in bare feet and expensive gowns. Men split off in groups with rifles at the ready. Horses neighed and stamped on the beach, frightened and confused.

She'd arrived in Mexico alone, broken, confused. She'd run across the country trying to find a way to get back to her life and had found problem after problem. Lies about who she was. Lies about what had happened in her past. Lies about everything. But Selena had never lied. Selena had never been anyone but herself. And she wasn't about to let someone else tell her how she had to act, who she had to be. Daughter of Felix Rios, king of the drug trade in the Yucatán. Half-sister to Miguel, a cruel, evil man who had wanted to use her to get what he wanted...power, money, fame. Her aunt had used her too. The DEA had used her as a lure, a way to get to Felix. She'd never even been someone they'd cared about. It had all been lies and more lies.

She marched on the sand. Her confidence building in the choice she'd made to return to the beach. To return to the fight. Not to run away any more. Not to let someone else pick up the pieces. She was going to fix it. She was going to take control. She was going to take her life back.

Her life in Arizona had been bucolic—sure, they'd been strapped financially, but they'd had friends, happiness, peace. Her mother had protected her from a chaotic, disastrous family in Mexico. She'd saved her from this life.

Miguel was dead in the ocean, drifting away, his body chum

for the sharks. That could've been her. She could've grown up spoiled and twisted without values without an understanding of what real love was all about.

Her mother had known this. Instinctively, she'd known. She'd had a terrible choice to make: stay in Mexico and risk her life and her child's life or flee her home country for the unknown. The law she'd broken seemed minor in comparison.

The anger toward her mother fell away. An understanding grew in her mind. A knowledge of why. She had to thank her mother for saving her from this madness. This horrible life.

Selena could choose for herself. Her father was an evil man. A truly bad man who'd taken his abilities and twisted them into a kingdom nobody with any integrity would want to rule.

Her birth certificate might say "Claudia Rios," but inside she was Selena Hernandez. The name and identity her mother had chosen. She was ready to fully own it.

If Wyatt was right, and she had to stay in Mexico for ten years, then goddamn it, she'd make it work. She'd find a way. She was strong enough. If any part of her was Felix, it would be that part. The determination. The strength. The stubborn bullish nature that she would make it no matter what.

The same idea had been in her mind when she'd left Mexico. Her mother was in jail, and she had been alone. She had wanted to do the right thing. That's all she ever wanted. Despite the craziness all around her, the bullets flying, the war playing out. She'd get her bag, her documents, and she'd do what she needed to.

"I know somewhere we can go." Selena, sopping wet and wearing a party dress, knew she'd left behind her clothes, her shoes and her bag in the tent in the jungle. "This way." She didn't know what they'd do after that point, but maybe Wyatt would think of something.

. . .

"WHERE IS MIGUEL?" FELIX APPROACHED IN A RUN FROM THE ruins, his suit jacket missing, his brow drenched in sweat and a pistol in his hand. His gaze played across Wyatt who stepped in front of Selena in a protective fashion. "And who is this?"

"We don't mean you any harm," Wyatt said, his voice low and warning. "We just want to leave."

"Miguel is waiting for you on the boat." Selena gently pushed Wyatt's arm away and stepped forward.

"Selena..." Wyatt warned.

She said the words calmly, soothingly. "Miguel has always been the one who would take over your empire someday. He wants it so badly." Selena said the words calmly, soothingly. "Go to him. Get away from here before they find you." She looked up at the ruins. The majestic structure stood strong. It had withstood centuries in this spot, and it would stand tall for many more.

"Is this your DEA agent?" Felix flashed a cold smile. "The one who set you up to fall into my hands?"

She took another step forward. "Let Wyatt go. He had nothing to do with this. He's an innocent man that got wrapped up in my problems. He's not DEA. He's just an embassy worker. A nobody. He can't hurt you."

Felix's features tensed. He pointed the gun straight at Wyatt. "Where is my son? What did you do?"

Selena's heartbeat grew sluggish at the sight of the gun. "He's on the sailboat, I swear." In a matter of moments, the fire burning below decks would find its way topside and Felix would turn his anger and fear on them.

"I don't believe you."

Screams of pain echoed from the ruins behind them. "Where's Gabriela?" Selena asked to distract. "Is she all right?"

"Fuck Gabriela." Felix's hand trembled.

Selena noticed a dark stain spreading across his shoulder.

"Where is my son?"

Suddenly, in the distance, the sailboat lit up the night. Orange flames climbed higher into the sky.

"What have you done!" Felix roared. His whole body flung back and he screamed to the sky. "You are a traitorous bitch. I've should've known a child of Pilar's could only be this way." He aimed straight at Selena's heart.

"Selena didn't do anything to him." Wyatt held up his hands and stepped in front of her. "I killed him."

"Wyatt, no!"

Felix, his face a dark mask of rage, pulled the trigger.

❦ 32 ❦

The bullet hit Wyatt's thigh with the force of a Mack truck.

He stumbled. Pain shot through his whole body. His mind lit up with an animalistic fight response. He lunged at the bastard who'd just shot him.

Felix had crumpled to the sand. "*Mi hijo*," he whispered.

The sailboat burned in the distance, lighting up the ocean with yellow, orange and red. Like the fires of hell.

"You've ruined everything." An attractive, older woman with a crown of bright white hair appeared out of the darkness. "I told you that *puta*, Pilar, wanted to ruin me—ruin us."

Felix kneeled in a daze. "*Gabriela, Miguel está muerto.*"

"We should have let *esta muchacha* rot. She did not deserve any consideration—we were perfect before she came along. Why couldn't you leave the past alone—a daughter." Gabriela spat on the ground. "Daughters are weak. Daughters are selfish."

"*Miguel está muerto*," Felix gnashed out between his teeth. "My son is dead—she is all I have left." His tortured eyes turned to Selena.

The older woman blinked rapidly. Then, her clin lifted into the air, and her nostrils flared.

Gabriela swung her pistol in Felix's direction. "You let her in even though I warned you she couldn't be trusted. Miguel warned you—Miguel." Her voice cracked. "You should have died in prison, *bastardo.*"

"Oh, God." Selena's eyes widened.

Time slowed down.

"Don't!" Selena lunged forward.

The gun went off.

Felix slumped to the sand.

Selena froze in mid-step.

"Shit." Wyatt stumbled. His leg lost all feeling. He didn't know if it worked any more. The blood poured out in a hot river down his thigh. His pants were soaked through.

Gabriela, eyes round and mouth agape, dropped her pistol and backed away. She looked in both directions, her face ashen.

Selena scrambled for the gun before Gabriela came to her senses.

Gunshots flew overhead in a loud *zing, zing, zing.* Wyatt could hear loud voices maybe fifty yards away. A whole crew of angry cartel men were ready to descend on them.

Gabriela held up her hands in surrender and then ran toward a group of cartel men. *"Ellos mataron al Señor! Con rapidez."*

Selena snapped out of wherever her brain had taken her. "We've got to run." Deep lines were etched around her mouth, and her hands trembled.

"I don't think I can." The pain grew unbearable.

"Get up. Get the hell up." Selena snarled at him and pulled on his arm with all her might.

"Leave me." He couldn't play the hero here. His wound was too severe. He'd done his job. He'd come back for her. He'd risked his life to save hers. "You run." He tugged his arm out of her grasp.

Her hands fluttered over his wound. In a voice choked with emotion, she said, "We've got to stop the bleeding." She ripped off a strip of the underskirt of her dress.

Wyatt instinctively pressed his hands against the hole in his leg. The warm blood oozed through his fingers. He felt light-headed and lay back on the sand. Although Gabriela and Felix's men weren't far away, he stared up at the stars and the bright silver moon. It would be so much easier to stay here on the beach and sleep. Maybe when he woke up all of this would be over, the men would be gone, and he would only be left with the sound of crashing waves.

Selena tugged at his leg.

Wyatt cried out from the instant shock of pain that jolted through him.

"I'm sorry," she soothed.

He felt an almost unbearable pressure bear down.

He screamed.

Selena had created a tourniquet of sorts high on his thigh.

"Get your ass up, Wyatt!" She knelt beside him, tears streaked her face. She urged him toward the edge of the jungle beyond the beach. "I'm not leaving without you."

Someone in the band of wild men shouted, "*Ahí ellos están!*"

"Come on!" Selena urged. "For me, please do this for me." She leaned forward and ran a hand through his sweaty hair. "Don't leave me alone, Wyatt. Please don't leave me alone." She kissed him.

He felt her tears on his face. Everything he'd ever wanted in life was about slip away if he let it. If he didn't get up and move himself into the jungle for cover, he'd be rounded up by those men, tortured, killed. Perhaps dangled from a bridge somewhere with a sign around his neck. The gringo who'd gone up against the cartel and lost. A warning to those out there who dared to stand up to them. Even an American with the full protection of the United States Government behind him couldn't escape the wrath of the cartel.

Her lips were soft and warm. He wanted more and more of them. Something worth living for...this woman, this beautiful girl who'd dropped into his life in the most unexpected way. If he wanted to believe his life could be joyful, a miracle, a never-ending adventure with the woman he loved, then it was worth it to try.

"Come on," she urged. Her face inches from his. "Come on. We can do this."

He gazed deep into her eyes. The warmth he saw there gave him strength. He fought to stand. The pain in his leg like fire.

"That's it, Wyatt." She glanced behind them. "They're coming. We have to go." She maneuvered under his arm, just tall enough to act like a crutch. He rested heavily on her shoulder. They moved as one. Each step more painful than the last. The blood oozed, but at least it had slowed. His pants stuck to his through-and-through gunshot wound sealing it off from further free-flow of blood.

He grunted, trying to hold back the tears of pain that threatened to spill. He had to do this...for her.

❦ 33 ❦

The dense jungle canopy absorbed all light, creating shadows and darkness deeper than the night. Dark with no moon. Dark with no stars. Dark that held snarls and cries and dangerous things.

They limped along through the tangle as quickly as they could, knowing armed men were not too far behind them.

Selena kept her mind off the serious wound Wyatt had suffered and thought about moving forward. The tent where she'd left her things, and then the parking lot beyond. If they could find a car with a key in it, Selena could drive them away from this place of horror. Deep in the trees, at least she felt safer. But the darkness made it impossible to move quickly. They stumbled over roots and branches. Wyatt grunted in pain.

She hated to hurt him more, but they had no choice. Gabriela and her men could catch up to them—panicked devotees of Felix Rios who might see her as the cause of all their problems.

"Where are we going?" Wyatt asked, his voice weak. His breathing came out in labored bursts.

Selena gritted her teeth and supported Wyatt. "Not much further." She hoped that was true.

The black all around had confused her. She didn't know if they were moving in circles or heading straight back to the ruins.

"*Detener! Manos arriba!*"

Wyatt immediately put up his left hand. His only free hand. "*No dispares!*"

A blinding white light shone in Selena's eyes. Her heart beat as rapidly as a bird's.

What was happening?

She backed away from the light in quick, jerky steps, bringing Wyatt with her.

A host of men in camouflage uniforms emerged from the jungle. They'd formed a circle around them.

No escape.

A flashlight played on Wyatt's leg.

"He's been shot."

English.

Selena had never been so relieved to hear it.

Melanie and James Brewster stepped into the light.

"You're okay." Melanie lowered a pistol that had been pointed at them and tucked it into a holster under her arm. "We've got you." She nodded at some of the military men. They moved forward to assist with Wyatt.

More men in protective gear fanned out into the trees, rounding up Gabriela and her crew.

Selena lingered near Wyatt. His face pale, his eyes partly closed.

"He needs help, Selena. Let us help him."

James flashed a badge. "We're DEA. Wyatt gave us the slip." He minutely shook his head. "Guess he was worried about you."

Selena stepped back into place as his support. They were safe. Her father was dead. Gabriela had been stopped. And she never had to worry about any of it ever again.

She followed the complement of soldiers into the jungle and left the battle field of Tulúm behind.

❧ 34 ❧

FIVE DAYS LATER

"Come on," urged Selena, as she stepped inside the cozy hotel room in Cancún.

Wyatt painfully maneuvered himself on crutches through the door. "Just because they kicked me out of the hospital doesn't mean I'm ready to run marathons."

Selena rolled her eyes. "We're five steps from the elevator."

He launched himself forward. "I don't know what the big rush is, anyway." Wyatt had been surprised when she'd showed up at the hospital that morning with his pain prescription filled, a handicap-equipped van with a lift in the back, and a Venti Mocha.

Selena pushed the door shut. "I've been going stir crazy in this room ever since Melanie dropped me off."

Gratefully, he settled onto the bed—one of two queens in a room with a gorgeous view of the beach. "Why didn't you go play tourist for a while?" He let out a breath. Although he didn't want to admit it, those few days in the hospital recovering from surgery had sapped his strength.

Selena slipped off her shoes and disappeared into the bathroom, leaving the door ajar. "I was worried about you."

His pulse fluttered in his neck. No one had ever told him that before. No one ever worried about Wyatt Demko. A loser. A loner. A disappointment.

"They wouldn't let me visit you after the surgery. Not family." Her voice echoed in the tiled space. "I wish I'd known how to explain."

"I can teach you." Wyatt imagined feisty Selena battling nurses in a Mexican hospital, and it brought a smile to his face.

Selena emerged from the bathroom wearing a fluffy white bathrobe. "I've been waiting for you." She padded toward him. "I couldn't leave without telling you how I felt."

His smile disappeared at the sight of her: slim legs beneath the short hem of the robe, a deep v-neck showing off her cleavage, and her heated gaze cutting right through him.

"Oh?" His breathing grew shallow. Memories of their one night together came flooding back.

"Yes." Selena took each crutch from him and leaned them against the dresser. "I had a lot of time to think about everything that's happened. What you did for me. How you risked your life for me when you didn't have to." She touched his bandaged leg. "Does it hurt?"

He shrugged.

As she leaned over him, her hair hung down and blocked her face from his view. He took in the smell of her: lavender and mint. A bare thigh visible in the gap of her robe.

He wanted her.

She skimmed her hand along the bandage, partially visible below the edge of his board shorts.

He gasped at the light touch.

"Oh, I'm sorry. I didn't mean to hurt you." She took a step back.

He touched her arm. "Don't leave." Wyatt had no idea if she'd be there tomorrow or the day after or the day after that. He couldn't stand the thought of it.

"What?" Selena smiled. "Why would I leave? I love you."

The words seared his soul. Spoken so quietly, so honestly—as if to doubt her would be absurd.

He pulled her onto the bed and kissed her. Her lips like two fresh slices of mango, sweet and moist. He nibbled at the edges of her mouth. Selena murmured something, and he kissed along her jawline and over the shell of her ear.

She reached for the tie of her bathrobe. Wyatt fumbled to help.

It slipped off her shoulders and gaped open to reveal her naked breasts—full and soft.

He cupped one in his hand. Heat hit his groin. He kissed her nipple, and she gasped.

This time, he wanted to go slowly. He wanted to explore her, taste her, learn every part of her.

She pulled his T-shirt over his head, and their bodies met, naked flesh to naked flesh. Only his shorts between them.

Wyatt hardened at the feel of her. This time he knew how special this woman was. How perfect. How strong. How amazing and crazy and gorgeous. In the motel in Mexico City, it had been pure lust. Bodies satisfying urges. The mystery of discovery. He learned how her body responded, the sounds she made, the smell of her, the feel of her skin, the touch of her hand on him and what it could do at just the right moment.

This time, it was so much more than that. He wanted to give her everything he had. Everything inside of his mind. He wished he had all the right words, knew how to explain it so she'd under-stand why this was different. They needed each other.

"Selena," he breathed, cupping her face in his hands. "I love you, too."

"I know," Selena whispered.

He marveled at how different his life had become in only a couple of weeks. A chance meeting on the street, two lost people finding each other.

He kissed her gently across her brow.

Selena snaked her arms around his neck and hooked a leg gently over his hip.

Although his leg complained at the movement, he ignored the pain. He could stand it a little longer.

"Does that hurt?" she asked, worry clear in her eyes.

The heat of her so close. So tantalizing. So impossible to stop. He needed her now more than air, more than life, more than his very soul. "You could never hurt me, Selena."

EPILOGUE
SIX MONTHS LATER

Selena held Wyatt's hand in hers, a small diamond ring on her left hand. They stood in front of the big screen that announced plane arrivals in Mexico City.

"Last time I was here I felt so alone," Selena said.

Wyatt squeezed her hand. "If I'd seen you here, I would've rushed to your aid."

"You would not." She laughed.

"If you were in that red skirt, yes, I would have."

Selena blushed. "I'm not so sure about that."

"I am." Wyatt spied the flight they were waiting for. "Looks like it was delayed a few minutes."

"Do you want to sit?" Ever since the shooting, Wyatt had been working hard to build up the strength in his left leg. Although he'd been in the hospital only a few days, he still walked with a bit of a limp.

"I'm fine." Wyatt grimaced.

"Come on. There's a bench over here." Selena led a reluctant Wyatt to a bench near baggage claim.

"I don't want my future mother-in-law thinking I'm some kind of weakling who can't take care of you."

"My mother isn't going to think that."

"How do you know?"

"She thinks you're amazing. I've told you already."

He tapped his injured leg. "I really wanted her to come after my leg had healed up completely."

"She can't help when the government decided to deport her."

Selena looked up. The crowd parted. Maria Hernandez—once known as Pilar Rios—entered into their field of view.

"Mama!" she cried out and ran to her.

"Selena!" Her mother burst into tears.

They embraced.

"I never thought I'd see you again," Maria said through her tears. "I thought you'd hate me forever. I'm so sorry about every-thing. I should have told you."

"No, Mama, no." The nervous energy she'd had since they left Wyatt's apartment earlier that day disappeared. Her engage-ment ring shone under the cheap fluorescent lighting in the airport terminal. "Thank you."

Wyatt remained a few feet distant to give the two women time to reconnect.

"Wyatt." Selena reached out a hand for him. "Meet my mother, Maria Hernandez."

Maria sized him up from head to toe. "So you love my daugh-ter, is that right?"

"Yes, ma'am." Wyatt straightened up.

As they exited the airport, her arms locked with Wyatt on one side, her mother on the other, they passed by a newsstand. A row of newspapers hung from the counter, and a picture caught Selena's eye. A very familiar woman—older, missing teeth, and a bright pink buff on her forehead—took up half the front page.

PATRICIA - Reina de los Mares?

"What does that say?" Selena asked, mesmerized by the photograph of one of her captors. Never found in the Battle of Tulúm. She, Silvio and Yolanda had managed to drive back into the jungle after receiving payment from Miguel the night of the fiesta. They hadn't been caught up in the firefight that had taken place that night.

Only a few remaining members of the cartel were at large, but Selena had never mentioned those three to the DEA after they'd made it to Mérida. She'd seen them as pawns in the drug trade, not active participants. Sure, they carried weapons and rode around pretending to be tough, but Selena had never really believed it.

"Queen of the Seas," Maria translated. "Does that mean something to you?"

"No, I just thought she looked familiar is all..."

Wyatt gave Selena a queer look. He knew there was more to the story than she was telling, but he chose to stay silent. They'd been through enough all those months ago. A few short days of intensity, of life-or-death struggle. Neither of them wanted to remember it, except for the time they'd spent together. The beginnings of their love for each other. The moment which brought them into each other's lives and changed it irrevocably.

As they hailed a taxi, Selena promptly forgot about Patricia and instead focused on where they'd take her mother to lunch. Then they could talk of wedding plans, visa possibilities, and what lay ahead for the three of them.

Twenty-four hours after Maria Hernandez had been deported to Mexico, she had reunited with her daughter.

THE END

Please consider leaving a review!

ABOUT THE AUTHOR

K. J. Gillenwater has a B.A. in English and Spanish from Valparaiso University and an M.A. in Latin American Studies from University of California, Santa Barbara. She worked as a Russian linguist in the U.S. Navy, spending time at the National Security Agency doing secret things. After six years of service, she ended up as a technical writer in the software industry. She has lived all over the U.S. and currently resides in Wyoming with her family where she runs her own business writing government proposals and squeezes in fiction writing when she can. In the winter she likes to ski and snowshoe; in the summer she likes to garden with her husband and take walks with her dog.

Check in with K.J. at her website to **join her newsletter mailing list** or for more information about her writing, her books, and what's coming next. www.kjgillenwater.com.

If you enjoyed this book, K. J. Gillenwater is the author of multiple books, which are available in print and in eBook format at multiple vendors.

- Acapulco Nights
  - Aurora's Gold
  - The Ninth Curse
  - The Little Black Box
  - Blood Moon

Short Stories & Short Story Collections:

•Skyfall
  •Nemesis
  •The Man in 14C
  •Charlie and the Zombie Factory

www.ingramcontent.com/pod-product-compliance
Lightning Source LLC
Chambersburg PA
CBHW071510110726
47908CB00003B/788